Awards and praise for Hannah Harrington's debut novel *Saving June*

A *VOYA* Perfect Ten title

Gold medalist in the Moonbeam Children's Book Awards for Young Adult Fiction—Mature Issues

"*Saving June* should become a movie someday— it even includes its own soundtrack."
—*VOYA*

"Harper's voice rings true, and readers looking for a mildly steamy romance (with more than a splash of alcohol, smoking and sex) won't be disappointed."
—*Kirkus*

"An incredible debut. Like the best of songs, it brings tears to your eyes and makes you smile. Like the best road trip stories, it takes you on a vivid journey that you don't want to end."
—Stephanie Kuehnert, author of *Ballads of Suburbia*

"With a powerful story, characters that truly come alive and a romance worth swooning over, *Saving June* is a fresh, fun and poignant book that I couldn't tear myself away from."
—Kody Keplinger, author of *The DUFF*

"Hannah Harrington weaves a fast-paced and heartfelt story about first loss and first loves. Readers will adore following a protagonist as real and raw as Harper Scott...a tender, funny and moving debut. I couldn't put it down!"
—Courtney Summers, author of *Cracked Up to Be* and *Some Girls Are*

"Wow. This novel truly blew me away... a beautiful coming of age story."
—*Reading Lark* blog

"We both absolutely loved this book. It was realistic, it was heart-wrenching."
—*Books to the Sky* blog

speechless

HANNAH HARRINGTON

Recycling programs
for this product may
not exist in your area.

ISBN-13: 978-0-373-21052-7

SPEECHLESS

Copyright © 2012 by Hannah Harrington

This edition published by arrangement with Harlequin Books S.A.

For questions and comments about the quality of this book, please contact us
at CustomerService@Harlequin.com.

www.HarlequinTEEN.com

Printed in U.S.A.

For Paula

in which
national geographic
inadvertently changes
my life

Keeping secrets isn't my specialty. It never has been, ever since kindergarten when I found out Becky Swanson had a crush on Tommy Barnes, and I managed to circulate that fact to the entire class, including Tommy himself, within our fifteen minute recess—a pretty impressive feat, in retrospect. That was ten years ago, and it still may hold the record for my personal best.

The secret I have right now is so, so much juicier than that. I'm just about ready to burst at the seams.

"Will you stop the teasing already?" Kristen says. We're in her bedroom where I'm helping her decide on an outfit for tonight—a drawn-out process when your wardrobe is as massive as hers. "It's annoying. Just tell me."

Kristen is not a patient person. I realize I've been pushing it by alluding to my newfound information over the past twenty minutes without actually divulging anything. Of course I'm going to tell her; she's my best friend, and I can't keep it to myself much longer without truly pissing her off. A pissed-off Kristen is not a fun Kristen. Still, it's rare for me to have the upper hand with her, so I can't help but hold it over her head just a little.

"I don't know," I say innocently. "I'm not sure you can handle it...."

She turns around from where she's digging through her closet and chucks a black leather sandal at me. I shield my face with both hands, laughing as the shoe bounces off one arm and onto the mattress. Kristen props a hand on her narrow hip and cocks her head at me, her glossy, shoulder-length blond hair swaying with the motion.

"You're building this up way too much," she says. She yanks out a shimmery red top from her closet before facing me again. "I bet whatever it is, it's completely lame."

"Well, in that case, I'll keep it to myself." When she glares at me, I just smile in return and say, "Don't wear that. That baby-doll cut looks like something out of the maternity section."

She hangs the top back up and comes over to the bed, flopping down on her stomach next to me. "Spill," she whines, the previous iciness dissolving into borderline desperation. This is as close as Kristen ever gets to groveling. "Otherwise I'm uninviting you from the party."

The threat can't be real—Kristen knows I've been looking forward to her New Year's Eve party for over a month now. She even helped concoct the cover story necessary to convince my mother to let me come over to her house despite the grounding I received after my parents saw my latest report card. Like I'm ever going to need geometry in real life anyway.

Even though Kristen can be...*touchy,* she wouldn't uninvite me from the party over something like this—but I decide it's better to cave already than to test her on it.

"Okay, okay," I relent. "I'll tell you."

She breaks into a grin and scoots closer to me. I like having her attention like this; Kristen is easily bored, so when I do get her full focus, it makes me feel like I'm doing something right. She is, after all, one of—if not *the*—most popular girls in the sophomore class, if you keep track of that sort of thing, which I do. She's used to people fawning all over her to get on her good side. I've been on her good side for almost two years now, and I intend to stay there.

I'd better make this good.

"So I met up with Megan today because she wanted me to help her pick out new shoes, right?" I start. "She also wanted to bitch to me about Owen, because he totally blew her off last weekend and they've been fighting a lot, and she's wondering if she should break up with him."

Kristen's mouth tugs into a frown. "Um, yawn. I already know this."

"I'm not done yet," I assure her. "Anyway, so Megan brings along Tessa Schauer, which…whatever. She's annoying, but I can deal. We shop for a while and everything's fine, and then I remember I need to call my mom about picking stuff up from the dry cleaners, except I'm an idiot who didn't charge my phone and the battery's dead. I ask Tessa if I can borrow hers since she's right there, and she hands it off and walks away. I call my mom, and then I'm about to give it back, but I decided to look through the pictures on the phone because I'm nosy like that, and…" I pause for a moment, just to draw out the anticipation.

"And…?" Kristen prompts. She's totally hanging on to every word.

"And," I say, "the first one I see? It's of Tessa. With Owen. Looking very…shall we say…*friendly*."

Her eyes widen. "*How* friendly?" she asks.

I dig my phone out of my pocket and toss it at her. "Look for yourself."

I watch in amusement as she fumbles with my phone, scrolling through my text messages. "Shut up," she gasps, looking back up at me. "You forwarded the pictures to yourself?"

"Duh."

"Won't Tessa know?"

I'm a little insulted by the question, to be honest. Of course I thought ahead. I'm not an amateur. "I deleted the sent texts," I explain. "She'll have no idea."

"That is…" Kristen pauses, and then grins up at me. "Totally brilliant."

I take the phone back and look at the screen, where the high-angled self-portrait of Tessa and Owen midkiss stares back at me. So tacky. Not just the picture, or how Owen's mouth is open so wide I can actually see his tongue entering Tessa's mouth (gross, gross, gross), but making out with your alleged best friend's boyfriend behind her back? That's just classless. I would never in a million years hook up with Kristen's boyfriend, Warren Snyder, while she's dating him. Okay, I would never hook up with him, period, because he's a sleaze, but that's beside the point. The point is, some things are sacred.

"She's a shitty friend," I tell Kristen. "I can't believe she did that to Megan." There's no way Megan will forgive her when she finds out. She's dated Owen for over a year, and Tessa's been her best friend for longer than that. An entire friendship down the drain, all because Tessa couldn't keep her hands off Owen. No boy is worth that. Not even Brendon Ryan, whom I would do a number of immoral and insane things for, and who is quite possibly the love of my life, even if he doesn't know it yet. We've been caught in a wildly passionate, completely one-sided affair since freshman year.

"Tessa Schauer is a slutty bitch. I hope Megan kicks her ass," Kristen says. "When are you going to tell her?"

"Tonight, probably." Megan and Tessa will both be at the party, so I'll have to find a way to corner Megan alone and break the news. Tessa will know it's me, even if I erased my tracks, but whatever. Who cares? Snooping on someone's phone is a far more minor offense than slutting around with your best friend's boyfriend. No one will have sympathy for her.

Kristen rolls off the bed and stands in front of her full-length mirror, fiddling with the ends of her perfect hair. "You know, you could have some fun with this," she muses.

I sit up. "How?"

"If you tell Tessa you know about her and Owen, I bet she'd do just about *anything* to keep you from sharing that with Megan."

"Like blackmail?" I frown. "I don't know…"

"I'm just saying," Kristen says, "I know for a *fact* that she has a fake ID. She was attention-whoring like crazy, showing it off to everyone who would listen in Econ last week. Maybe you could convince her to hook up the two of us with our own."

Interesting idea. Except—

"What would we do with a fake ID?" I ask. Buying booze is the obvious answer, but while Kristen might pass for twenty-one with the right push-up bra and a pair of heels, there's no way I could I am much less…*developed* than her.

"Well, I could go to Rave with Warren, for starters," she says. "You only have to be eighteen to get in."

Rave is this nightclub in Westfield, the next town over. Warren turned eighteen last month and went there to celebrate, and wouldn't shut up about it for two weeks. I have to admit, it would be interesting to see what all the fuss is about.

And if it's important to Kristen, then it's important to me.

"I'll see what I can do," I tell her, and by the way Kristen smiles at me, I know that was exactly what she wanted to hear.

six hours later

I don't know how I'm going to talk myself out of this one.

My phone buzzes insistently in my hand, like it knows I'm trying to avoid it. A glance at the front screen confirms my impending doom: MOM flashes there like it's mocking me. Crap.

Kristen nudges me in the rib cage with her elbow. "Who the hell is calling you?" she demands. "Everyone worth knowing is already *here*."

It's true; the party is in full swing, the room filled with half of Grand Lake High's student body—well, the half that matters, anyway—and loud music. It's no secret Kristen Courteau throws the best parties. Absentee parents, an older brother who has no problem supplying minors with alcohol, a big house with a top-notch stereo system—it's everything a group of rowdy sixteen-year-olds could ask for.

On this couch I'm packed in tight like a sardine, stuck between Kristen and Brendon Ryan. Brendon Ryan, the last person I want knowing that my mother is calling to check up on me.

"It's my mom," I explain, leaning my head close to hers to be heard over the racket and praying that Brendon is too absorbed in downing his beer to pay attention. "She'll be pissed if I don't answer."

"Then answer it," Kristen says, like it's that simple.

"And have her hear all *this?*" I shake my head. "She'll kill me!"

"Fine, then *don't* answer it." Kristen rolls her eyes and knocks back the rest of her drink. Somehow she manages to look good doing even that. "I'm getting more beer," she informs me, peeling herself off the couch and dancing her way across the room to the cooler and abandoning me to resolve this problem on my own. Sometimes Kristen can be such a bitch. If she wasn't my best friend, I'd probably hate her.

Next to me, Brendon curls his hand over the cap of my shoulder and leans in close to my ear. Normally I'd be thrilled because a) Brendon Ryan is touching me, b) his near proximity means I can smell him, and c) BRENDON RYAN IS TOUCHING ME OH MY GOD (!!!), but I can't even savor the moment because I'm too panicked. Also, tonight he reeks too much of beer and cloying cologne. This is a disappointment because I always assumed that a perfect creature such as Brendon would smell of spring rain and mountain breezes and other heavenly aromas.

"Hey," he says, his breath warm against my ear, and oh, yeah, that's enough to send my already racing pulse into overdrive. "I bet if you go down the hall it'll be quieter."

It's a no-brainer suggestion, really, but in that moment, I feel like Brendon is a certified genius for coming up with it. Maybe it's due to the fact that when I'm anywhere within a six-foot radius of Brendon I lose all ability to think coherently. Well, okay, the Jell-O shot I kicked back ten minutes ago probably isn't helping matters.

"Yes," I finally choke out once I realize I've spent the last several seconds staring into his brain-melty hazel eyes with my mouth hanging open like the love-struck idiot I am. "Good idea."

I push myself off the couch, stumble past the cluster of barely clothed freshman girls writhing to some electro dance remix—nasty—and don't stop until I've reached the end of the hallway. Of course, even down here I can feel vibrations from the stereo's pulsating bass. My phone stopped ringing a while ago. Great. Now I need to come up with an excuse to explain why I didn't answer Mom's call right away. One that does not involve divulging that I'm at a New Year's Eve party with a bunch of intoxicated minors.

It's so stupid. One lousy grade and my parents act like it's the end of the world. A D- in geometry is not going to ruin my entire life. But of course they don't see it that way. The only reason I was allowed over to Kristen's at all was under the pretense that we'd be babysitting her younger cousins. If Mom finds out what's really going on, there'll be hell to pay.

I open the hall closet and lock myself inside; at least the door blocks some of the sound from the raging party. My phone starts ringing again—Mom, of course. I push aside a broom handle and answer it with the most nonchalant hello I can muster.

"Chelsea," she says, and by the way she says my name alone, I can perfectly picture the pinched expression on her face. "Why didn't you pick up before?"

"Um.. " I rack my brain for the first believable excuse. "My phone was at the bottom of my bag, and I couldn't find it in time. You know my purse…it's like a black hole."

"Uh-huh," she says. I can't tell if she's skeptical or if I'm just paranoid.

I perch awkwardly on the edge of a cardboard box, keeping one eye on the door. "So, what's up?"

"I just thought I'd ask if you could pick up a gallon of milk before you drive home tomorrow morning." She pauses. "How is the babysitting going?"

"Fine," I say, though of course as soon as the word leaves my mouth, something crashes in the hallway. I cringe and press a hand to my forehead. This is just perfect.

"What was that?"

I recover without missing a beat. "Oh, just one of the kids causing trouble," I say. "Probably should've skipped the candy after dinner—sugar overload." I let out a laugh and hope it doesn't come out too forced. "Actually I should probably go help Kristen wrangle them before they destroy the house."

"All right," Mom says, so oblivious I feel kind of bad. But only for a second. Then I'm just relieved that she actually buys my story. "Just make sure to pick up the milk tomorrow."

"Right. The milk. Got it." I need to wrap up this call ASAP before someone gives me away. "I'll talk to you later, okay?"

Mom says, "Have a good night, sweetie," before hanging up. And I'm in the clear.

Or, almost. I wriggle out of the closet and shut the door behind me, yanking my skirt down and raking my hands through my hair. I spent two hours wrestling with a flat iron to make it straight, and it's already getting all poofy and gross. Great. I try to smooth it down as best I can, cursing genetics for the millionth time in my life for not gifting me with thin, silky hair like Kristen's.

"Chelsea?"

I whip around to see Tessa Schauer standing there, peering at me with raised, overly plucked eyebrows. Usually when

Tessa looks at me it's for approval, or else a little fearful, but right now there's just mild curiosity written across her face.

I don't like it.

"What?" I snap, and she cringes just the slightest bit. That's better.

All the bronzer in the world can't hide her sudden blush. "I was just wondering what you were doing in the closet," she says.

"None of your business." No way am I letting Tessa know I'm the kind of loser who needs permission from her parents to do anything. As far as she's concerned, I do whatever I want, whenever I want.

"Jeez, no need to bite my head off," she says. "It was just a question."

"That's funny, because I have a question for *you*," I say. "What's it like to stab your best friend in the back?"

"What are you talking about?" she scoffs, but I can see the guilt flicker in her eyes. She's not that smooth.

"I know about you and Owen," I tell her. Tessa's eyes go wide, and I take a step closer. "Did you really think you could keep it a secret?"

She backs up, flustered. "I don't know what you mean," she lies. "Are you drunk?"

"Don't play dumb with me," I retort. "What do you think Megan's going to say when she finds out? Her boyfriend and her best friend. Talk about a knife in the back."

Finally Tessa drops the innocent act, her jaw tensing with anger. "She won't believe you."

"Pictures don't lie," I point out.

Realization dawns on her face. "You snooped on my phone."

I smirk at her. "You should be more careful with your indiscretions," I say, and pull my phone from my pocket. "What was the point of pictures anyway? Were you going to post them to your Facebook and let Megan find out that way? Maybe I should save you the time and just forward them to her right now...." My thumb hovers over the keypad.

Tessa dives for my phone, but I snatch it back out of reach. Does she seriously think she can wrestle it from me? She really is a low-class bitch.

Now her anger gives way to panic. "Please, don't tell her," she begs. "It was so stupid of me, I know, but he said he was going to dump her anyway, and it was just a few times, and..." Her voice wavers. "Please, you can't tell her—"

"Chill out," I snap, just so she'll stop this sniveling display of desperation. The secondhand embarrassment is killing me. "You look so pathetic right now."

"I know you don't like me, Chelsea," she says, wiping away a stray tear from under one eye. "But please, don't do this. Megan's my best friend."

"Maybe you should've thought about that before you stuck your tongue down her boyfriend's throat."

Tessa flinches. "You can't tell her," she says again. "You *can't*."

"Okay," I say.

"'Okay'?" she echoes. Cautious optimism creeps into her voice. "So you won't say anything?"

"As long as you do something for me."

By the time I return to the living room, Kristen's over in the corner, wrapped around Warren. I don't have to look around to know there's more than one girl in this room staring in envy. Warren's a senior, star of the basketball team, tall with broad shoulders and just enough stubble to make him look older and more mature than he is. And Kristen is—well, Kristen. Blonde, blue-eyed, curvy in all the right places and skinny in all the others, so pretty it hurts. Standing next to her is always a blow to the self-esteem.

I'll never know exactly why Kristen made me her project, but she did. All through middle school I'd been intimidated by her from a safe distance, until eighth grade, when the seating assignment for biology designated us as lab partners. Not only did Kristen acknowledge my existence, but somehow over the course of the year, she started inviting me over to her house and to the mall, passing me notes between classes, saving me a spot at her lunch table, and before I knew it we were friends. Not just friends, but best friends.

Being Kristen's best friend has its benefits—everyone knowing your name, invites to just about every social gathering (or at least all the ones worth attending), and a built-in social circle. The same social circle that includes Brendon Ryan, who could easily be my soul mate. That is, if I could get him to notice me.

I turn my head and there he is, refilling his cup of beer at the table with Natalie Thomas glued to his side. Ugh, I can't stand Natalie. She used to be Kristen's best friend, before I came along; she'd never say it to my face, but I know she secretly resents me for that. She's such a hanger-on, one with a notorious habit of flirting with all the guys within a five-mile radius—regardless of whether they have girlfriends or not.

Tonight she's donned this bright neon-green glittery dress that would cause irreversible retinal damage to look at directly, and it comes down only to the very tops of her thighs. So, so trashy. She makes me want to vom.

Brendon Ryan is too good for her. Brendon Ryan is classy. He wears preppy polo shirts and button-downs with sweaters over them and styles his dark blond hair perfectly so it looks messy, but in a purposeful way. He's student council president and always raises his hand in class before speaking, and instead of chewing gum he prefers mints, which he carries around in this tiny tin case. I've been in love with him ever since the first week of freshman year when he turned around in the seat in front of me in homeroom and offered me one, flashing that dazzling smile of his. Everything about Brendon oozes effortless cool. Unlike all the try-hard jocks Kristen and I tend to associate with.

If Natalie thinks she has her sights set on Brendon, she has another think coming.

I march right up there and position myself between the two of them. It's a tight squeeze, but one I manage to pull off by pretending I am in dire need of more pretzels.

"Hi!" I say to Brendon.

"Hi," he says, smiling. "How'd that phone call go?"

"I managed to pull it off. Thanks to you."

Natalie leans over to me as I pop a handful of pretzels into my mouth. "You're really pigging out there, aren't you?" she comments. "Try and leave some for the rest of us."

"I see someone left the gates open," I mutter under my breath. I study her botched blond dye job, as tacky as the rest of her look, and add, "Wow, Natalie, I didn't know brassy roots were in this season. Is trailer-trash chic back in style?"

Natalie scowls at me in return. "I'm surprised you have an opinion," she says. "Aren't you supposed to just be Kristen's little mouthpiece? Enjoy it while you can—she'll throw you away like she does everyone else soon enough."

"Hmm, shouldn't you be stocking up on more hooker heels?" I shoot back. I let my eyes travel down to the ones she has on and smirk. "Leopard print? Keeping it classy, I see."

She glares and makes an annoyed sound in the back of her throat, but it does the trick—she spins around and stalks off, wobbling. Whether that's due to her drunkenness or the height of her stupid heels, I can't be sure.

Brendon looks at me, miffed. "That was kind of rude."

"Me or her?" I ask.

"Both, actually."

"She started it," I reply. "Besides, maybe I'd be nicer to her if she dressed a little better." It would also help if she stayed away from Brendon and didn't get her slutty germs all over him. Natalie is the kind of girl who can give you an STD from eye contact alone.

"I think she dresses just fine."

Warren's voice from behind me makes me jump a little, and I whirl to see him standing there with Kristen and his friend Joey Morgan. Kristen smacks him hard on the shoulder, and Warren in turn grabs her in a greedy kiss, which she readily reciprocates. Gross. Those two are always slobbering all over each other. Get a room already.

"I don't know, man," Brendon says. "Personally I prefer something left to the imagination."

He winks at me, and the surge of butterflies in my stomach is so strong I think I may throw up right there. I need something to calm my nerves. The most obvious remedy is more alcohol. They don't call it liquid courage for nothing.

Two Jell-O shots later and I'm thinking about what Natalie said—about me being Kristen's mouthpiece. I know that's how I'm seen, and if I'm being honest with myself, it's kind of true. It's no secret that Kristen is the ringleader of our social group. The real thing that's bugging me is what she said about me being tossed aside. Being Kristen's friend is a balancing act, yes, but it's one I've pulled off for a few years; if she wanted to get rid of me, she would've by now.

I don't know why Natalie's stupid comment is annoying me so much. After all, it's *Natalie;* her opinion doesn't matter.

Brendon hands me another shot, and I notice his outstretched arm is a perfect golden tan.

"*God,* you're tan," I tell him, running my fingers over his wrist and marveling at the deep red-brown shade. His skin feels hot to the touch, and the butterflies in my stomach flutter again.

"Yeah." He laughs. "I spent Christmas in Miami with my grandparents."

"Oooh, nice!" I look at my own arm and cringe. "I'm so *pasty,*" I moan, and Kristen laughs.

"You're such a ginger," she says. She lowers her voice like she's confiding a secret. "Still, it could be worse. So I'm in the locker room before P.E. the other day, right? Steph Lidell comes in and starts changing right next to me, and she takes off her sweater, and I am, like, *blinded* by *orange.*"

This isn't news to me. Steph sits in front of me in Geometry, and whenever she passes back papers, I get a full view of her streaky orange hands. Still, I know better than to point out that it's totally old news. Kristen doesn't like being one-upped when she's telling a story.

"It's already bad enough that she has that fried, bleached-out hair, but a gross spray tan? *Really?*" Kristen shakes her head sadly. "It was horrible. I mean, she's like seven feet tall! So she's just this giant orange giraffe who smells bad. Like some weird combination of mustard and sweat or something. Seriously, I almost passed out." She laughs, then sighs and adds, "I swear, it was tragic."

"*Seriously* tragic," I agree, tipping the Jell-O shot back until it slides down my throat, weirdly warm and cold at the same time. These things are like ninety percent vodka. As it hits my stomach, I shake my head hard and grimace.

Joey claps me so hard on the back I nearly choke. "You drunk yet, Chelsea?"

Yes, actually, I am. More than a little. I turn around to face Joey, and the room spins around me. Maybe that last shot wasn't such a good idea. I'm really feeling it now.

Joey slides his hand up and hangs his arm loosely over my shoulders. I hope he doesn't think we're hooking up tonight. I've made out with him a few times, but never actually enjoyed it. Kristen keeps pushing me toward him, though, with the hope that if I start dating Warren's best friend we can all go out on double dates. I might be on board with this plan if I found Joey even remotely attractive, but to me he's just another beefy, boneheaded jock. He's definitely no Brendon Ryan. The fact that he's pulling me in under his sweaty armpit makes me want to puke.

No, wait, that's the alcohol.

"Um…" I shrug out from under Joey's grip. "I think I'm gonna—" I stop and clutch one hand over my swirling stomach.

My nausea must show in my face because Kristen laughs and says, "Oh, my God, if you puke on my carpet I'm going to be *so* pissed!"

Brendon looks at me, concerned. "Are you okay?"

"I'm fine," I insist. My stomach, however, does not agree. "I just need to… Bathroom. Bathroom would be good."

I bolt out of the room, shove past two juniors molesting each other on the staircase and take the steps two at a time. When I reach the top, I see a line of bored-looking girls outside the bathroom. Yeah, I don't know if I can wait that long. I'm definitely not willing to take the risk.

There's another bathroom in the guest room, I know, and Kristen won't mind if I use it. I rush to the end of the hallway and throw open the door without a second thought. Before I take more than a step in, I'm stopped in my tracks by what I see. Someone else is already in here.

Two someones.

I've never seen guys together. Not like this. The two boys are entangled, one lying on top of the other, panting hard. The dark-haired boy on top has his hand in the hair of the blond boy underneath him. The telltale sound of jeans being unzipped makes me gasp; the blond boy must hear it, because his head jerks up and his eyes meet mine, and I realize I know him. It's Noah Beckett. We're not friends, exactly, but we're in the same grade. I sat next to him in Spanish last year. He used to let me borrow his pencils, and now he's making out with some guy I don't recognize in my best friend's guest room.

Suddenly my nausea is the last thing on my mind.

I'm still processing the sight in front of me when Noah sits up, looking panicked. Instinct kicks in and I back out hastily, knocking my shoulder hard against the door frame. Noah calls after me, but I ignore him, stumble down the hallway and down the stairs, where I lean against the banister, trying to catch my breath.

Noah Beckett is gay? I never would've guessed. To me he was always just the kid who rides around on his skateboard in the school parking lot. I think he's on the soccer team or something. He's the kind of affable guy who hangs out with a lot of different groups and gets along with just about everyone. Who blends in with the crowd. I've never really noticed him before.

Well, I don't think I'll have a recognition problem now. "Feeling better?"

Brendon approaches me with a cautious smile, like he's afraid I'll hurl all over his shoes at any given moment. Not a total impossibility. At this rate, I'm pretty sure my hand on the banister is the only thing keeping me upright.

"Uh—" Why is it that I always sound like such an idiot around Brendon? Seriously, I am incapable of forming a complete sentence in his presence, even when I'm stone-cold sober. It's kind of pathetic. Okay, a lot pathetic. I breathe out and try to focus. "Where's Kristen?"

"In the kitchen, I think," he says. His brow furrows. "Is something wrong?"

"No," I say, "I just—I need to talk to her."

I find her in the kitchen surrounded by half of the basketball team. The guys are all rummaging through her cabinets looking for snacks. Kristen's lucky her parents are out of town; this place is going to be a disaster area come tomorrow morning. I'll probably have to help her clean it up, too. Somehow I'm the one who always ends up cleaning out the vomit-ridden toilet bowls.

"Kristen!" I say, louder than I mean to. Everyone's head swivels around to look at me as I wobble up to her on unsteady legs. Balance is a tricky concept at the moment.

Kristen looks up at me over her cup of beer, one part amused, one part embarrassed. "God, Chelsea, you're a hot mess." Which is pretty lame of her, because her cheeks are apple-red and her eyes are just glassy enough to let me know she's only a fraction less drunk off her ass than I am.

I ignore the insult and grab her arm urgently. "Kristen," I say again, "you're not going to *believe* what I just saw."

This catches her attention, and everyone else's. Warren

closes the refrigerator door and looks over at us, and Brendon comes up next to me. Joey hops off of the counter and crosses his arms. Everybody's gone quiet, wondering what I'm going to say. And really, this is the best gossip I've heard all year. Considering the year is less than an hour from being officially over, that's saying something.

I don't know what I expected to happen when I told everyone. I guess I thought it'd be a funny story, or at least a memorable one. It'd be the kind of thing where later, every so often someone could bring it up by saying, "Hey, remember when Chelsea walked in on Noah and that random guy macking on each other?" And that'd be the point where I'd jump in and give my firsthand account, and everyone would be both amused and scandalized, and maybe Brendon would be bowled over by my charismatic storytelling skills and declare his undying love for me on the spot. Or something.

I didn't realize Kristen would have the reaction she does—which is less laughing and more one of extreme disgust, like I just told her that her guest room has a cockroach infestation. Once I spill the details, she gives a full-body shudder, mouth hanging open with a mixture of shock and revulsion.

"Oh, my God. Oh, my *God! Ew!*" she exclaims, appalled. "He got *fag* all over my *sheets!*" She says it like being gay is a highly contagious epidemic or something. My stomach drops, and I open my mouth to say something.

Before I can, Derek Connelly, the team's small forward, laughs. "That dude?" he says. "Seriously?"

Warren stalks over to us, one fist clamped tight around a bottle of beer and the other clenched at his side. "Whatthefuck?" he slurs. Redness creeps up his neck and flushes his whole face. "That fucking— I swear— I'm gonna—" He doesn't finish the thought, but somehow I don't think the rest of that sentence would be "give him a hug." Warren is about as af-fectionate as he is articulate.

"Seriously. What. The. Fuck," Joey echoes, useless as al-ways.

"Who was he even *with?*" Kristen asks me.

"I… I don't know," I say uneasily. "I don't think the other guy goes to our school." This conversation is not going the way I imagined it would.

"Who the fuck does he think he is?" Warren growls. He wipes the sweat off his upper lip with the side of his fist. "All right, where's the fag? I'm gonna go talk to him."

"Fucking right," Joey agrees.

The two of them push their way out of the kitchen and head for the staircase. I trail after them and manage to catch up halfway through the living room, nearly bowling over five people in the process.

"You guys, don't." I reach out, snagging Warren's shoulder.

Except because I'm so trashed, I stumble and almost fall down. Joey and a few other people see and laugh. Brendon, though. Brendon isn't laughing.

"Look," I say, "they're leaving anyway. Just leave them alone, okay?"

I point to where I can spot Noah's shock of white-blond hair. He hurries to the front door, red-faced, with a cute black-haired boy behind him. The black-haired boy seems to be dragging his feet, intent on going at a leisurely pace, his fingers wrapped around Noah's wrist as they move through the throng of people packed at the bottom of the staircase. Noah stops and says something to him, the words impossible to make out over the music and the conversation. The boy says something back, and Noah frowns, tugging the boy's hand, and they disappear through the door together.

The irony is that if I hadn't been drinking, I probably wouldn't have spoken up at all—not right there in front of anyone; I would've waited until it was just Kristen and me alone. And I definitely wouldn't have touched Warren—he's not the kind of guy you pal around with.

Of course, if I hadn't been drinking, I wouldn't have needed to find a bathroom so badly and I wouldn't have seen what I did.

Warren shakes me off with a scowl, and I fall sideways into Kristen, who laughs and props me up against the wall.

"You're *sooooo* drunk," she says. "Oh, my God."

"They're fucking holding hands? Shit." Warren spits into his plastic red cup—so many kinds of gross—before he nods at Joey and says, "You coming?"

And Joey says, "Fuck, yeah," because Joey is an idiot.

"You guys." I push myself off the wall. "You guys, seriously. Don't. Just leave it, okay? Okay?"

"Don't worry," says Warren, "all we're gonna do is teach them a little lesson." But his smile is all wrong, twisted, and there's something else in his voice, too, warning me not to push it.

And so I don't. Because it's easier. It's easier to let them go.

My plans to have Brendon sweep me off my feet at the stroke of midnight are thwarted when my nausea catches up to me, and I instead ring in the New Year vomiting my guts out in the bathroom. I must pass out sometime after that, because I wake up the next morning curled around the base of the toilet the same way you'd curl yourself around another person. Kristen didn't even think to wake me up and help me into the bedroom, and now I have a sore hip and a crick in my neck. Not to mention a severe case of dry mouth.

I use the counter to pull myself to my feet then turn on the tap. As I scoop the cold water with both hands and splash it over my face, I try to piece together exactly what happened last night. I remember Warren and Joey taking off, but everything after that is a little fuzzy. It's kind of freaking me out; I've never gotten that drunk before. Never to the point where I can't remember what happened the next day.

Things start to come back to me when I rub my face dry with the thick terry-cloth towel hanging on the rack. Kristen cajoling me into one more shot even though I was already falling-down drunk; jumping up on her coffee table to dance until I fell off and landed on some freshman girl; Brendon— oh, God. Brendon. I'm pretty sure I totally threw myself at him in the most embarrassing manner possible.

"Yup, you totally did," Kristen informs me cheerfully after I've managed to stumble down to the kitchen and collapse in the nearest chair. She sets a mug of water and two Advil in front of me—which for Kristen is as considerate as she gets. "You kept rubbing up on him and babbling about how hot his box of mints is. He was so weirded out. It was pretty hilarious."

"I'm sure," I mutter. It would've been nice if Kristen had intervened to spare me the humiliation, but I guess she was too busy getting a kick out of the situation.

She picks up the empty beer bottles littered on the table and takes them to the sink. "Cheer up," she tells me. "At least you weren't *abandoned* by your supposed *boyfriend*."

An unsettled feeling twists in my gut. "He didn't come back last night?"

"No," she scoffs. "Fucking jerk. Probably went off to hot-box his truck with Joey. I swear—" She's cut off by her phone

on the counter ringing. She grabs it with a sigh. "That's probably him. He better *grovel*."

While she takes the call I swallow the Advil, downing all
of the water in the mug in a few long gulps. My head is totally throbbing. I feel like death warmed over. No, scratch
that. Like death left out on the counter for two days and then
reheated in the microwave for thirty seconds. That's exactly
how I feel.

There's an issue of *National Geographic* lying half-open on
the table. I pick it up and leaf through it idly. I'm not a big
recreational-reader type, other than celebrity gossip blogs and
Us Weekly, but Kristen's a talker, and I'm sure she'll be arguing with Warren for a while before he gives in and promises to buy her something shiny in exchange for bailing. The
magazine is open to a striking photo of an old Buddhist monk
swathed in a yellow robe kneeling in prayer. Below the picture is a profile on the monk, who'd taken a vow of silence
and hadn't spoken a word in sixty years. I guess the idea was
that by not speaking and staying in a constant state of con-
templation, it made him closer to God, or enlightenment,
or whatever.

I'm too preoccupied skimming the article and nursing my
hangover to eavesdrop on Kristen's conversation, but then
she lets out an especially sharp *"What?"* that makes me snap
to attention. When I look at her, she's speechless, eyes wide
and mouth hanging open. But she turns her back to me and
lowers her voice so I can't hear whatever it is she says next.
It isn't until she hangs up the phone and drops into the seat
next to me, the shocked expression etched into her features,
that I get an answer out of her.

"What's going on?" I demand.

She drags her eyes off the phone in her hand and meets my gaze. "Noah Beckett is in the hospital," she tells me.

"Wait, are you serious?" Kristen just nods, and my mouth goes dry again. I wrap my hands around my empty mug and ask, "What the hell happened?"

"He was in the parking lot of the Quality Mart, and he… he got beat up really bad," she says. She pauses for a long time. "I guess he's unconscious."

My heart kind of stops, thinking about Noah like that. Who would do that to him? And then I realize.

I don't want to ask the question because I'm so afraid I already know the answer, but I have to. "Did Warren and Joey do it?"

Kristen doesn't say anything, but she doesn't have to. The look on her face says it all.

"Oh, my God," I breathe, slumping back in my chair. "Oh, my *God*." I cover my mouth with one hand. "I thought they were just going to talk to him!"

"You can't say anything." Kristen's tone has a careful edge to it.

"But—"

"I mean it," she says, more emphatically this time. "I'm not kidding. If anyone asks, nothing happened. You don't know anything. Got it?"

I stare down at the open magazine, but the words there are a jumbled mess. I can't wrap my mind around this. I'm an expert at finding out secrets, but keeping them —especially a secret of this magnitude—is something else.

"Yeah, I got it," I say. "Nothing happened."

Except I know better. We both do. Warren and Joey are behind this. They have to be.

Kristen wants me to pretend like last night never happened. Like I should just push it out of my mind and ignore the fact that her boyfriend put a boy in the hospital. I drive home in a daze, trying to do just that. But no matter how loud I crank the radio, I can't escape my thoughts, and they keep circling back to Noah. What the hell was Warren thinking? I know he was kind of drunk, and I know that he's not the nicest guy under sober conditions, but still.

I promised Kristen I wouldn't say anything. If I do, I'm going to be in so much trouble—a kind of trouble I can't even fathom. My parents will kill me. Kristen will disown me. Everyone will hate me. Besides, why should *I* have to be the one to rat them out? There were other people at that party who heard my story about Noah, who saw Warren and Joey get mad and leave. They have to know. Or they will, soon enough, once word spreads about what happened. So why should the responsibility to tell fall on *my* shoulders?

All the rationalizing in the world isn't making me feel better about this decision.

Mom's doing dishes when I walk into the kitchen. Dad sits at the table, reading the newspaper. It's so perfectly normal I want to cry. I lean against the doorway and watch them, swallowing against the crater-size lump lodged in my throat.

"How was your night, kiddo?" asks Dad.

I shrug one shoulder. "Fine," I lie.

"You're awfully quiet," Mom says. She wrings the sponge and raises an eyebrow at me. "Did you get the milk?"

Oh, shit. I totally did not even remember she asked me to pick that up.

"Sorry," I mumble, rubbing my forehead with one hand. My head is *killing* me. "I forgot about it."

"Chelsea." Mom sighs. "I ask you for *one* thing, and you can't even—"

"I *forgot,* okay?" I snap. "*God.* I said I was sorry."

Dad shakes out his newspaper and lays it flat on the table. "Don't worry about it," he says, standing up and coming over to me. He plants a kiss on the top of my head, and I hold my breath, hoping the three mouthwash rinses and obscene amount of Kristen's perfume I doused myself with are enough to mask any lingering smell of alcohol.

It must be, because he doesn't comment on it. "I can make a grocery run," he offers. Always the peacemaker.

Mom sighs again, louder this time, and I take it as my cue to slink upstairs without further interrogation. I shut the door and toss my purse onto my bed. The issue of *National Geographic* comes tumbling out—I snuck it in my bag before I left Kristen's. I couldn't ask to borrow it because she'd think I was a freak, but I really did want to finish reading that article about the monk.

I flop down on my bed and fumble through the pages until I find it. Being silent for sixty years—I can't fathom it. Hell, I can't fathom being silent for sixty *days.* Even sixty minutes would be tough. This monk guy, his silence is used to better himself. My silence about Noah—it's the opposite. It's because I'm a coward.

I don't want to think about this anymore, but even when I pull a pillow over my head and squeeze my eyes shut, I'm consumed with the memory of Noah's eyes, the way they'd been filled with shock when I opened that bedroom door, and then panic as he realized what I'd caught him doing. And with whom. I wonder if that's the same look he had when Warren and Joey kicked the shit out of him in that parking lot.

When I found Noah—them—on the bed together, Noah's

mouth had opened like he was going to say something, but I'd turned and hightailed it back downstairs as quickly as possible. Maybe he was going to say "Wait," maybe he was going to ask me not to say anything about what I'd seen. Or maybe he wasn't going to say anything at all, realizing that kind of request was futile, even if I was there to hear it.

After all, everyone knows Chelsea Knot doesn't know how to keep her mouth shut.

I go to pull another pillow over my head, but my hand instead curls around my ratty stuffed dog, Nelly. It's pretty lame to sleep with a stuffed animal when you're sixteen, but I never could bring myself to get rid of her when I finally became too old for toys. Dad gave her to me when I was seven years old and had to get my tonsils out. I hug Nelly tight to my chest, smoothing out her matted gray cotton fur with one hand.

Yeah, I can do this. I can play dumb like Kristen said. No one has to hear it from me. I can stay quiet, even if no one else steps forward. Even if it means Warren and Joey get away with this. Even if Noah never wakes up.

What if he doesn't? And what if no one points the finger at Warren and Joey? If that happens, can I really live with myself?

I already know the answer to that. I lie there for a while with Nelly tucked under my chin, trying in vain to come up with other options, some way out of this that leaves me unscathed, but they all circle around to the same conclusion. Kristen'll be furious with me, I know it, but...but she'll understand. She has to understand. I can't *not* say anything.

The walk downstairs is like trudging down the Green Mile. Mom and Dad are in the living room, cozied up on the couch watching television.

"Mom?" I say, voice shaking. "Dad?"

They both twist around to look at me, and their expressions of content transform into identical looks of worry. It'd almost be funny if it were any other situation.

Dad mutes the television. "What is it, honey?" he asks.

I take a deep breath. It's now or never.

"I have to tell you something."

THREE DAYS LATER

day one

RAT.

   The word is scratched across my locker in fat black marker for everyone to see, lettered in abrupt, messy slashes, like whoever wrote it didn't even pause, didn't have to think twice about what they were doing. I can feel the eyes of everyone in the hall boring into my back; hear their titters behind me, providing the soundtrack to my humiliation. Blood rushes up to my face and turns my pale skin as red as my hair. The familiar hot prick of tears stings behind my eyes, waiting for their cue to spill over.

   Well. This semester is gonna suck.

   I stand there and stare at the new label I've been branded with, forcing myself to suck in deep breaths through my nose in the vain hope it will help subside the urge to burst into tears. I can't say anything. The article, folded neatly and tucked in my front pocket, is a constant reminder.

   In an effort to keep myself from crying, I start reciting times tables in my head, except I suck at multiplication and lose track by the time I get to four times six. Okay. We'll go with the prompt: rat. List all animals that start with the letter R. Rabbits, raccoons, roaches, rhinos, rams, ringworms, roosters, rottweilers (do dog breeds count?), reindeer...oh, and can't forget red hawks—like the Grand Lake High Red Hawk. Our school mascot. Is there even such a thing as a red hawk? I'm dubious. If there is, I've never seen one in Michigan. Whatever. The Red Hawks, our basketball team, are definitely animals, and I'm making up the rules, so I say it counts.

This little game does the trick, and once I'm confident in my ability to stave off the tears, I calmly spin my combination into the lock and pop it open. My geometry book is right where it should be, on the top shelf, so I slide it into my backpack and shut the door. Everyone is looking at me, waiting for my reaction. They probably think I'm about to collapse into sobs and have a meltdown of epic proportions. Part of me is dying to do just that, but I know it's exactly what they want; they're hungry for it. That is, after all, the goal of a public shaming. Everyone loves kicking the popular girl the second she's been knocked off the pedestal.

No way am I giving them the satisfaction. These are the same people who two weeks ago envied me and clamored for my attention, and now I'm supposed to, what? Get on my knees and beg for their forgiveness? Embrace the role of whipping girl they've designated for me? That is so not happening. Their opinion of me never mattered before, and it's not going to matter now. Nothing has changed. I'm still the same Chelsea Knot. Bow down, bitches.

I stride down the hall with my chin tipped up defiantly, ignoring the pressing stares. As I come up to the corner, at the edge of my vision I see Kristen huddled with a few other girls. I can't help but slow down and sneak a glance. Since school started up again, she's studiously avoided me, and I stopped trying to call after leaving her a week's worth of pleading voice mails that went unanswered. I've tried telling myself that it's only time she needs, that maybe the shock of her boyfriend's arrest hasn't worn off yet, and once it does, she won't hate me for doing what I did. She'll understand. We're best friends.

When I approach, she looks the way she always does: immaculately put together, with every strand of her glossy blond hair perfectly in place, her makeup flawlessly applied. She's wearing this creamy cable-knit sweater matched with a black skirt, more modest than her usual wardrobe, and when she sees me, I catch her midsmile. Her expression is almost demure. For a brief, shining second I think it's going to be okay. She's going to be on my side.

But then her face changes as she sees me. God, that *look*. She's staring at me like I'm a bug she'd squash under her heel if it wouldn't make such a mess.

She levels an icy glare at me as I pass and sneers. "What are you looking at, bitch?"

And that's it. The final judgment. She might as well have stamped *SCUM* on my forehead.

The other girls around her giggle nervously, Tessa and Natalie among them. Now that I'm out of the picture, the pecking order has changed. They'll all be vying for my old rank. I wonder which one of them will be bestowed the honor.

What everyone else thinks doesn't matter, but what Kristen thinks does. I can't pretend otherwise. I knew she'd be mad, but I also thought she wouldn't throw so many years of friendship out the window. But that look on her face...my slim hope that her anger wouldn't last dissipates, crushed to dust in some imaginary fist.

Tears, again. I fight them down and hurry around the corner without a word. At least I know where Kristen and I stand for good. Kristen, my supposed best friend. Former, now, I guess. What was I thinking? Warren is her boyfriend. I told the cops what he and Joey said at the party, after they found out about Noah from me. What they said about teaching him a lesson. And now they've both been arrested. It doesn't matter if it was the right thing to do or not. Of course she hates me.

I should've expected this. I really did expect it, on some level. I just didn't realize it was going to be so hard.

Mr. Callihan gives me a funny look when I hand him the note before class.

"A vow of silence?" he says dryly.

I nod, fiddling with the strap of my bag. Mr. Callihan has never liked me much, but that's okay because I don't like geometry, either. It's my worst subject, and the most boring. I typically sit in the back next to Megan and talk to her as much as I can before Mr. Callihan threatens me with detention. My hope is he'll be so keen on the prospect of me shutting up during his lectures that he won't ask a million questions about why I'm keeping quiet. The last thing I want to do is try to explain. It's why I came prepared with the note.

"Well." He sighs. "You're lucky I don't grade on class participation."

I take my usual seat next to Megan, who is diligently copying down the warm-up problems in her notebook, all of her attention focused on what she's writing. She glances at me as I swing my backpack onto my desk, and then just as quickly averts her eyes again. I know she has to have heard what happened; everyone has. It even made the front page of the *Grand Lake Tribune*. Sure, the article didn't include the dirty details or mention me by name, but too many people witnessed my scene in Kristen's kitchen to keep my role in everything under wraps, and I'm sure Kristen didn't hesitate to fill in the blanks with her own revisionist history designed to paint her in the most flattering light. And I know the gossip grapevine well enough to know how fast that story would've traveled.

Geometry goes okay, all things considered. Everyone acts like I'm invisible, which isn't so surprising. All of my friends hate me now for turning in two of our own, and everyone else hated me already. The few who didn't have no doubt heard the story and blame me for what happened to Noah. Mr. Callihan doesn't call on me, but when the bell rings and I pack up my stuff, I can tell he's watching.

Invisible is preferable to what I get in next period, American Lit. Mrs. Finch is far less accommodating of my voluntary silence. When I show her my note at the beginning of class, she sends me straight to the guidance counselor, Ms. Davidson.

The only time I've ever set foot in Ms. Davidson's office was to fix my schedule—freshman year I'd picked French for my mandatory language credit without consulting Kristen, who'd chosen Spanish, so I went and convinced Ms. Davidson to let me switch over. Even though I'd been kind of excited about taking French, imagining that one day I would utilize it while showing my spring collection during Paris Fashion Week, it was more important to share as many classes with Kristen as possible. High school was now; my career in fashion design would come later, and there was always Rosetta Stone.

Ms. Davidson sits behind her desk and reads the note I provide, *hmm*-ing under her breath. She's quiet for a while, longer than what's necessary to read my explanation. Poor Ms. Davidson. I can tell she's mentally reviewing all of her training and schooling to see if there's something she's learned that is applicable to my situation, some proper protocol for dealing with the voluntarily mute. I'm pretty sure they don't make pamphlets for that.

"Chelsea," she says finally, "what is it you hope to accomplish with this?"

I shrug one shoulder and stare up at the ceiling. Even if I could explain it to her, I don't want to. She wouldn't understand. I don't know what the big deal is. No one wants to hear what I have to say anyway. Not Kristen, not my teachers. Not even my parents. After I explained to them what happened that night, they looked so completely let down by me I thought I would be crushed under the weight of their combined disappointment.

Running my mouth has hurt enough people already—the least I can do is shut up. Why can't everyone see I'm doing the world a favor?

Ms. Davidson sets my note down on her desk and folds her hands on top of it. "Well, I can't force you to talk to me," she says. "But this kind of behavior is unhealthy and unacceptable. And unreasonable. You can't shut out the world. Your teachers need to you to communicate." She pauses. "I'll have to speak to your parents about this. In the meantime, you should return to class."

I can't help but smile a little in triumph as she writes me a hall pass. I may not have won the war yet, but I've won this battle.

She hands over the pass and says, "If you ever want to talk, my door is always open."

Yeah, that'll happen.

Back in class, Mrs. Finch calls on me to answer some question about *Of Mice and Men* and symbolism or something. Not only do I not know the answer, but even if I did, she already knows I'm not going to say it out loud. So I sit there and look at her and do nothing.

"Chelsea," she says warningly, and everyone in the class starts whispering, like, *ohmygodlookathersheissuchafreak*. Finally she sighs. "I'm issuing you a detention," she informs me, and the murmurings grow louder.

I haven't had detention since freshman year when I got caught cheating off Ashley Ziegler's algebra exam. And Mondays are the days of meetings for the school paper, right after school—I've been a contributor since the start of this year. Mrs. Finch knows that; she's the one who runs the meetings. She's a stickler for attendance. Miss one meeting and you're booted from the staff, unless you're on your deathbed or something.

I guess this means I can say goodbye to my one extracurricular activity. Dammit. I open my mouth to protest, and then promptly shut it again. Whatever. I don't *need* to work on the paper, even if I really like doing it. I'll find something else to occupy my free time. I'm not letting her—or anyone else—get to me.

She signals for me to come up to her desk. I stand there, ramrod-straight, holding out my hand as I wait for her to write up the detention slip. Once she's handed it to me, I take it and march back to my seat, leveling a defiant glare at everyone who stares. Of course, now that my weird silent freak status has been established, people don't hold back. Whenever Mrs. Finch turns her back to the class, rubber erasers go flying, bouncing off my head and shoulders. I don't have to turn around to know where the assault is coming from. Derek and Lowell are both on the basketball team, too. They were at the party. They know what happened.

When class ends, Lowell walks by and shoves the books

and papers off my desk. I don't know why someone wrote *RAT* on my locker when Lowell is the one who looks like a rodent. Beady eyes and pointy nose and thin mouth. The only reason anyone gives him the time of day is because he can shoot a stupid basketball and always knows where to score the best weed.

"Finally decided to keep your mouth shut, huh?" he says with that rodent smirk.

I shoot a quick glance to Mrs. Finch, but she's sitting at her computer, clacking away on the keyboard, totally oblivious. Even if she was looking, she wouldn't be able to tell anything out of the ordinary was going on. It would look like I was talking with friends, Lowell leaning his palm casually on my desk, Derek flanking my other side. I'm trapped.

"We all know your mouth's only good for one thing," Derek chimes in, "and it's definitely not talking."

I'm kind of taken aback, despite everything, because— because Derek was my friend. Yeah, Lowell's always been a creep, but Derek's always been a decent guy when he's not hanging around getting high or drunk with Lowell and Warren and Joey. We run in the same circles. He's the kind of guy who wouldn't mind if I copied his homework or asked to borrow a pencil, someone I'd wave hello to when we crossed paths in the halls. I even helped set him up with Allie Dupree last year after I figured out he was crushing hard on her and he asked me to find out if the feeling was mutual.

And now he's standing in front of me with the cruelest smile I've ever seen. Carelessly cruel, which is maybe why it hurts the way it does. I train my gaze straight ahead and sit statue still.

Lowell shoves his face in front of mine so I have no choice but to look at him. "I think Derek's right," he says, all mock serious and wide-eyed. "Hey, maybe at lunch, you can come by our table and suck my dick. Then Derek's. Then everyone else's. Think you owe that much to the team after costing us our two best players, don't you?"

If I were speaking, I'd retort that the very idea makes me want to vomit, and inform them that contrary to popular belief, guys *do* talk, and from well-placed locker room sources, I am aware that neither have impressive dick sizes anyway. I'd watch that comment land and saunter away, secure with the knowledge I'd one-upped them both.

But I'm not speaking, and I'm not used to being on the receiving end of this kind of harassment, and after everything else—my locker, Kristen, the detention—I'm not equipped to fight back. It's taking every ounce of resolve I have not to crumble under their sleazy smirks.

I will not cry. I will not cry. Dammit.

Derek and Lowell laugh, and I carefully stand up, collect my papers and shove everything in my bag. I don't look back as I walk out, and I don't stop walking until I'm in the bathroom, locked in the second stall. I sit on top of the toilet seat, drawing my bag onto my lap and wrapping my arms around it. My whole body shakes.

All I want to do is scream, but I can't. I can't. I made a promise to myself. Talking is what led to this mess in the first place. If I hadn't said anything, no one would have found out Noah is gay, and Warren and Joey wouldn't have beat him unconscious. If I hadn't said anything to the cops, they wouldn't have been expelled and arrested, and I'd still have all my friends. My biggest worry would be the state of my hair at this point in the morning, or what I should use as the topic of my next column in the school paper, not wondering how I will possibly survive the rest of this semester.

I close my eyes and take deep breaths as the door swings open and two girls come in, chatting away about a Spanish grade, unaware of my presence.

"Hey, did you hear about Chelsea Knot?" one of the girls suddenly says. I recognize that voice; it's Allie Dupree, Derek's girlfriend. I hold my breath and listen hard.

"No," the other girl says. "What about her?"

"Derek's in one of her classes, and I guess she's refusing to talk. Like, at all," Allie explains. "She's like a mute or something now."

"She probably just thinks she's too good to speak to anyone," the other girl says.

"Wow, you really don't like her."

"Chelsea Knot is a total bitch." The words ring a little louder than they normally would, bouncing off the tile floor and walls. "She's the one who told everyone that time I got my period and stained my jeans. It was mortifying."

I vaguely recall this incident, but cannot for the life of me remember the name of the girl. My stomach twists and I try to push the feeling down. It's not my fault the girl made the mistake of wearing white jeans that week. Besides, it was *funny*. Can't she take a joke?

"She's so stuck-up, always acting like she's better than everyone else in this school," the girl whose name I don't remember continues.

"Except for Kristen Courteau," Allie points out. "Any farther up Kristen's ass and she'd be able to see her tonsils."

"Poor Kristen," the other girl coos. "I can't believe all that happened at her house."

They continue talking, but their voices fade as they exit the bathroom, the door swinging closed behind them. I release a long, shuddery breath, willing my heart to stop beating so fast in my chest. Part of me wants to race after them and tell the two of them off, but the larger part of me is rooted to the spot, unable to move, and relieved they didn't realize I was in here the whole time.

I guess I should get used to this feeling of being invisible. Almost everyone's acting like I don't exist at all, and the people who've acknowledged me—well, I wish they hadn't. For once in my life, I wish everyone would just forget about me.

Ms. Kinsey is totally that cliché free-spirit art teacher you're always seeing in movies. You know, with the crazy long curly hair and hippie skirts and Birkenstocks, and when it's warm, she takes us outside to sit on the grass and sketch trees and shit. Last year a rumor went around that she's a lesbian. I didn't believe it until this one time Kristen and I went to the dollar theater across town and saw her there, holding hands with this really tall, willowy woman with short hair. Kristen thought it was both hilarious and gross, and spent an entire week cracking lesbian jokes at Ms. Kinsey's expense.

Ms. Kinsey is a freak show, but she's not so bad compared to my other teachers. I mean, she's totally ridiculous and over-the-top, but even though she's been teaching at Grand Lake for a long time, she's not jaded and bitter like most of the veterans. And she's always nice to me, even after I almost started a fire with the kiln last year in Intro to Ceramics. I'm not great with pottery, but I do enjoy drawing; I spend enough time sketching out different outfit ideas in my free time to pull out a halfway decent rendering of a flower vase or a bowl of fruit when necessary. Of course, Ms. Kinsey grades on such a wide curve that my actual skill doesn't matter anyway. If I could ace Ceramics with my lopsided candle holders, I can no doubt pass General Art Studies. I can tolerate Ms. Kinsey's obnoxious hippie persona in exchange for an easy grade.

I duck into the art room early, not wanting to linger in the halls and risk running into Kristen or Derek or Lowell or anyone else interested in making my life a living hell. It's a long list. Going to the cafeteria for lunch was like being behind enemy lines. Everywhere I turned, there was someone glaring or pointing and whispering. I ended up sitting at the table where the Special Ed kids eat, and even they ignored me. Talk about humiliating.

Art is one of my only new classes. Last semester I had Keyboarding, a subject so tedious the only reason I didn't kill myself to spare me the agony of Mr. Newkirk's monotone was that I had Kristen to talk to. Thankfully she's not taking art. No one I am—was—friends with is, as far as I know. At least I hope.

The art room is empty when I get there, save for Ms. Kinsey, who is erasing a chalk depiction of a pineapple off the board. This is the only room in the school equipped with an old-fashioned chalkboard; every other classroom has one of those glossy white dry-erase boards.

"Good afternoon, Chelsea!" she chirps pleasantly. So pleasantly I'm actually startled. "It's good to see you. How are you doing today?"

Terrible. Horrible. Like I want to crawl under a rock and die.

Ms. Kinsey flashes me one of her full-on, thousand kilowatt sunny smiles. She's the first person today to look like she's glad to see me, and I feel a sudden, unexpected surge of gratitude toward her.

I smile a little and shrug, digging through my bag for my note. I can't find it—though I do come across the detention

slip and mentally berate Mrs. Finch for being such an up-
tight bitch. Finally I walk up to the blackboard and take a
piece of chalk.

I can't talk.

Ms. Kinsey frowns. "Oh, what's the problem? Are you
sick? Is it laryngitis?"

I shake my head and write on the board again.

I've taken a vow of silence.

I turn to see her reaction. She reads what I've written and
then looks at me again, smiling.

"That's very interesting," she says, and she sounds like she
actually *does* find it interesting, not like she's mocking me.
"What inspired this?"

I pull the *National Geographic* article from my pocket and
hand it to her. She unfolds it, eyes scanning the wrinkled page,
before her face lights up like the Fourth of July.

"Brilliant idea, Chelsea!" she exclaims. "I think it's great
that you're on this voyage of self-discovery. If more people
strove for spiritual enlightenment, the world would be a much
better place for it." She squeezes my shoulder with one chalky
hand. Even though she's totally off base (I'm not exactly sure
what "striving for spiritual enlightenment" entails, really),
after a day of no one being nice to me, I could just hug her
anyway. Which is proof that I am totally losing it.

Other students start filtering into the classroom. I hastily
wipe off the board and make a beeline for one of the workstations. The good thing about art class is that it is devoid of
jocks and most populars. I'm here only because it's the easiest
elective available, and it sure as hell beats Shop (such a mis-
leading title!) or Personal Finance (my only interest in money
is spending it, not budgeting it).

If previous experience is any indication, the art freaks will be too consumed with fostering their existential angst and crafting abstract pieces out of coat hangers, Styrofoam, magazine cutouts and black paint (to symbolize their dark, tortured souls, of course) to heed me any attention. A few weeks ago I was comparing schedules with my friends and lamenting the fact that none of them had this class, but considering my new circumstances, I'm relieved. The tardy bell rings, and I think maybe, just *maybe,* I'll finally be able to actually relax.

And then Sam Weston walks into the room.

My heart plummets to my feet, and for an awful moment I am convinced I am going to either pass out or throw up in front of everyone. I've been so preoccupied worrying about Kristen and the others that I hadn't even thought to prepare myself for running into Sam. Sam, who I don't know a lot about, but the one thing I do know is that he is best friends with Noah.

He rubs a hand over his rumpled, wavy dark hair and scans the room from behind his black framed glasses, searching for a seat. I do the same, realizing with growing dread that the only space available is at my workstation. When he catches up to my realization, his gaze flicks to mine for a second, and I look away, silently willing him to sit somewhere else, *anywhere* else. It doesn't work. My avoidance of eye contact doesn't deter him from walking over and setting his backpack on the seat next to mine.

Why? Why is this happening to me?

Oh, right, because God hates me and wants me to suffer. Obviously..

I'm careful to keep my eyes on my sketchpad as Ms. Kinsey explains our first assignment. We're supposed to imitate another artist's style. Awesome. Who am I supposed to at-

tempt, Monet? Van Gogh? That'd be nothing short of a train
wreck. Maybe the flower lady—what's her name? Oh, right,
Georgia O'Keefe. Yes, that's exactly what I should do. Paint
big flowers that look like vaginas. It's not like I haven't already alienated myself from the student body enough. Why
not go for broke?

It's less nauseating to think about flowery vaginas than it is
to focus on what I am so acutely aware of—Sam's very, very
near proximity. But as Ms. Kinsey drones on (and on, and on,
and on), I can't help but wonder if he's going to try anything.
At any moment he could make a nasty comment, tell me to
fuck off and die, or do something worse, like mess with my
stuff. Or with me. The art room has plenty of arsenal: scissors,
permanent markers, superglue, X-Acto knives. Oh, God, I
didn't even *think* about X-Acto knives. I'm going to have to
channel Jason Bourne now if I want to survive high school.
Assess the situation! Know your exits! Everything is a weapon!

If I'm lucky, Sam'll just give me the cold shoulder like everyone else. Even though I don't know him very well—or
at all, really, aside from sharing a few choice classes over the
years—he's never come across as a particularly potent brand
of douche bag. But then, neither did Derek, so what do I
know about anything?

When Sam's elbow accidentally knocks against mine, I
nearly jump out of my skin. So much for playing it cool. He
glances at me with big blue eyes, clearly surprised by my crazy
overreaction, but doesn't say anything. I blush and try to re
turn my attention to whatever Ms. Kinsey's still discussing.

"…and four weeks from now we'll have the presentations,"
she says.

Oh, right, the project. I'm looking forward to it so much I
could just shoot myself in the face in anticipation. Ms. Kinsey

beams brightly at me, and I struggle to look less outwardly like I feel, which at the moment is borderline suicidal.

"So why don't you go ahead and partner up, and you can start deciding who you want to choose as your subject."

Wait. Partners? What?

Please, please, *please* tell me I heard that wrong.

I didn't. Everyone in the classroom shuffles around, making the migration to other workstations, meeting up with the partners they arranged via silent hand signals and elbow nudging during Ms. Kinsey's ramble. Everyone except me, of course. And, oddly enough, Sam. I notice he hasn't moved from his spot. Doesn't he have friends?

I try to remember who I've seen him with in the past. Noah, mostly. And I know they hung out with a lot of groups, but I can't think of any specific one—they're not art freaks, or super academics, or straight edge, or burnouts. I've seen them both skateboarding, but they don't hang out with the skaters, either. *Definitely* not the jocks, even though Noah plays soccer. They just…floated from group to group. Somehow they still managed to be friends with practically everyone. Cool but still accessible. Which is the reason Noah was allowed to come to the party in the first place.

I chance a glance at Sam as he drums his fingers on the countertop. He sees me watching and stops abruptly.

"Uh…" he starts to say. He looks everywhere else before he settles his gaze on me, and then he does the hair rubbing thing again, like it's a nervous tic. "It looks like everyone else paired off. Guess that leaves us."

Sam doesn't look happy about it, but he isn't looking at me like he wants to stab me in the face with his pencil, either, which isn't something I can claim with the least bit of confidence for anyone else in this class. If he can handle this, so can I.

He flicks open his sketchbook to a fresh page. I notice there are a bunch of other drawings on the ones before it, but he flips past them too fast for me to see what they are.

"I don't know if you had any ideas," he says, "but I was thinking maybe something more modern. Like Salvador Dali." He writes the name down on the pad.

I'm not really crazy about the idea of recreating dream-scapes with melting clock faces—that is way beyond my skill level—so I make an apathetic face at the suggestion.

Sam notices my unenthused expression and mutters, "Or not," crossing out the name sharply. He drops the pen onto the sketchpad and looks me straight in the eye. "You know, I realize this isn't exactly a dream collaboration for either of us, but it'd be nice if you'd contribute a little something more than a judgmental glare."

I'm considering how to respond to this without actually responding when Ms. Kinsey flutters over to our station. She looks over Sam's shoulder at our blank page of brainstorms.

"Need any help?" she asks.

We both shake our heads.

"Think we can handle it," he tells her, but he doesn't sound like he believes it.

"I just want you to know," she says to me, "that I am very much willing to work around your spiritual commitment. All I ask is that you find another way to participate if you aren't going to speak. Use your imagination! Be creative!"

From the way she says it, I can only assume she's expecting me to break into an interpretive dance for our presentation. Which is just not going to happen in this lifetime. Or any other.

I give her a thumbs-up that far overstates my enthusiasm for her suggestion, and Sam looks at me with raised eyebrows.

"'Spiritual commitment'?" he echoes, bemused.

"You didn't tell him?" Ms. Kinsey says. "Well, of course you didn't *tell* him!" She laughs at her own joke, turning to Sam with a big smile. "Chelsea here has taken an oath of silence."

"You've—*what?*" He gapes at me like a floundering fish, processing this piece of information, and then turns to Ms. Kinsey. "How am I supposed to do a project with someone who won't talk?"

"There are many forms of communication," she says airily. "I know you'll find a way to make it work while still respecting her spiritual beliefs." She pats him on the shoulder, sauntering off as he stares after her with an annoyed look.

I grab the pen from him, scratch out a sentence on the clean sheet and hold up the pad.

I'm silent, not stupid.

"Yeah, okay, if you say so." He snatches back the notebook. "Let's just get this over with."

We spend the rest of the period going back and forth, trying to brainstorm artists, Sam voicing his ideas and me writing down mine. He doesn't once stray from the topic at hand, and I'm certainly not about to bring Noah's name into the conversation. Sam was right; we just need to plow through this and get it done.

Eventually we settle on Jackson Pollack (my idea). I think it's a solid choice—Sam likes modern art, and I like the idea of doing something easy like indiscriminately slashing paint across a canvas. But when at the end of class we go to inform Ms. Kinsey of our selection, she tells us someone else in the class has beaten us to the punch.

"I'm sorry," she says with a frown, glancing down at her notebook, "but it looks like you'll have to come up with someone else." The bell rings, and she smiles again. "Oh, by the way, Chelsea, would you stay for a moment? I have something for you."

I nod, surprised, and Sam looks at me and shrugs.

"We'll talk about the project later," he says. He rolls his eyes. "Or, I guess, not talk. Whatever."

After everyone has shuffled out of the room, Ms. Kinsey goes to one of the supply cabinets and pulls out a small whiteboard and a dry-erase marker. She hands both to me and says, "I was thinking this might solve some of your communication hurdles."

I'm touched by the gesture. I uncap the marker and write *Thank you* on the board.

"You're very welcome, Chelsea," she says. "But keep in mind I'm not technically allowed to just give school supplies away, especially with the art budget being what it is. So consider it a loan." She smiles, reaching out to squeeze my shoulder. "Until you find your voice again."

I'm almost late to detention because I'm too busy scrubbing the vandalism off my locker. All I have is a wet paper towel and hand soap, and the marker's dried already, so it's slow going. After some time I've rubbed it off enough so that there are only a few black smears left. Not perfect, but it'll have to do.

When I get to the detention room to sign in, I immediately spot Brendon Ryan sitting in the front row. I'm surprised by his presence—Brendon is hardly the detention type. All the teachers adore him, just like the rest of the world. He looks just as startled when he meets my eye, blinking a few times before his mouth twitches into a half smile. He's probably amused by the memory of how I acted on New Year's Eve, the pinnacle of pathetic drunken desperation. Still, I can't help it; my heart flips in my chest at the sight of him, the way it has for the past year, the way it has as long as I've been stupidly in love with him and his stupid face.

The problem, of course, is that Brendon's face isn't stupid at all. It's gorgeous. Like the sort of Abercrombie model, statuesque perfection that would leave Michelangelo in tears. I want to lick his high-set cheekbones. I want to run my hands over his chest to see if it's as hard as it looks. I don't even want to make out with him—I mean, I do, obviously, of course, but really I'd settle for just tracing his perfect lips with my finger. Or running my hands through his gorgeous blond hair over and over for hours. Or—

Okay, this could go on, but I'm actually starting to creep myself out, and the point remains. Brendon is gorgeous, and even more so because he doesn't seem to notice exactly how good-looking he is. Maybe he just doesn't care. He's that fucking cool.

I tear my eyes off him and hastily duck into a seat on the other side of the room, way in the back row, next to a short, petite Indian girl with long, black hair that falls all the way to her waist. There's a lone apple sitting in the middle of her desk. I watch as she stares at it intently for almost a full minute, then reaches out and rotates it about forty-five degrees to her right. A minute later, after some more staring, she spins the apple slightly again.

What a freak.

I turn my attention back to Brendon. My enormous crush on him might've meant something a few weeks ago. Actually things had been going well in that arena—up until Kristen's

party. I could tell he wanted to kiss me that night. Um, before I ran upstairs to puke, that is, and instead stumbled into
Kristen's guest room. Before I decided to out Noah to everyone within earshot. Brendon's body language was clear as
day. He was totally into me.

Probably.

It doesn't matter now. He's just like everyone else; I might
as well not exist, unless someone needs a spitball/eraser/
pencil/food/sexual harassment target.

That doesn't stop me from spending all of detention staring
at the back of his dumb/gorgeous blond head, willing him to
turn around and smile at me, which is one of my most absurd
fantasies. Right up there with owning a pet unicorn or mar-
rying Prince Harry. It's just never going to happen. I don't
know why I'm torturing myself like this. I'm such a masochist.

I take out a notebook and a pen and doodle the outlines
of models, drawing different dresses—some of them angu-
lar with low necklines, others with big, swooping skirts. My
mind and eyes keep wandering back to Brendon, though, and
soon enough my outfit doodles turn into me doodling a trail
of broken hearts along the margin. When I realize what I'm
doing, I stop myself and scratch the hearts out so hard my pen
tip almost tears through the paper, my display of aggression
causing the girl next to me to glance over. I ignore her and
rip the page clean out of the notebook, crumple it in my fist
and shove it into my backpack.

There are only two and a half years left of high school. I
can make it alone. Once I graduate, I'll never have to see any
of these losers ever again. I will find a way to move to a new,
big city where no one knows who I am or what I've done,
leave all this behind me, and become the fashion designer

I've always dreamed of being. I'll be able to block Kristen and Noah and this entire mess from memory.

Until then, I will just show up and shut up and grit my teeth and get through this. Whatever it takes.

"She needs to see a doctor," my mother says at dinner.

Of course that's what she says. Therapy is my mother's solution to everything. I'm sure she thinks there'd be peace in the Middle East if every country were forced to sit down on a stiff leather couch with a box of Kleenex and talk about their feeeeelings.

Actually...has anyone tried that yet?

Ever since my mother got home from work, she's been hounding me. Ms. Davidson made good on her threat and apparently spoke to her about my insubordination issues. She also recommended counseling. I'm not crazy; I'm perceptive. What comes out of my mouth is the root of my problems, so the solution is for nothing to come out. Ms. Davidson said I couldn't shut out the world, but my question is, why can't I do just that? It's what the world wants. It's the only way to keep myself out of trouble.

Mom probably wouldn't be on my back so much if I'd just owned up and confessed my true motivations behind the vow, but instead I'm passing it off to my parents as an experiment. It's just the easier explanation, and I know if I was honest, she'd take it as some personal parental failure even though it has nothing to do with her. I can tell she doesn't believe me, though, by the way she's staring like I'll crack under the pressure of her intent gaze if she just waits long enough.

I sigh loud enough to get my father's attention and roll my eyes, just to garner some *jeez, this isn't a big deal, must be Mom's time of the month again, huh?* solidarity. It works like a charm. He cracks a small smile at me.

"Isn't sighing almost the same as speaking?" he teases.

I scribble on the whiteboard Ms. Kinsey gave me—the one I've resolved to cart around with me at all times—and show it to him. *My vow, my rules.*

He chuckles. "Fair enough."

"Frank," Mom says warningly. She hates when he humors me. She's not big on humor in general, really. She's into managing a floral shop, which is what she does for a living. And being a florist is *very serious business* in her world. God forbid you don't discuss the art of flower arrangements with the utmost reverence.

"I don't see the big problem," Dad replies. "I think it's important to nurture creativity, and if this is how Chelsea decides to...*express* herself, then we should be supportive."

I smile at him to show I appreciate his principled stand, even though I was banking on it all along. See, Dad has this stiff office job where he wears a suit and sits in the most depressing cubicle ever for eight hours a day and tries to sell office chairs over the phone to people who don't want to buy anything in this economy anyway. He's got to hate it. I've seen pictures of him when he was my age; he rocked long hair and wore these crazy sunglasses and played drums in a band. There's even this cassette tape of their recordings he keeps in his closet. I listened to it once, but it was all endless jamming that can only sound genius if you're seriously stoned. All of the lyrics revolved around a) getting high and b) sticking it to The Man. He's still a hippie at heart, and as someone who went from fighting The Man to working for him, I'm sure he secretly thinks my vow is "rad" or whatever slang word he thinks is hip.

"'Expressing herself'? How? By *not expressing herself at all?*"
Mom harrumphs and drops her forkful of tofurkey. I swear
I'm the only kid not on television who is actually subjected
to the evils of tofu on a regular basis. My mother's been having a two-year-long love affair with organic foods. It's tragic.
For me, I mean. "That's it. I'm scheduling an appointment
with Dr. Gebhart tomorrow," she declares.

"Irene, come on. It's just a harmless social experiment,"
Dad says. "It's a phase. She'll get over it soon enough. Why
not let her have a little fun?"

"This isn't her 'having fun.' It certainly isn't healthy behavior," she insists.

I really hate how they're talking about me like I'm not in
the room. I pick up the board and write, *I'm sitting right here
you know.*

Ooh, on second thought, maybe not a smart move. Because
now that Mom is looking at me, she's really *looking* at me.

"If you choose not to act like an adult," she says with a
cool stare, "you do not get to partake in adult conversations."

And you know, that's the last straw. There's only so much
condescension one girl can take in a day before reaching her
breaking point.

I slam my chair back from the table so hard all the dishes
rattle, and then storm up the stairs to my room, making sure
to stomp as hard as I can on each step. It's very six-years-old of
me, I realize, and probably won't help my "please stop treat-
ing me like a damn child" case, but I'm too pissed and upset
to care. God, everything just *sucks* today.

As I go to shut my door, I hear Mom and Dad downstairs,
arguing. I listen just long enough to hear my name thrown
around before flinging myself dramatically onto the bed and
staring at the ceiling. When I was thirteen, Dad painted it

dark blue and stuck on those glow-in-the-dark plastic stars, so when all the lights are off, it's like being in a planetarium. A pretty crappy imitation of a planetarium, but whatever. I count each one and list something that is pissing me off: Lowell. Derek. Mrs. Finch. Tofu. My mom. Jell-O shots. Warren. Joey. Whoever invented markers. The list of everything I hate at this very moment could fill an entire galaxy.

I can't help but wonder what Kristen is doing right now. And how she is, really. Is she upset? Is she worried about Warren? Has she cried? Is she thinking about me? Or was I ever really only a placeholder, someone completely disposable, like Natalie said?

I'm not great at a lot, but I'm good at being Kristen's friend. Or, I was, until I messed it all up for myself on a stupid whim. I liked it, being in her orbit. Girls wanted to be us. Guys wanted to date us. Even those who hated us wanted a look. I loved that, loved that I mattered, that people were jealous. I loved turning heads. It didn't matter if most of them were looking at Kristen; I was in their line of vision, and that totally counted for something. Being on the radar at all. It made me more than average. It was everything to me.

I don't know who I am without Kristen. I don't know if I want to find out.

I'm interrupted from my thoughts by a knock at the door. Obviously I don't answer, so it opens on its own. I twist around to see Dad in the doorway.

He hovers for a minute and then clears his throat. "Hey, kid. Can I come in?"

I nod. He walks across the room and sits at the foot of the bed, pushing my feet to one side for room. I lie there and look at him. His shoulders have this tired slump to them, and there are tired lines around his eyes. He looks old. Drained. It makes me wonder how he ever had the energy to do things like paint my ceiling.

"How was school?" he asks softly.

I shrug, pulling my sleeves over my hands. I'm not going to burden him with my problems. This is my hill to climb alone.

"Don't worry about your mother. I talked her down from siccing Dr. Gebhart on you. You have to understand, she's just worried," he says. He puts his hand on my shoe and squeezes. "And I worry, too. Things have been stressful lately. For all of us."

Is Noah's father doing the same thing right now, sitting by his bedside and offering comfort? Did he even know his son was gay before I said anything? Does it matter to him?

I fish the whiteboard from the floor where I'd dropped it. *Would you care if I was gay?* I write.

Dad blinks a few times. "Are you? Is that what this—?"

I tap the board again with my marker tip. I want to hear his answer first.

"No," he says quickly. "Of course not. Who you love… that isn't important. It doesn't change who you are, or how much we love you. Nothing could change that."

I knew that's what he'd say. Still, it feels nice to hear it regardless.

I erase the board and write, *I'm not gay. But I'm glad it wouldn't matter.*

He looks at it and smiles a little. "We just want you to be happy. You know that, right?"

Yeah. Yeah, I know.

I nod, and he drops a kiss on my forehead, sets his palm flat on the top of my head for a moment before he starts to leave. "Stay sweet," he says on his way out, the same thing he always says to me. He hesitates, lingering at the doorway. "What happened to that boy... You did the right thing, Chelsea."

I feel like such an idiot. I don't even care if I did the right thing—it doesn't feel like the right thing. It feels like I screwed myself over. One stupid moment of fleeting conscience and I've lost all I care about. Maybe I could try groveling for forgiveness, hope it would get me back into everyone's good graces, but the thought of it alone is nauseating. Natalie might think I'm just Kristen's little minion, but I'm not.

I don't know exactly what I am, but I'm more than that. I know that much.

day two

The next day, Mrs. Finch issues me another pretty pink detention slip. She also keeps me after class because I clearly have not been berated by her enough. I wait until the rest of the students have cleared the room before I reluctantly walk over to her desk.

"Chelsea, I obviously can't force you to participate in class," she says, "but for every day you refuse to contribute, I can—and will—give you a detention." She pauses to press her lips together for a moment. "Do you understand?"

I stare at her stony-faced.

She sighs with a curt nod. "Very well, then."

If Mrs. Finch thinks the threat of detention is enough to deter me, she really doesn't understand the scope of my stubborn streak.

No Brendon in detention this time, but the Indian girl from yesterday is there again. I sign in and sit down next to her. Today she has a single orange on her desk, but she isn't looking at it. Instead she's knitting something out of teal and purple yarn while reading a folded up newspaper. The only other person I know who knits is my grandma Doris. But this girl is good at it; she moves the needles in smooth, quick motions, in and out, in and out, not even looking down at her work as she reads. It's oddly fascinating to watch.

I pull out my geometry assignment and get to work. Or I plan to, anyway, except five and a half problems in, the numbers start blurring together. I end up doodling spirals all over the page while I stare into space. I don't mind detention, really. It's boring, yeah, but it's not like I have anything better to do. There could be way worse punishments. Mrs. Finch can suck it.

The girl next to me shifts in her seat, the chair legs scraping against the floor, and I glance up just in time to see the orange roll off her desk and toward mine. I put my foot out to stop it, then bend down, pick it up and extend it back to the girl.

"Thank you," she says brightly. She takes it from me and peers at my open textbook. "Hmm. Asymptotes are so depressing."

I stare at her, trying to figure out if she's actually serious. She looks like she is.

"The curve goes toward the line, you know, and they get closer and closer, but they never get to touch," she explains. She shrugs. "It's just sad, is all." She holds out the fruit. "You want my orange?"

I shake my head. The detention teacher shoots us a stern glare from behind her book.

"I'm Asha," the girl hisses out of the side of her mouth, when the teacher's buried her nose back in her trashy romance novel.

I look back down at my textbook, pretending to be absorbed in the nonsensical formulas and graphs displayed before me, but I can feel her gaze on me, like she's expecting a response. I consider ignoring her; it's what I would've done before. Normally I wouldn't bother with some geeky freshman loser dressed in the most unfortunate fuzzy purple sweater I've ever seen in my life. I don't associate with freaks.

Except this particular freak won't stop staring at me, and it's a chore to act like I'm concentrating on this math homework, so I write *I'm Chelsea* on the whiteboard and slide it to the corner of the desk so she can see. Maybe now she'll leave me alone.

Asha nods knowingly. "I know. I've heard of you," she whispers.

Oh, great. Is she going to give me a hard time, too? Even the freaks hate me.

She rummages through her backpack and tears a blank page from one of her notebooks. She scribbles something down and then passes the sheet of paper to me.

You're the girl taking the vow of silence, right?

News travels fast.

I hand the paper back and start returning to my homework, except Asha keeps writing, and a minute later she pokes me in the shoulder with the corner of the page. I take it back, assuming that she's written a profanity-laden attack on my character, but when I look down, that's not what I see. And she doesn't *look* mad or mocking—there's something weirdly sincere about her.

Since she doesn't appear hostile, I decide to humor her. What can it hurt?

I hear things. People say a lot in front of me because they don't think I'm listening.

~~What else have you heard?~~ Don't answer that. So what are you in for?

I punched a teacher in the face.

Seriously?

No, but it sounds cooler than having a bunch of tardies.

Point taken.

Hey, your answer to problem number four is wrong. To find the domain you need to set the denominator to zero.

Wow. I was not even close.

Not really, no.

It goes on like this for a while, until the teacher glances at the clock and says, "All right, you're all excused."

Everyone clears out of the room like it's on fire. Asha is the only one who takes her time packing away her knitting needles, zipping up her bag and tucking the newspaper under her arm. Now that we're both standing up, I can tell exactly how short she is. I mean, I'm no giant, but I tower over her by a good three or four inches. Her sleek black hair sways back and forth as she walks in front of me out the door. I wonder how she deals with it—it must take forever to wash, and even longer to brush. I have enough trouble keeping my own tamed, and mine only goes a little past my shoulders. It's flaming red and wavy, and no matter how much product I use, it always ends up looking wild and tousled within an hour of drying. Ridiculous.

Asha and I head in the same direction, and we end up walking side by side through the parking lot together. Outside the weather is clear and cold. There's snow blanketed on the grass; it'll be there for another two months, at least. Michigan winters are like that. Last year there was a blizzard in April, bad enough to close the schools. Usually I'm eager for all the snow to melt, for spring to start and the birds to sing and the flowers to bloom, all that jazz, but today I'm glad for this miserable weather. It suits my perfectly miserable mood.

"I love winter," Asha announces out of the blue, winding her scarf tight around her neck. "I get to wear all of the stuff I knit. I need to buy some new boots, though. My old ones fell apart."

I let my gaze travel down to Asha's feet; she's wearing scuffed-up black ballet flats. Her feet must be freezing. Asha seems unperturbed by this, though.

"So I guess I'll see you around," she says cheerfully. "Good luck with the vow!"

She starts down the sidewalk, but I touch her arm and grab my whiteboard.

Want a ride home?

I can't let her walk in those shoes. It's just too pitiful.

"I have to go to work," she says. "Over at Rosie's. You've heard of it?"

I nod. Rosie's is the little diner in the center of town, right on the strip by the lake. We don't usually eat there—Kristen always thought of it as a magnet for the "undesirables," which I guess is her word for anyone below her family's tax bracket—but I pass by all the time.

I can drive you.

"Really?" She beams. "That'd be great!"

My car is my baby. It's an old-school Volkswagen Beetle my parents gave me for my birthday two months ago. Dad took me to the used-car lot and did all the haggling; he's big into cars, and everything I know I learned from him. By the time I was twelve, he'd taught me how to change a tire, switch out the oil, add more steering fluid, name all the engine parts. Stuff like that.

The first thing I did when I got the car was swing by Kristen's house. She was totally unimpressed. "You got it in yellow?" she'd said, her mouth turned down with distaste. "It looks like a taxi." She acted like it was the tackiest thing she'd ever laid eyes on. I went from feeling excited to wanting to crawl under a rock in five seconds flat.

I don't know why I'm thinking about that right now.

We're heading toward my parking spot when a voice calls out from behind us.

"Asha!"

It's Sam. He's on his skateboard, rolling in our direction, pushing off the pavement easily with one foot. Who skateboards in the winter? The parking lot is clear of snow, but it's still odd. He skids to a stop a few feet away, surprise registering on his face when he notices me standing there.

Asha turns around and smiles. "Hi, Sam," she says. "What're you still doing here?"

"Library research. Thrilling stuff, I know," he replies. His gaze flickers to mine and then back to Asha's. "What about you?"

"Detention," she says brightly. I can't help but smile a little at her nonchalance.

Sam's eyebrows shoot skyward. "Why, Asha, you little deviant. Guess I should go before your bad influence rubs off on me."

He starts skating past us, until Asha reaches out and grabs his backpack handle, yanking him to a stop. He laughs and pops his board up with one foot. It's kind of cool. I don't know how to skateboard, or even use Rollerblades. My mom is paranoid because growing up, she knew a boy who had an in-line skating accident and hit his head on a rock and died, so she never let me learn. She doesn't trust anything with wheels. It took weeks of convincing to even talk her into letting me take the training wheels off my bike.

"Hey, when are you gonna make my scarf?" Sam asks Asha.

"You still have to pick out the colors," she says. "I was thinking red and blue."

"Nah. Too Captain America for me. I'm more of a—"

"—Batman? Black and gold?"

"Green Lantern, maybe. Green and silver."

I sit back and listen to them debating superhero colors. They don't seem to be bothered by me being there. Not even Sam. If he's unhappy with my presence, he doesn't let on.

I wonder if he knows how Noah is. If he's any better. No one's told me, and even if I was talking, I wouldn't ask. Even though I'm dying to know. It just…it doesn't seem like it's my place. Or maybe I'm just scared to find out if he's not doing well. That would make things even worse for me than they already are. If the vitriol aimed at me is already this bad, I can't imagine what it'll be like if Noah doesn't recover.

I look past Asha and Sam and toward my car. Weird…it looks like there's something on my windshield.

I let them continue with their bantering and walk up to the car, and that's when I see it. Someone's thrown eggs all over the front window, the yolk running down onto the hood in a sticky yellow mess. I walk around only to find the word *BITCH* spelled out in shaving cream all over the back. It's like I've been sucker-punched. My bag drops to the ground at my feet.

"Chelsea? What's wr—" Asha's voice cuts short as she comes up beside me, eyes widening.

"God." Sam stops cold, skateboard in both hands, and shakes his head. "Who would do this?"

I'm not sure why he's so shocked. I don't bother pointing out that the suspect list would include probably half the student body—including him. I can come up with twenty names off the top of my head. It'd be easier to narrow down who *wouldn't* do this.

"Come on," Asha says gently. She puts a hand on my arm. "I'll help you clean it off."

Sam sets down his backpack, takes off his jacket and unzips the hoodie underneath it. "Here," he says, handing me both. "Use this. I'll check and see if there's any other damage."

He checks all the tires while Asha uses his hoodie to wipe off the shaving cream. I grab my squeegee from the backseat and scrape the eggs off the windshield. It takes a while because they're all crusted and frozen and gross.

"Why don't you pop the hood?" Sam asks.

I go into the driver's seat and push the release, then go back outside and lift the hood all the way. Sam comes up beside me to peer at the engine. His arms stick out of his black T-shirt, pale and skinny. He's shivering.

"Doesn't look like they messed with anything else," he says. "You okay to drive?"

I nod, close the hood and hand him back his coat. He slips into it and turns up the sheepskin collar. My whiteboard is still in my hands; I write on it and show him.

Thanks.

A weird look passes over his face, like he doesn't know how to take my gratitude. "Don't mention it," he says. He turns to Asha, who is pinching the shaving cream-covered hoodie by the tips of her fingers. "Hey, just so you know, I'm covering Andy's shift tonight."

They work together? Well, that explains their friendship. Asha frowns. "Is he sick or something?"

"No," he says. "He texted me to say he's supposed to stop by the hospital. Noah woke up last night."

My heart jumps into my throat. Noah woke up? Sam shoots

me a meaningful look, and my fingers curl tighter around the whiteboard. I don't know if he wants me to feel relieved or guilty. I'm both, really. But it also makes me feel even more foolish. If Noah's going to be totally fine, what was even the point of saying anything? If I'd waited, he could've just pointed the finger at Warren and Joey himself, assuming he doesn't have amnesia or something, and spared me all of this.

"That's great," Asha gushes, bouncing on her heels. "I was going to knit him a hat, but I don't know what size his head is, so I'm working on a scarf instead."

"I'm sure he'll love it," Sam says with a grin. He starts to take his hoodie from her, but I hold up a finger to stop him.

Let me wash it for you.

He looks surprised. "Um. Okay. If you want."

I do want to. I want to wash his hoodie, and tell him to tell Noah—well, I don't know what I'd say to Noah if I had the chance.

Pretty sure I won't have to worry about that. No way is Noah going to ever want to see me face-to-face. On second thought, maybe I should cross my fingers for that amnesia.

I drive Asha to the diner, and she spends the whole time talking. About her knitting. About how she waits tables and Sam is a cook, and this cool guy named Dex owns the joint, and she really likes the job. About how she earned so many tardies for first period health class because her father makes her walk her little brother Karthik to the middle school every morning, and he is always running late.

She won't shut up, but I can't really be annoyed because I'm pretty sure she's just trying to distract me. I appreciate the sentiment. I'm still a little rattled from what whoever did to my car. I keep wondering how far this will go. Messing with my locker, messing with my car, verbal intimidation—what's next? Cutting my brakes? Roughing me up in the parking lot? I don't think anything that extreme will happen, but obviously the past week has, if nothing else, shown that I severely underestimated what it's like to be on the receiving end of Kristen & Co.'s bullshit.

Not talking leaves me a lot of time alone with my thoughts and ever-growing paranoia. I've never been like this. So inside my own head.

As we near the lake, Asha directs me down the street to the diner on the corner. I pull up against the curb and put my car in Park. Rosie's doesn't look like much from the outside, just a small, cozy gray building with a red neon sign out front, the *E* flickering on and off intermittently.

"Thanks for the ride," she says as she unbuckles her seat belt.

I take my board from where it's resting on the seat divider. *Anytime.*

"Well, my sentence is up, so I guess you'll be on your own tomorrow."

I can handle it.

She pushes her hair behind her ears and smiles. "I'm sure you can."

I wait until Asha runs up to the entrance, and she turns to wave before disappearing inside the doors. I wave back, and then sit there, idling, lost in thought. I'm in no hurry to go home. It'll just mean sitting around, stuffing my face with tofu while Mom threatens to have me committed or something, and then dragging myself to bed, where I'll toss and turn, staring at my alarm clock and dreading school.

Maybe I'll do my homework for once. Actually look at the Steinbeck reading Mrs. Finch assigned. What a novel concept.

When I go to pull back onto the street, I notice she left the newspaper sitting on the passenger's seat. The comics section stares up at me, and suddenly I'm hit with the idea.

I totally know what our art project is going to be.

day three

"Charles Schulz?" Sam says. "Really?"

We're the only ones in art class actually discussing the project, I'm pretty sure. There was an awkward moment at the start of class when I pulled out his hoodie, freshly cleaned and smelling like Mountain Spring detergent. He just mumbled thanks and dived into talking about the project. Everyone else around us is talking and laughing and throwing shit at each other. Stay classy, Grand Lake.

I roll my eyes and snatch his sketchpad out of his hands.

Skeptical is not a good look for you.

He grabs it back. "I'm just saying—" he starts to say then stops. "You know what? It's too weird having a conversation with no one. It makes me feel a little like the schizophrenic dude outside the Save-U-More who yells at the ice freezer. So I'm just going to continue this discussion via note-writing, okay?"

do comic strips even count as art?

Of course they do. Don't be so prejudiced. Art encompasses more than old oil paintings and stupid abstracts. Open your mind!! Be creative!!

you sound like ms. Kinsey.

Ms. Kinsey would never call abstracts stupid. Besides I choose to take that as a compliment.

you would. so—charles schulz? really?

Broken record much? Come on, it would be fun!!!! Different!!!! EXCITING!!!!!

your abuse of exclamation marks and capslock is not really selling me on this.

I need to express my enthusiasm somehow.

try using your words.

I am. Just not with my voice.

is it hard? not talking?

Yes. No. Sometimes. Not really. Except for the early onset of carpal tunnel. Like now. Owwwww. ☹ Going 2 use shrthnd frm nw on k?

k. so y no talking? isn't writing the same thing?

No. I have to think about what I write b4 I put it on paper. I don't want 2 say the wrong thing. No 1 wants to hear it n e way. Me + talking = BAD NEWS.

Sam pauses for a long time, twirling the pen around in his hand.

saw noah last night. he's going to be o.k.

I look at him and then back down at the page. Part of me is glad he's sharing this information with me, but part of me wants to know why. Is he trying to make me feel better, and if so, why the hell would he do that? He has every reason in the world to hate me. The pen hovers over the pad as I try to figure out what to say next.

Charles Schulz. We're totally doing it. OK?

o.k. you win.

★ ★ ★

The most awkward part of my day comes after my second-to-last class. And that's really saying something, since there is so much awkwardness spread out throughout the day—from avoiding Kristen and all the jocks in the hall, to finding a safe haven at lunch, to dealing with the ritual embarrassment of Mrs. Finch doling out my daily detention slip. Yup, lucky me received another one today, all shiny and pink. I'm convinced she gets a twisted satisfaction out of dispensing these punishments. My best defense is to act like I don't give two shits.

I'm also crazy worried about my car. I almost didn't drive to school today, but I was afraid my parents might notice and ask questions. Mom would totally flip out and ship me off to a boarding school or something; Dad would probably inflict bodily harm on the perpetrators, less so in honor of my dignity and more for the sacrilege of damaging a vehicle. Especially one he paid for.

Even if I told my parents about the locker vandalism and the car defacement, and they told the school, it wouldn't help anything. They wouldn't catch whoever did it, and it would only add fuel to the fire. I've accepted the fact that I'm going to have to suck it up for however long it takes people to get over this, even if that means spending the next three years watching my back. I can only hope I don't develop a crippling ulcer or die of a heart attack from all the stress in the meantime.

The sad thing is I thought this was going to be my year. Getting my license, having a car of my own, partying it up with Kristen and Warren and Derek, hanging out every weekend and going to dances and prom and living the high life, as it were. Maybe landing a boyfriend of my own for once instead of being Kristen and Warren's third wheel.

I'm reminded of this as I walk out of my last class and see the big blue banner advertising the upcoming Winter Formal stretched across the wall. And Brendon standing underneath it, bent over the drinking fountain. I stop dead in my tracks, disrupting the chaotic flow of traffic and causing some upperclassman with the body of a cinderblock to bump into my back.

"Watch it," he mutters, pushing past.

Whatever. The guy has this weird faux-hawk/mullet thing going on, so I just can't take him seriously.

You know who has perfect hair? Brendon.

I really need to get over this swoony phase. I need to move on and accept that it is never going to happen. I blew it. He hates me. We are never going to date. He is never going to walk down the hall holding my hand, or ask me to the prom, or kiss my neck, or anything. He won't even look at me! And, not to brag, but I am something to look at, dammit. I'm not gorgeous like Kristen, but I've been known to turn a head or two in my time.

These days the only heads I turn are the ones who want to glare at me.

Brendon wipes his mouth off with the back of his hand, turns around and—oh. Eye contact! Eye contact! Houston, we have visual!!

Oh, God, what do I do now? Think, dammit, think! Suddenly, inexplicably, I'm raising my hand in a wave. Brendon, frozen in place, looks at me like a deer caught in the headlights of a semi barreling forward at one hundred miles per hour. So then we're both just standing there, six feet apart, gawking at each other like idiots.

The warning bell rings, loud and shrill. We both jump, startled out of this weird transfixed staring contest. Brendon's face burns bright red, and he hesitates, looking like maybe he wants to say something. But he doesn't. Instead he hurries off and merges into the stream of stragglers rushing for last period, disappearing down the hall in the opposite direction.

God, he must hate me for embarrassing him with my come-ons at the party. I've been so preoccupied dealing with the repercussions of ratting out Warren and Joey that it's easy to forget everything else that happened. To him I'll always be the ditzy alcoholic slutbag who tried to jump his bones that one time.

Even if I could explain myself, what would there be to say?

Last year I went to every school-sanctioned dance, except for the senior prom, of course, which isn't held in the gymnasium anyway but at the one nice hotel Grand Lake has in midtown. But as for the rest—Homecoming, Spring Fling, End-of-Year—you name it and I was there. Well, at least for part of it, anyway, since usually about an hour after arrival Warren would inevitably get bored and want to leave, and since he was our ride, that meant we all had to go. So we'd all pile into his truck and head over to Kristen's.

The dances themselves are lame. Student Council is in charge of organizing them, and all they do is throw up some streamers in the gym and pay some of the tech kids to DJ. Really it's just an elaborate excuse for all the guys and girls to grind on each other to that month's Top Forty until it gets so obscene the chaperones intervene.

What I like about the formals most is looking for new dresses. That search for the perfect one. I like scouring through celebrity gossip magazines and blogs and taking cues from what the stars are wearing to premieres and award ceremonies. Of course no way can I shell out for Vera Wang or

Oscar de la Renta or Chanel, but I've learned that if you look hard enough you can find cheaper alternatives. I sort of have this dream of one day writing for one of those magazines, being the person who critiques celebrity fashion; Mrs. Finch even let me publish a few Fashion Dos and Don'ts columns in the *Grand Lake High Gazette.* I've never told anyone about that career goal, though, not even Kristen—she got all pissed when I wrote about frosted lipstick being a fashion "Don't," since she loves it, and then told me someone who wears gold shimmery eye shadow isn't one to talk. I still don't understand what's so wrong with gold eye shadow, but I threw it out anyway.

By the time I get home from school, all I want to do is zone out, so I go upstairs and sit in the middle of my bed with my laptop, opening all of the celebrity blogs I read religiously. I scroll through a set of photos of Kate Hudson wearing this dress that reminds me a little of the one I bought for this year's Homecoming, a low-cut silver number plated with tiny glittery sequins. It was flashy and over-the-top and made me look not unlike a disco ball, but it was the kind of dress you wear to have fun in, to stand out, to say, *hey, take a look at me,* and people did.

Of course, it was effectively ruined when we went to Kristen's after and Joey pushed me into her dirty swimming pool. Ass.

For the Winter Formal, I'd go with something less outlandish and more elegant. Probably a solid dark color, with maybe a few rhinestones on the collar, or sequins down by the hem, but nothing extreme. Something classic.

If I was going, that is. Which I'm not. Obviously. I don't have a death wish.

I'm just about done reading the comments section when

I notice one new email sitting in my in-box. I switch to the window, fully expecting a piece of spam touting penis enlargements or Russian mail-order brides, and instead see a message from Kristen waiting for me. My heart picks up speed in my chest like I just downed a shot of Red Bull. Could it be? Is she reaching out to me to make an apology, or an offer of amends? There's no subject line to tip me off on what it could possibly say, so I hold my breath and click on it.

I just thought you should know I heard about your little silent act, and I think it's pathetic, just like everything else about you. Don't think you're anyone special. No one misses having you around. Everyone only ever tolerated you because of me, and now they all know the true Chelsea Knot. I'm just sorry I ever wasted any time on you at all.

And if you think this week has been bad, just wait.

For a few minutes all I can do is stare at the computer screen, reading the email over and over like if I do that enough times it'll somehow make sense. At first I have this weird feeling like someone just punched me in the chest, and I think I might cry, but something hard knots itself in my stomach as I read the words again. I want to grab my laptop and hurl it across the room. I settle instead for slamming it shut with more force than necessary, clenching and unclenching my hands until they stop shaking.

I leap off the bed and pace around my room, trying to calm myself down. I can't believe Kristen is actually threatening me. I can't believe she's implying she orchestrated everything that's happened to me since my return to school. Okay, on second thought, I can totally believe it—I know firsthand what she's capable of—I just never thought I'd be on the receiving end of it.

I end up staring into my closet at the dresses from days of yore hung in their plastic dry-cleaners bags. I picked all of them out with Kristen. Actually almost *everything* in my closet was picked out with, or by, Kristen. It was one of our unspoken rules that all outfits were subject to best-friend approval. And Kristen tended to exercise her veto power. Excessively. Which is why, I realize, I don't own anything I truly like. I only own clothes I *think* I should like.

For instance, why is there so much pink here? I don't like the color pink. I don't look *good* in the color pink. But a third of my closet is devoted to pink sweaters and blouses and skirts. All because Kristen always insisted it was "my color."

I have red hair and pale skin. Pink totally washes me out. I look *ridiculous* in pink.

When I was thirteen, my dad painted my ceiling blue because that's what I wanted. Not because someone else suggested it, or thought it should be that color, but because *I* liked it. The same way I was so in love with my yellow Beetle, before Kristen berated it to my face.

How did something as simple as deciding what I like become so freaking complicated?

Before I realize it, I've torn every article of pink clothing off the hangers and tossed it all into a pile behind me. It feels...good. Liberating. Why should I wear a color I hate? It isn't like it'll change Kristen's mind, or make people like me, or make my life at all easier. These past few days I've tried to blend into the walls by hiding in too-big sweaters and jeans, make myself as unnoticed as possible, but obviously that isn't helping.

So maybe it's time to stop working around other people's expectations.

I go through the rest of my closet and my entire dresser, pulling out anything I don't like anymore, or never liked in the first place. Over half of my clothes end up in the DO NOT WANT heap. I don't stop there—I sort through all my makeup, my jewelry, my shoes, the girly magazines stashed under my bed. By the time I'm done, my room looks like it was ravaged by a level-five tornado.

I throw everything I'm getting rid of into garbage bags. Most of it can go to Goodwill. The magazines I'll dump. Clippings of articles I've written for the *Gazette* are taped up by my mirror; there are photos, too, snapshots of Kristen and Warren and Derek and our whole group, hanging out on the quad, partying at Kristen's, group shots of us all in our formal wear for Homecoming, that I carefully peel off the wall. I stuff it all in an empty shoebox and shove it all the way in the back of my closet shelf, where I won't have to be reminded. Out of sight, out of mind.

Mom finds me in the basement as I'm piling the garbage bags next to the dryer. She folds her arms and watches, waiting for me to acknowledge her presence. Once I've stacked the last bag, I turn and look at her. She has the same hair as me, red and wild, but she always pulls it back in a tight knot. A few wisps have escaped the elastic and frame her face.

Mom's side of the family is Irish to the bone. The story goes that some great-grandmother of mine came to the States in a potato boat or something. She has three brothers, two sisters, a million cousins, and among them you'll find all of the stereotypes: Catholicism, raging alcoholism, legendary hot tempers. It sure makes holiday get-togethers interesting. Dad's one of those American mutts who cites about fifteen European countries as his heritage. Apparently none of them were strong enough to battle out the Irish in the gene pool.

"What are you doing?" she asks.

Crap. My whiteboard's upstairs and neither of us knows sign language, so that leaves me limited options. I tear open one of the bags, point to the clothing, and then shake my head, trying for my best *DO NOT WANT!* expression. I also attempt mimicking handing a folded pair of studded jeans to a grateful jeans-deprived poor person, which my mother understands about as well as you'd expect. Meaning, not at all.

Ah, well. I can just store it all down here for right now, and if by some miracle life returns to normal, I'll drag it all back up to my room. I'm not holding my breath waiting for that to happen, though.

Mom exhales in exasperation. "Stop this nonsense and just talk to me!"

For a second she looks so hurt that I feel kind of bad about it. I mean, it's not like I decided to do this to punish her. And it's not like I can explain my real reasons to her. "You see, Mom, your darling daughter never knows when to shut the hell up and has a habit of saying things that land people in jail or in comas, or else mortifies them with what may quite possibly fall under the legal guidelines of sexual harassment, and the only way my so-called friends will listen to anything I have to say is if I kneel at their feet begging for forgiveness, which isn't going to happen in this lifetime, so it's easier not to say anything at all." Please. If I said all that, she'd skip Dr. Gebhart and go directly for the straitjacket.

"Chelsea." Mom's arms drop to her sides, and she takes a step toward me. "Tell me what's wrong. Tell me so I can fix it."

I waver for a minute, wondering if I should just give in and tell her what she wants to hear. Since it seems like she just wants to hear *something,* anything at all. I even open my mouth, the words forming somewhere in my throat, but when I try to actually speak, it's just...like my vocal chords are paralyzed or something. Nothing comes out.

"What I don't understand is why you would go to that party in the first place," she says. She sighs again and walks over to the dryer. "And then I think about everything else you must've been doing behind our backs. I'm smarter than you give me credit for, Chelsea. I knew things...happened, things I figured I was better off not knowing about. Like the drinking. The boys. But I thought we raised you better than that."

I want to tell her that it isn't like that. So I drink, sometimes, but it's not like— It's just a social thing. A fun thing. I'm not like her cousin who got so drunk at Thanksgiving he passed out in the driveway. And as for the boys, well, there isn't much to talk about in that department. The most I've done is make out with Joey a few times, mostly because Kristen kept pushing us together. But kissing Joey wasn't even enjoyable. It was actually a little gross. Nothing like movies make you think.

Anyway, after what happened on New Year's, I'm never going to drink again. And probably will never kiss anyone ever again, either. Chances are I'll die alone. Surrounded by cats. Oh, God. I can see it all so clearly. I'll be the crazy cat lady chasing kids off her lawn with a broom.

"I told your father this would happen," she continues.

"We should have pulled you out of that school. Those kids are barbaric." She rearranges the fabric sheets boxes absently, and I notice the slight tremor in her hands. She's really worried about me. I feel that twinge again, the guilty twist in my gut.

I always wondered what it'd be like to grow up in a big family like my mom did. She and Dad made a conscious decision for me to be an only child. Yeah, there are perks—like never having to share my room or toys or attention. But it might be nice, in times like these, to have someone to confide in, or at least commiserate with. Maybe an older sibling, someone who would be able to tell me that all of this high school stuff doesn't matter. That things will get better. My parents can tell me as much as they like, and maybe they're right, but I'm never going to fully believe it.

The thing is, despite everything going on—I don't want to change schools. It feels too much like running away. Let the jerks that vandalized my locker and my car and harassed me think they can just run me off that easy? No. I'm not going to end up as one of Kristen's little victims. I know the games she plays; she expects me to cave under the pressure and come begging for forgiveness, but it's not going to happen. I'm not like those other girls she can scare into submission.

When Mom looks at me again, her eyes are a little glassy, like maybe she's going to cry, but I can't tell for sure. It might just be the lights down here.

"I know I can't change your mind," she says. The slightest of wry smiles appears on her face. "You get your stubborn streak from me."

I smile back as much as I can, hoping it'll tell her without words what she desperately wants to hear. That this isn't her fault. It's like what those cheesy action-movie heroes always say before they finish taking out the bad guys: I started this, and I'm going to finish it. Except even in the movie of my own life, I've never been the heroine. I've never been Action Girl. I've only ever been Kristen's supporting character.

day four

On the drive to school the next morning, in an effort to psych myself up, I blast Eminem at full volume. I got this album when I was, like, nine. I had to beg Dad to buy it for me on the down-low, since Mom had a ban on me owning any music she deemed inappropriate. Eminem definitely fell in that bracket. But Dad's always been a softie, and even though he's all about Led Zeppelin and Eric Clapton himself, he likes to think he still has the kind of antiestablishment streak that would allow him to procure contraband music for his only daughter.

What's really hard is overcoming the temptation to sing along. Sure, no one would know but me, and it's doubtful I'd hurt anyone by spitting out lyrics alone in my car—no matter how vulgar they may be—but when I said I have something to prove, I didn't mean only to the kids at school. I have something to prove to myself. That I'm not who everyone thinks I am. That I can stick to this.

Listening to Eminem makes me feel like a badass. Or at least as though I have the potential for badassery. I mean, the way he sings, it's like he'd probably punch out a puppy if it looked at him wrong. Obviously I'm not glorifying animal cruelty here, I'm just saying, I could use some of that attitude. It's better than the attitude I have now of just letting everyone mess with me all the time.

I pull into my usual parking spot and leave the car on until the current song finishes, and when I walk through the school doors, I try holding on to that newfound sense of I-don't-give-a-crap. My first test is the fresh graffiti on my locker, the word *BITCH* etched in black marker. For a second I flinch inwardly, stung, but then I'm just annoyed. Bitch? Really? Whoever is behind this is in dire need of a thesaurus. The level of creativity is tragic more than anything.

I decide not to bother cleaning the slur off my locker this time. I even take a red marker out of my locker and dot the I with a heart. I'll wear it as a badge of honor. Yeah, that's right. You think I'm a bitch now, Grand Lake High? You ain't seen nothing yet.

"Chelsea?" Asha pops up behind me, clutching some notebooks to her chest and smiling wide. Her face falls as she notices the defacement of my locker. "Who did that?" she asks.

I snap the lock shut and shrug my shoulders. I'm not going to waste time caring about it. I lean back against my locker and level Asha with a questioning look. She still hasn't explained why she's talking to me.

She seems to understand the implied question. "I'm on my way to Advanced Algebra," she explains, gesturing down the hall. "I saw you as I was walking and just thought I'd say hi." She grins again. "By the way, I was going to ask you—"

"*Excuse* me."

I look up in time to see Kristen shoulder her way past Asha, hard, sending her stumbling into the bank of lockers. Her books fall from her arms and her notes flutter to the floor.

Tessa trails after Kristen, laughing. "What reeks?" she asks, her nose wrinkled. She eyes Asha up and down. "It smells like curry."

I instinctively put myself between her and Asha, opening my mouth to respond with something like *All I smell is bitch-assery and acne cream,* but then I close it when I remember I cannot, of course, say anything. Still, I do a pretty mean glare, and for a moment Tessa's smirk falters. Asha doesn't react, just calmly bends down to collect her scattered papers. I kneel down and help, ignoring Kristen and Tessa's looming presence. Just as I grab one of Asha's math worksheets, Kristen steps on it, causing the paper to tear in half as I pull upward.

"Oops," she says flatly.

I rise to my feet so we're face-to-face. I'm so angry I'm shaking with it. The urge to haul off and punch her in the face is strong, but I swallow the temptation; I don't even know how to throw a punch, and while it might feel satisfying in the moment, it won't solve anything. The worst is the way Kristen stares back at me, so unaffected and *smug,* like she knows I can't touch her.

"What are you going to do? Glare me to death?" she drawls. She looks from me to Asha and back again. "This is sad, even for you. Do you really have to drag the queen of the loser brigade down with you?" Her tone goes ice-cold. "Don't you think you've ruined enough lives already?"

"You better watch your back," Tessa warns Asha. "Chelsea will throw you under the bus in a heartbeat. *Trust me.*" She casts a bitter glare my way just in case I didn't get the intended message. I'm itching to spill to her who was *really* behind the blackmailing, but there's no way she'd believe me over Kristen anyway.

Asha tucks some loose papers inside her binder and smiles at them, big and fake. "Thanks for the super helpful advice," she says. "I'll take it into consideration." She starts down the hall, barely slowing to glance back at me over her shoulder. "Coming?"

I take one last look at Kristen before turning and falling in step beside Asha. My heart is still pounding like crazy as we disappear around the corner out of their sight. When Asha stops at the water fountain, I lean against the wall with my eyes closed, taking deep breaths and trying to calm myself. I hate that I'm letting them get to me this much when I promised myself I wouldn't. I hate that I just stood there and let them talk to Asha like that.

The worst thing is knowing they're right. Asha might be a loser, but she's been nice to me, inexplicably so, and she doesn't deserve to deal with what'll come to her just by being in my orbit.

"You're not ruining my life."

I open my eyes as Asha wipes her mouth off with the back of her hand. She must see the uncertainty on my face, because she smiles at me, equal parts grim and reassuring.

"You don't really believe I think the girls who just body-checked me into the lockers, called me a loser and ripped up my homework have my best interests at heart, do you?" she says.

I dig my whiteboard and marker from my bag. *They're not going to leave you alone if they see you with me.*

"So?" she says. "In my opinion, if those girls hate me, that only means I must be doing something right." The warning bell rings, and she sighs. "I should get to class. See you later."

I don't run into her again until lunch. I'm holed up in the library, the easiest place to be alone without drawing attention to myself or worrying about anyone bothering me. Every computer is taken, so my genius plan to waste the hour surfing the web is dashed to the rocks. Instead I plop down at an empty table and pull out my lunch—a bag of pretzels, bottled water and a Snickers bar, courtesy of the first-floor vending machine—and my geometry book. I can't believe this is my life now. Spending lunch in the library. Doing homework. Ahead of time. Homework I cannot even understand. Oh, parabolas, why must your formulas elude me so?

"That looks nutritious."

I look up to see Asha sitting across from me. She has a brown-paper-bag lunch spread out in front of her: a diagonally cut peanut butter and jelly sandwich, a little bag of crackers, some apple slices and a can of iced tea, along with her knitting.

I have no idea how long she's been sitting there. Did I really get that absorbed in my geometry homework? Wonders, they will never cease.

Asha sees my look and casts her gaze down at the tabletop. "Sorry, am I interrupting?" she asks. "I can go if you want."

She pushes her chair back and stands, but I shake my head, motion for her to sit down and close my textbook. Parabolas can wait. Asha beams, sitting again and unwrapping her sandwich.

"How's it going?" she asks.

I gesture to my homework and point a finger gun to my temple.

She grins. "Having some trouble, I take it?"

I pull out my whiteboard and write, *Only always*, and she laughs.

"You know, I could help you with it sometime," she says. "I'm pretty good with numbers."

I am more than willing to use this reluctant camaraderie to my benefit. Maybe I can get a good math grade out of it. That'd be something.

You free after school?

Asha makes an apologetic face. "Can't. I have to work," she explains. But then her eyes brighten. "Hey, why don't you come with me? Thursdays are slow anyway, and I get a break, so I could help you out. And I bet I can get you a free sandwich. Sam makes amazing tuna melts. I mean, I haven't tried them because I'm vegetarian, but everyone says they're awesome."

What about your boss?

"Dex won't care, trust me. He's really laid-back. You'd like him."

I consider my options. Hanging out at a diner does sound pretty sweet compared to the alternative—moping in an empty house until my parents come home from work. The prospect of eating something not made from tofu is too enticing to pass up. What's the worst that could happen?

O.K.

Asha's face lights up. "Perfect!" she exclaims. "It'll be fun, I promise." She grins and passes me an apple slice.

I bite into it, grateful, and for the most fleeting of moments I forget how depressed I'm supposed to be.

Asha meets me after detention, and we drive to Rosie's together. She's particularly bubbly today. Or maybe I've just forgotten what it's like to be in such a good mood that you feel the need to dance in your seat to the radio.

"You like rap?" she says over the music. "That is awesome."

Kristen would not find that awesome. And she definitely would not find Asha's dorky car dancing awesome. At least, not post-Warren Kristen. Pre-Warren Kristen was different. Less concerned about looking like an idiot. We used to choreograph silly dance routines in my bedroom, using hairbrushes for microphones. Those days are long over.

Asha doesn't stop dancing as we enter the diner. She even does a little twirl on her way up to the counter, leans across it and hollers, "Hey, Dex! I'm here!"

"My savior!" An older guy—late twenties, probably—pops his head over the counter. He has long hair, like my dad's in those old pictures, and a bunch of tattoos up and down his arms. There's also a big black star inked on his neck. He sees me hovering and grins. "*And* you brought me a customer? Damn, you really know how to score the brownie points. Speaking of brownies…"

Asha gasps. "You *better* not be teasing me."

"Of course not. I would never joke about a subject as sacred as baked goods." He brings out a brownie on a napkin. "Fresh out of the oven."

"You rock so hard," she says. She turns to me. "Chelsea, you *have* to try this."

I break off a piece and pop it into my mouth. It *is* good. Melt-in-your-mouth good, warm and chewy and delicious. I give Asha a thumbs-up to express my approval.

Dex cocks his head to the side. "Have I actually rendered someone speechless with my baking?" he asks. "That may be a first."

"Don't be so quick to flatter yourself. Chelsea doesn't talk," Asha explains. "She's taken a vow of silence."

Okay, now I'm blushing. I hate having to explain this. People probably think I'm just being an attention whore, and it is so not about that. Or people just think I'm a freak. Which… maybe I am. But I'm still not comfortable with letting my freak flag fly, so to speak.

But Dex doesn't miss a beat. "Very cool," he says, not sarcastically at all, then to Asha, "Sam's pulling stock from the freezer, and Andy should be here in an hour or so. I'm going to hole up in the office and make some calls to vendors, so come back and grab me if you need me."

"Sure thing," she tells him, walking around behind the counter. "It's cool if Chelsea hangs out?"

"As long as she doesn't break anything," he says with a wink, and then disappears down the side hall.

I sit down on one of the stools and sling my bag onto the counter as Asha smoothes her long hair back into a ponytail.

"I'm going to go load up the dishwasher," she tells me. "We don't really have one specific person who buses, so whoever has a minute just takes care of it. Noah was usually the one…"

She trails off, and at first I'm confused, but it takes only a second to put two and two together. Noah must have worked here, too. That explains the other day, when they mentioned that guy having to cover kitchen. And he's Sam's best friend, it's no surprise they'd work together.

This has to be a joke. Maybe I've underestimated Asha, and the only reason she's been friendly to me is that she's setting me up for humiliation. I can think of no other possible reason why she would invite me to Noah's workplace, a place full of people who know and, presumably, care about him. And anyone who cares about him likely hates me.

I grab my whiteboard and write furiously.

Why did you invite me here?

She frowns. "So I can help you with your homework. We talked about this."

This was a bad idea.

"Why?"

You know why.

"What do you mean?" she asks, but in a careful way that leads me to believe she knows exactly what I'm talking about. I don't want to have to spell it out for her, literally.

How much do you know?

She hems and haws before she answers me. "I heard what you did at the party," she admits. She can't look me in the eye as she says it. "Did you know what would happen? When you—told people what you did?"

I shake my head, because it's true that I didn't, but I don't know how that makes any difference. I should've known. I shouldn't have been such an idiot to not realize what would happen.

Why are you being nice to me?

"I don't know." She goes quiet for a minute. "I guess I just… I don't think you are what people say you are."

How would you know that?

"You turned your friends in to the cops," she says. "That's something."

Yeah, but what she doesn't know is that I question my decision every day. I busy myself with rubbing my board clean so I don't have to look at her and see that hope in her face, the hope that I'm this good person she imagines me to be, when I know the truth.

Asha's face flushes. "I'm sorry. I didn't know you'd be upset," she says. "You can leave if you want."

She disappears into the back, leaving me there to stay or go. Staying is a bad idea, I know. I start to grab my backpack so I can leave, but then I think of what Asha said, how she doesn't think I'm the person other people say I am. Her words gnaw at my gut. I know I'm not that person, but it's comforting to know someone else sees me as something more than a bitch or a backstabber.

Besides, I can't deny the fact that I could really, really use her help with my homework.

I sit back down and slide out my geometry book from my bag. It couldn't hurt to stay for a little while. If things get weird, I'll just take off. No harm, no foul.

I flip the book open to tonight's assignment. I hate math. I hate formulas and functions, especially when letters get involved. It's so confusing. I don't know how I'm supposed to relate to numbers. How learning any of this will ever come in handy in real life. Like, will I one day be in the grocery store, comparing the prices of toilet paper, and desperately need to find the square root of x in order to get the best deal? I highly doubt it. Geometry just feels like a waste of time.

My whole *life* feels like a waste of time.

I'm staring at the open page so hard my eyes cross when Sam walks up with a metal tub of sauce. When I see him, I jump a little, causing the stool to squeak as it turns. He looks even more startled than I feel.

"Chelsea? What are you doing here?" he blurts out.

I feel my face burning red. I point one hand to the left, where Asha went, and Sam follows the gesture with his eyes, seeming to connect the dots.

"Excuse me," he says flatly, and takes off in that direction.

As soon as he's out of sight, I jump off the stool and follow without thinking, hovering by the double doors leading to the busing area. I crouch behind a cart of clean dinner trays and spy through the dirty circular windows, catching a glimpse of Sam marching up to Asha, who is stacking some dry dishes into a rack. I can hear every word.

"You brought her here?" he exclaims. "What were you thinking?"

"Give her a chance," Asha says.

"It's not me I'm worried about," he says. "If Andy sees her, he is going to freak out."

Okay, who the hell *is* Andy, and why would he care about me being here?

Asha sets down the last plate and looks up at him. "I just think she could really use a friend right now."

"And you're volunteering for the position," he says skeptically.

"I don't think she has anyone else," she tells him. "Everyone is mad at her."

"I'm not saying we should be gathering the pitchforks or anything, but come on. Did it ever occur to you maybe she deserves it?"

"You don't know, Sam. It's not just about Noah…it's about her ratting out those basketball players. There were these girls today, and they said these awful things to her… I mean, *really* awful. Then one of them said something to me—"

"*What?* Who?"

"It doesn't even matter," she continues, "but Chelsea got in the girl's face, and she didn't say anything, obviously, but I could tell she was mad about it. And someone wrote something nasty on her locker. And you saw what they did to her car, and I *know* you don't think that was deserved. I just want to be nice, okay? Can you please have my back on this?"

There's a lengthy pause, and I hold my breath, trying not to make any noise that will give me away, desperately waiting to see what Sam will say to that.

"All right," he says softly. "Just…be careful, okay?"

"I will," she promises. "Will you do me a favor?"

"Depends. What is it?"

"I told her you'd make her a tuna melt. On the house."

Sam groans. "The things I do for you, Asha."

I decide I've heard enough. I bolt back to my stool, settling on it just as Sam reappears. He gives me a long, considering look, like he's warring with himself on how to deal with me.

"Asha says I owe you a tuna melt," he says. He's not smiling, but he doesn't sound angry. "Sound good?"

I nod, and he turns his back to me to grab ingredients. I shouldn't have stayed. Now I know why Asha is being nice—I'm her charity project. It's embarrassing, and idiotic because if she knew me at all, what I'm really like, she would hate me, not pity me. She's too nice for her own good.

The way Rosie's is set up, the grill is right there so you can see your food being made in front of you. I watch as Sam quickly assembles the sandwich then slaps it on the grill. After a while he flips it with the spatula and cooks the other side. His movements are smooth, practiced, like he's done this so often he could do it in his sleep.

Asha reemerges just as an elderly couple walks through the door. She skirts around the counter, snatching two menus, and goes to greet them. Sam flips the tuna melt onto a dish and pushes it toward me.

"You're gonna love it," he says. "I'm famous for my tuna melts."

So Asha said. When I take my first bite, I totally get the ringing endorsement. It's so good I actually moan a little. Embarrassed, I clap a hand over my mouth.

Sam looks over from wiping down the grill and grins. "Told you."

More people start filtering into the diner as the evening goes on. Asha's kept busy, alternating between seating patrons, bringing out drinks and busing tables. Every time Sam finishes cooking, he yells "Order up!" and sets out the dishes where Asha can reach. It is way more interesting to watch him than it is to focus on my homework.

About an hour later, a boy rushes through the door, half running into the kitchen and yelling, "I know, I know, I'm late, goddamn car wouldn't start, but I'm here, I'm on it."

"Don't swear in front of the customers," Sam chides him.

"Like they give a fuck," the boy mutters under his breath. He looks toward one of the booths with a wide smile. "Hi, Sally!"

I swivel the stool around to see an older woman waving at him cheerily. When I turn back to the counter, the boy is staring at me with frightening intensity.

And that's when it hits me.

This is the boy. The boy who was with Noah at Kristen's party.

"Why the hell is she here?" he asks.

I'm frozen in place. All I can do is stare back at him, my stomach in my throat.

"That's Chelsea," Sam explains. "She's—"

"I know who she is," he snaps. He hasn't taken his eyes off me for a second. "I'm asking what she's *doing here.*"

Oh, God. Oh, God, I might actually throw up. This is too much.

"Andy, come on. Be cool, okay?" Sam assures him. He puts his hand on Andy's back and gives him a little shove. "Go ring up the customers. I just boxed their order. It's cool."

The look on Andy's face tells me it is anything *but* cool. But after a lingering second he tears his piercing stare off me and moves to the register at the other end of the counter.

I gaze down at my open textbook, my eyes blurring with

unshed tears. My breath comes out all shaky and uneven. I can't even be justifiably upset at his reaction—Andy has every right to hate me. I'm fuzzy on some of the details, but when the cops interviewed me, they did say he was inside the convenience store when Warren and Joey pulled Noah out of that car.

If he'd been there—if he hadn't gone inside—it could've just as easily been him. It could've been even worse.

I should leave. I should find a bathroom to throw up in. I should—

"Hey." Sam throws a straw at me so I look up. His face is soft and serious. "Don't worry about Andy. I'll talk to him later. Explain things."

Explain what, exactly? Nothing's changed. Nothing will undo what I did. And how am I supposed to ever make that up to Andy? To Noah? To anyone?

Where do I even start?

Normally I would call it a night and duck and run, but I can't find an opportunity to make a sly getaway when I keep catching Sam looking at me and when Asha walks by me every few minutes. Besides, I'm Asha's ride home, and even I know stranding her here would be a shitty thing to do. So I stay, struggling through the first few problems of my geometry homework until I give up the pretense of understanding anything and start sketching out random outfit design ideas instead.

Asha, true to her word, spends her break sitting next to me and explaining how to graph parabolas.

"Since *a* is positive, it opens upward," she says. "So you make the chart, then take the interval and plug the numbers into the equation." She scribbles a few numbers in my notebook. "And all you have to do is solve for y, find the points and draw them in. See?"

This is her third attempt to explain this problem to me, and I'm only just starting to get it. I can't believe how patient she is with me, considering she's been running around here like a crazy person all night. When her shift ends, I hang back awkwardly as she goes to say goodbye to Sam, who is closing with Dex and Andy. Andy hasn't even looked at me since our first interaction. That's okay with me. It's not like I have anything to say to him, either.

As we drive toward Asha's house, she rolls her head back against the headrest and sighs. "Usually that wouldn't be so rough," she says. "But we're pretty understaffed right now—" She stops and looks at me cautiously. "Sorry, I'm not trying to, you know, make you feel—"

I cut her off with a shake of my head to let her know that it's okay. I know she's not *trying* to make me feel guilty. It doesn't matter. I still do.

"I really liked having you there. And not just for the transportation," she says. She turns her head away from me, toward the window. "I don't really have a lot of friends. Yeah, Sam is great—everyone I work with is, really—but at school, people think I'm… I don't know. Weird, I guess. Most of the time I'm okay with that. But sometimes—it's just, it's nice, hanging out with you, is all."

I drive in silence, thinking about what she just said. I don't know Asha well enough to consider her my friend, and honestly, even now, as nice as Asha is, it still feels bizarre to socialize with someone I never would've given a second look a few weeks ago. Like some part of me feels this is just temporary. I guess I had convinced myself that eventually everyone would get over what happened, and I'd be accepted back into the fold—but that prospect is looking dimmer and dimmer as time goes on. And after receiving Kristen's scathing email, which makes me see red even just thinking about it, I'm not sure if I really want that anymore. Maybe some bridges are better left burned.

"You should come again tomorrow," she says. "I could help you with your geometry some more. If you don't have anything better to do."

Andy will probably be there. I don't know if it's fair of me, to be hanging out at Rosie's, like I'm trying to rub my presence in his face or something, when he's so obviously angry at me. But then I think about Asha, how she really *wants* me around. I know it'd be better if I kept to myself—for both of our sakes, and Andy's and Sam's. But being alone sucks. It sounds like Asha knows that firsthand, and that's why she's offering her friendship. I don't know if I have enough pride to turn that down, no matter who it's coming from. Even with what happened with Andy, today was the best day I've had since New Year's. It seems like that's something I should hold on to. That I *need* to hold on to. I turn my head and nod. And the pleased look on Asha's face tells me I've made the right decision.

day five

Friday used to be the best day of the week because it hailed the start of a weekend of partying and shopping and blowing off homework in favor of hanging out with Kristen and everyone else. Now Friday is my favorite day for a different reason. It means I get two full days of blissful peace where I don't even have to *think* about school.

This Friday will be longer than usual due to another detention, courtesy of Mrs. Finch. All of my other teachers have, if grudgingly, accepted my silence, but she has not. Every day she comes up to my desk first thing, asks if I've decided to participate, and when I just stare at her with my jaw clenched, she writes up the detention slip and sets it in the middle of my desk for everyone to see.

On my way out of her room, Lowell stuck a wad of gum in my hair and I had to spend fifteen minutes in the bathroom picking it out best I could, warding off the amused looks other girls gave me at the sink as I held my hair under the tap. It was disgusting and humiliating and I wanted to scream, but I just settled for pulling my hair back in a bun to hide the wet spots.

Halfway through Geometry, I catch Megan staring at me.

It's the first time she's made eye contact this week. Her expression is unreadable, so I try for a small smile, testing the waters. Megan is a sweet person, and we were friends before; maybe she hasn't made a snap judgment about my involvement in what happened. Maybe we can still be friends.

The cold look she shoots me in return kills that short-lived hope.

She leans toward me and hisses, "I know you knew about Owen and Tessa."

My stomach twists. I've been so caught up in the Noah situation that I almost forgot about that.

"You were supposed to be my friend," she says, her voice tight and strained with a mixture of anger and hurt. "You should've told me. I had to find out from some girl in my science class. She showed me the picture of them on her phone. You know, the picture *you* spread around."

My eyes widen. The pictures are still on my phone, but I haven't sent them to anyone.

"I guess everyone was right about you," she mutters.

Mr. Callihan stops midlecture to clear his throat pointedly, and Megan leans away from me. She stares straight ahead, and I know that once again, I no longer exist to her.

I'm too busy processing this latest information to pay attention to the rest of Mr. Callihan's diatribe. It doesn't take a rocket scientist to realize what had to have happened. It was Kristen. She must've sent the picture and told everyone I did it—a perfect way to turn Tessa and Megan against me for good. Knowing I have literally zero way to defend myself against her accusations.

This must be phase one of Kristen's retaliation. And I *know* this isn't the end of it.

When I see Brendon at lunch, I'm not sure if it's going to make my Friday better or worse.

He's standing in front of the library double doors, riffling through his backpack. I'm supposed to meet Asha for another tutoring session. Part of me wants to flee the moment I spot him there, but the only way out is if I turn around abruptly and backtrack. I'm still considering my options when Brendon glances up and sees me. He looks uncertain, but since I have him inadvertently cornered, he can't really ignore me.

"Hi," he says, zipping up his backpack.

I try for a disarming smile and hope he doesn't notice the way I'm staring. I can't help it. Why does he have to be so pretty?

"I heard about your…thing," he says. "The no talking?"

There's an awkward moment where I'm just looking at him. Obviously I can't really respond to that, can I?

"I heard you joined a cult, and that's why you're doing this." A smile flits over his face, a little uneasy.

So that's what people are saying, huh? The rumor mill must be in overdrive—certainly Kristen's taking care of that much. I wonder what else is being said about me. I'm sure I could take a wild guess and not be far off the mark.

"I didn't do anything," he says. At my completely confused look, he elaborates. "That day I got detention. Some girl asked me to borrow a pencil during a test, I handed one to her…my Civics teacher gave us both detentions. Total overreaction." He pauses. "I just remember you looked surprised to see me there, thought you might want to know why."

Of course when Brendon gets in trouble, it's not really trouble. I knew he was too straitlaced to do anything wrong. I nod slowly, not sure how else to react to this. I feel like I should be coming up with some way to extend this interaction, but part of me wants it to end as soon as possible to kill the painful awkwardness of it all.

"Um. So." Brendon swings his backpack onto his back and shifts uncomfortably. Clearly the novelty of a one-way conversation has worn off. Or maybe he believes I really *am* in a cult. "Guess I should probably...yeah."

He ducks his head and hurries off, and I turn to watch him disappear into the sea of students. Just as he rounds the corner, Asha comes walking up to the library. She looks from Brendon to me with a knowing smile.

"You like him, don't you?" she says, head tilted to one side.

I give her an incredulous look. What is this, middle school?

"I don't blame you. He's cute." She snags my arm and tugs me toward the library. "Come on, no more time for swooning. Parabolas await!"

Oh, my life.

"Tell me I'm not the only one counting down the minutes until school lets out," Sam says, collapsing onto the stool next to me in a dramatic fashion, half sprawled over the art table.

It must be a long day for him if he's commiserating to me, of all people. I know the feeling. This has been the longest, most hellish week of my entire life.

I pull a sympathetic face and write on my whiteboard. *You are not alone.*

"I think I'm going to need the weekend just to recuperate from all the studying I did this week," he says "I had two major projects due and four big tests. That's inhumane." He sighs, pushing his head up and propping it against his open palm. "Asha told me you're coming to Rosie's again."

I nod warily. While he acted okay with making me the tuna melt and for most of the night, I still remember his conversation with Asha. I know his tolerance toward me is only because she asked for it.

"Listen," he says, leaning closer to me, "I told Asha I'd give you a chance, because she asked. But if you're going to be hanging around, I need you to be honest with me about a few things." His eyes narrow. "You're not messing with her, are you?"

I shake my head hard. I don't even know how I *could* mess with Asha. Hasn't he noticed that I'm in no position to screw anyone over? I'm the lowest of the low.

He studies me carefully. "I hope not," he says. "Asha is a good person. Better than most. She's not like you."

That stings. I frown and reach for my whiteboard. *You don't know me.*

"You're right," he says. "But I know Asha. She sees the good in people, even when she probably shouldn't. She's the best friend you can have, not just some consolation prize. She doesn't know how to be mean. If you act like you're her friend, she's going to believe you are. If you're just using her to help yourself get a good grade and then drop her, she's going to be upset. I don't want to see her get hurt."

I can't pretend his concern isn't warranted. After all, my main motivation for spending time with Asha so far has been for help with my homework. But at the same time, I can't deny that there's something about her I genuinely like, too. Sam is right—Asha doesn't know how to be mean. When she says something, she means exactly what she says. She isn't like Kristen, where cutting criticisms are disguised as compliments, where everything has a double meaning. It's refreshing to be around someone I can take at face value.

Asha is the only person who is nice to me, I write, turning the board for him to see. *I don't plan to screw that up.*

He stares at my words for a while before he clears his throat. "Good," he says softly. "Now that that's out of the way, I have a few more questions for you."

I sit up straighter, bracing myself for the worst.

"What's your favorite color?"

Okay, that's the last question I expected. I was thinking something more along the lines of *Why are you such a bitch?* or *How dare you?* or something else dripping with disdain and accusation.

"You were right when you said I know nothing about you," he explains. "So let's remedy that. We'll start off easy. Tell me your favorite color."

I try to hide a grin as I write on my board. *Guess.*

"Oh, I see how it is. You're going to make this hard for me."

I like to keep an air of mystery.

"I'm sure you do," he says with a smile.

A smile? I'm so surprised I almost fall off the stool. It's a nice one, too. Kind of lopsided, but cute. The fact that it's so unexpected makes it even better. I return it with one of my own, a real one, and I feel the tension between us fading like a slowly deflating balloon.

Sam even walks me to my locker after class. He doesn't say anything about it, just does it like it's a perfectly normal thing to do. I appreciate the company, if only because listening to him talk helps distract me from worrying about who I might possibly run into. I text Dad to let him know I don't know when I'll be home since I'm being tutored after school, which isn't really a lie; Asha said she'd help me out again. That girl is on a diehard mission to drill geometry into my head.

"Okay," Sam says, leaning into me as some freshman barrels past us on the staircase, "favorite Peanuts character."

He spent all of class playing this game with me—trying to guess things about me without me speaking. All I have to do is shake my head or give him the thumbs-up when he guesses correctly. So far he's found out that my favorite color is green, my favorite vegetable is carrots and my middle name is Rose. That last one took a *lot* of guessing on his part.

"Let's start with the obvious," he says. "Charlie Brown."

I shake my head.

"Snoopy?"

Nope.

"Okay... Linus?" No. "Peppermint Patty?" No. "Marcie? Pig-Pen? Lucy?"

No, no, no.

Sam grins. "Damn. I thought it would be Lucy. You seem like the Lucy type."

I shoot him a withering glare. Lucy? Really? The girl who yanks away the football and is bossy as hell?

"Fine, fine, not Lucy then." He pauses, considering, and then snaps his fingers. "I got it. Woodstock?"

I grin and flash him a thumbs-up. I can't believe it took him so many guesses. I mean, who *doesn't* love Woodstock? He's adorable.

"All right, I have one last question for you," he says. "Asha's birthday is tomorrow. I'm taking her ice skating. Do you want to come?"

I'm so caught off guard by the question that I almost trip over one of the steps. I barely manage to stop myself from falling flat on my face by grabbing on to the handrail.

"Asha asked me to invite you. I realize it's probably not the level of cool you're accustomed to when it comes to social outings," Sam says. "Your crowd's idea of a fun time is probably driving around bashing mailboxes with a baseball bat."

I want to resent his assumption, but the truth is Warren and Joey drove Kristen and me around town at three in the morning doing precisely that like five times over the summer.

Ice skating. Okay, not really my thing, but it's for Asha, and a way to prove I'm not just using her. I look defiantly at Sam and nod.

"You'll come?" He doesn't bother to conceal his surprise.

I nod again, more firmly this time, and Sam blinks once, but then shrugs.

"Okay," he says. "I'll pick you up around noon."

We finally fight our way through the steady stream of students and stop at my locker. Sam leans against the one next to mine. He looks like he's waiting, or like he just wants to chill out. I stand there and wait for him to say something. It's not like I expect him to keep me company or whatever.

"Guess I'll see you after school," he says, after he realizes I'm just staring at him. He does this awkward mock salute thing and walks away. He is such a dork. It's sort of endearing.

I see him later at Rosie's. When I walk through the door, he's cleaning off the grill, his back to me. He glances over his shoulder when the bell chimes and flashes me a quick smile. I smile back, starting to approach him, when Asha calls my name.

"Chelsea!" She waves me over to the booth where she's sitting. "How was detention?"

I make a face and slide into the seat across from her, pushing my bag aside. The hour I spent in the detention room after school seemed to crawl by at a torturously slow pace. I really hope Mrs. Finch gives up on this punishment method soon. If not, she may just break me yet.

Asha and I sit in a booth, rolling silverware as she explains quadratic expressions, while Sam and Andy cook behind the counter.

I avoid Andy as much as I can. It's not too hard, since he seems to be doing his best to avoid me, too. The only time he acknowledges me is when he comes over to wipe off the table next to ours. His eyes meet mine for a fleeting second, his mouth pulling down with displeasure. He looks surprised, like he didn't expect me to show my face here again.

To be perfectly honest, I'm sort of surprised, too.

"I got this, Andy." Another girl, tall and curvy with a tiny diamond stud in her nose, comes up to him and swats him in the arm. "Get your ass back in the kitchen."

Andy rolls his eyes. "Bossy, bossy." He tucks his rag in his apron pocket and heads back behind the counter.

"Hey, Asha," the girl says then cocks her head at me. "Who's your friend?"

"This is Chelsea," Asha explains. "Chelsea, this is Lou. She's Dex's other half."

Lou laughs. "I think my official title is Head Bitch in Charge." She smiles at me. "Do you want something to drink?"

I feel myself blushing, but Asha, thank God, steps in for me.

"Chelsea doesn't talk," she says. She looks at me. "You want a Coke?"

I nod, and Lou grins again, even wider this time. "I'll be right back," she says.

After Lou has walked away, Asha explains that she's Dex's girlfriend. "She waits tables, but she's basically a comanager. She and Dex have been together forever," she tells me. "They're, like, made for each other. It's ridiculous."

When Dex comes in later, he goes straight to Lou, kisses the top of her head and smoothes a hand down the back of her old-fashioned gingham dress, which she paired with black fishnets and neon-green high-tops, a combination that sounds crazy in theory but one she manages to pull off with flair.

I really like this. Sitting in the middle of this frenzy of activity, watching everyone run the diner. Dex heads up the register, ringing up customers and taking order slips from Asha and Lou, attaching them to the ticket rack and sliding it toward Sam and Andy. Sam and Andy work in tandem, passing cooking utensils back and forth, trading off on orders. Everyone has their duty to make things work smoothly.

And even just sitting there, it's like I'm somehow part of it, even though I'm not, really. I'm just an observer.

day six

I haven't been ice skating since Beth Murkowski's birthday party in the fourth grade, and I'm not sure that even counts since it was on the pond in her backyard and I had to borrow her sister's pair of skates that were three sizes too big. Needless to say, that experience ended in many bruises and tears. I'm skeptical of my ability to get through this without inflicting some horrible injury on myself or innocent bystanders, but Asha assures me on the car ride over I'll be fine.

"It's not that hard," she says. "One foot in front of the other!"

Yeah, easy for her to say. She clearly has experience, if the pair of beat-up baby-blue skates resting in her lap is any indication.

"Don't worry, I promise not to laugh when you fall down," Sam promises. He pauses before he adds, "Much."

If this seat belt allowed me to reach over and smack him, I would. Unfortunately I'm left to glare at the back of his head.

As soon as we get to the rink, Asha takes off for the ice while Sam and I wait in line for skates. When Sam approaches the counter and asks for size seven skates, I can't help but think of what people say about how the size of a guy's feet correlates to the size of their dicks—or is it hands? And then I realize I'm thinking about Sam's dick and it's getting kind of embarrassing.

I'm still staring at his hands when Sam steps aside and says, "Chelsea?" I realize he's gotten his skates and it's my turn now.

"What can I do for you?" the guy behind the counter asks.

I don't have my whiteboard with me, or any writing utensils, and I don't know how to mime "ice skates" in an effective manner, so I flounder for a few seconds before looking to Sam for help.

Thankfully Sam steps up to the plate. "She needs skates," he explains.

The guy raises his eyebrows at Sam. "Is she deaf or something?" he asks.

"No," he says. "She just had her tonsils taken out. She's still recovering." The lie comes so smoothly from Sam's mouth I'm caught off guard. He throws a sympathetic arm around my shoulder, pulling me in close. "But she insisted on coming anyway. She's a brave little toaster, this one."

This explanation seems to placate the guy. When he asks me what size I need, I hold up six fingers, pay for the skates with cash and then head down to the rink with Sam. We sit on the benches, pulling on gloves and strapping on our skates, and I unsteadily follow him into the rink.

The second I step foot on the ice, I nearly slip, but Sam grabs my arm to prevent me from falling flat on my ass.

"Easy there," he says. "I've got you."

He gently pushes me toward the wall so I can hold on to the railing. I cling to it for dear life. Out of the corner of my eye I see Asha whiz by, unbelievably fast and effortless, like skating is the easiest thing in the world. How does she do it? I can barely stand on the ice without tripping over myself.

"We'll take it slow," Sam says. "Hold my hands."

I hesitate, every instinct screaming at me not to let go of the railing since it's the one thing keeping me up, but I slowly convince myself to extend one hand to take his and then the other. I'm gripping his hands so hard it should be painful, but if it is, Sam's face doesn't show it.

"All right, now I'm going to move backward, and you're going to follow me. Okay?"

He doesn't wait for an answer before he begins to glide backward. My body leans forward to keep hold of his hands, my legs refusing to move until they have no choice. As soon as I attempt to skate toward Sam, I immediately trip and tumble face-first onto the ice in the most comically ungraceful manner possible, an embarrassing, crazy flail of arms and legs, landing hard on my elbows. It hurts, but not nearly as much as my pride does at the moment.

"Yikes." Sam skids to a stop in front of me, trying not to laugh but only half succeeding. "Teaching you to skate may be more difficult than I thought."

I'm too busy pulling myself onto my knees and rubbing my elbows to glare at him properly. I never should've agreed to this. All I'm doing is making an idiot out of myself. Hasn't my dignity taken enough of a blow these days without me contributing to it of my own volition?

Upon seeing my sulky expression, Sam gives up all pretense of containing his laughter. "Aw, come on, you're okay," he says. He extends an open hand down to me. "Get up and try again."

After a moment's more of moping, I take his hand, letting him assist me to my feet. This time he goes more slowly, helping me inch along the ice. After a little while I start to get the hang of it—it's like Asha said, one foot and then the other.

"There you go!" Sam says, his voice a little more enthusiastic than what is warranted. "You're getting it!"

I start to gain a little confidence, and with it speed, pushing off the ice with a little more gusto. Just as I think I've figured it out, however, I lose my balance and stumble forward into Sam, toppling us both to the ice in a tangle of limbs. I land right on top of his chest, so when he laughs, I feel it reverberating through me, and I can't help but laugh, too. Sam's eyes widen like he's startled by the sound. Our faces are so close together, and looking at him looking at me, I'm suddenly, painfully aware of the rush job I did on my makeup this morning. I must look like such a mess.

Sam's laughter fades, slowly replaced by an awkward smile, his eyes locked on mine. He reaches one gloved hand up to brush some of my hair behind my ear, and my breath catches in my throat at the contact.

"You should smile more often," he tells me. "It's a good look for you."

I know that a normal person would've gotten to their feet by now, and this has officially passed the welcome sign to Awkward City, but I'm so struck by the look on his face that I can't bring myself to pull away yet.

"Wow, you two really suck."

The sound of Asha's voice defuses the moment like a bucket of cold water poured over my head. I look over to where she's standing with both hands on her hips and push off Sam quickly, struggling to my feet. I'm not sure whether to be disappointed or grateful to Asha for interrupting.

"Hey, we can't all be Michelle Kwan," Sam retorts, sitting up on his elbows.

To his credit, he sounds completely unfazed by what just happened, so maybe I really was imagining things. He stands up, brushing off his knees while Asha skates around him, throwing in a few graceful spins. I like watching her move. She seems so sure of herself out here.

She skates over to me and snatches my hand. "Come on, skate with me," she urges. My eyes widen, and she smirks. "I'll go extra slow, I promise."

I allow Asha to drag me for a while, until I get into the rhythm enough to keep up with her snail's pace, and we glide along semismoothly. Sam catches up and skates backward in front of us. Showoff. Every so often Asha breaks away to zoom around the rink and do a few twirls and spins, or she and Sam will race around, or they'll skate tight circles around me, laughing.

I fall down a few more times, and they both laugh, but every time I do they help me up again, so I can't be too annoyed about it.

"This is for me?"

Asha is marveling at my gift to her like I purchased a diamond necklace or something. I nod as I sip on what's left of my Coke, the straw making gurgling sounds. We're seated in the rink's small eatery, stuffing our faces with nachos and hot dogs. Crap food compared to the diner, but once the free skate was over, we were too hungry to drive over to Rosie's and wait.

I figured now would be a good time to give her my birthday gift. I don't know why she's so impressed; I didn't exactly have a lot of notice, so I just dug out one of the half-finished denim clutch purses I'd pieced together from my bin of sewing projects and completed it last night. All it took was sewing in the snap buttons—tedious, but not too difficult—and then cutting and sewing on the shoulder strap. I didn't even wrap the stupid thing, just stuffed it in a gift bag with some tissue paper.

Whatever. I've only known the girl for less than a week, I figured I'd already put in more effort than anyone would rightfully expect.

"I love it! Homemade gifts are my favorite," Asha says, examining the little purse more closely. "I can't believe you made this! It's so cool. You'll have to teach me sometime." She turns to Sam, beaming. "Isn't it cute?"

"Adorable," Sam agrees. He's looking at me as he says it, eyebrows raised like he's impressed but doesn't want to show it too much.

Somehow that look makes me feel like I've passed a test I didn't even know I was taking.

day seven

Sunday is my most relaxing day of the week. I don't have to deal with a million people expecting me to talk. I don't have to explain myself to anyone. Mom is mostly out of the house, working at the store, and Dad camps out in front of the television watching sports. I use the time to finish reading *Of Mice and Men,* which turns out to be just as awful as I thought it would be. I hate stories with dead puppies. So depressing.

After I've finished the book—well, after I've thrown it across the room—I spend some time at my sewing table, digging through my big bin of various fabrics and old, abandoned projects. I'm terrible at finishing anything; what I try to sew never looks the way it does in my head, and I end up ditching most of my work with the intent to pick it up again later. Except then I get distracted by a new idea, and the vicious cycle continues anew. Asha's purse was the first project I've completed in months.

I find a pair of old jeans I'd saved to convert into a denim skirt and work on it for a while, figuring out the measurements and trimming off the pant legs. I get annoyed removing the inseam stitching, though, and decide to set it aside, knowing I'll probably never touch it again. Coming up with ideas is much more fun than trying to make them reality.

I flop back on my bed, staring at my ceiling, which is quickly becoming a favorite pastime since I have no actual life to speak of. I fish my phone out of my purse and scroll down to Asha's phone number—she gave it to me earlier, told me if I needed help with geometry I could always text her. I type *hey* and click Send.

A few minutes later my phone receives a new text.

Hi! Homework trouble?

nope. just bored. of mice & men is a terrible book.

Steinbeck depresses me.

ugh i know right? one dead puppy is one too many.

Lol. Hey I'm about to walk over to Rosie's for a shift. Talk to you later?

It could just be residual effects from the combination of finishing such a depressing story and being defeated by a pair of jeans, but I don't really want to be alone right now with the dread that comes from knowing tomorrow I'll have to drag myself back to school. That must be the reason I ask Asha if I can pick her up and tag along to Rosie's. She agrees, and it takes me only a minute to grab my bag and car keys and rush out the door. Dad doesn't notice my exit—he probably won't even realize I'm gone, and who knows when Mom will get home from work.

Asha's already waiting for me in the driveway by the time I pull up to her house. She bounds down the icy walk to the car and dives into the passenger seat, rubbing her hands together to warm them up. She doesn't say anything as we drive over to Rosie's, just hums some unfamiliar melody underneath her breath while gazing out the window, lost in her own little world. It's so weird to me how she seems so damn *bubbly* all the time.

Maybe that's the effect spending time at Rosie's has on people—everyone there today is in a good mood. I don't see Sam at all, and I find myself a little disappointed about that. Asha catches me scanning the area behind the counter and must know what I'm thinking.

"He worked earlier today," she explains as she ties on her apron. "Don't worry. Dex will fix you something."

Dex looks up from where he's cooking meat on the industrial stove. "You hungry?" he asks, and before I can shake my head, he turns his back to me. "You look hungry. Tonight's special is goulash. It's a new recipe, and if you allow me to test drive it on you, it's on the house."

I apparently don't have a say in the matter, because he starts fixing it before I can communicate any affirmative answer. That's okay; my stomach is actually rumbling with hunger and the delicious smells of his cooking only make it growl louder. By the time he serves me the bowl, I'm all but salivating.

Dex watches me like a hawk as I lift the spoon to my mouth and take my first tentative bite. I've never had goulash; it tastes similar to beef stew, except better, thick and warm and a little spicy. I grab a pen from my bag and scribble on a napkin.

I want you to feed me forever!

I slide it across the counter to him, and he laughs as he reads it.

"I'll take that as a stamp of approval." He grins. He turns to Asha and says, "I like this girl. She can stay."

day eight

I'm almost feeling good when I get to school on Monday. Refreshed. Rejuvenated. I park my car in the student lot and walk toward the school with a little swing in my step.

And then I run into Derek and Lowell.

They're both standing at the edge of the parking lot, looking straight at me. I freeze for a moment. No one else is around. No one to witness whatever is about to happen. I hate the helpless feeling that crawls its way into my stomach.

As I come up to them, I veer to the right, trying to walk past, but Lowell steps in front of me, blocks my path.

"Hey," he says, and when I keep walking, more sharply, *"Hey."*

I stop and look at him. I try not to let it show the way my heart is beating, fast and hard, like it's trying to free itself from my chest.

"What's that?" Lowell cocks his head to one side, gaze sliding down to the whiteboard tucked under my arm, and before I can jerk back, he reaches out and snatches it from me. "Hey, Derek, catch."

He throws it over my head to Derek. I lunge for it, but

Derek jumps back, holding it out of reach and laughing at my attempt.

"Oh, what do we have here?" Derek says. He snaps the marker from its holder and scribbles on the surface. When he flashes the board for me to see, I'm met with the ugly words *STUPID WHORE,* made even uglier by his harsh scrawl. The same scrawl I've seen on my locker. "I think you should wear this around your neck or something. Like, as a sign. Give us all some fair warning."

I know I can't force him to give it back.

I know I can't show a reaction in front of them, because that will only egg them on.

I do the only thing I can think of. The one thing I know will piss them off the most.

I smile.

They both stare at me like I've been sent from some alien planet, which is how I know I've thrown them for a loop. It's the smallest of victories, but still a victory, nonetheless. Derek tosses the whiteboard carelessly, sending it skittering across the sidewalk.

"Whoops," he says, voice dripping with sarcasm.

Lowell gives one last glare and mumbles, "Fucking freak."

He hocks some spit at me. Thankfully his aim is terrible, and the spit only makes contact with the toe of my shoe. They both laugh like it's the most hilarious thing ever and head into the building. Assholes.

I gather the whiteboard off the pavement and rub the spit off my shoe in some snow, my body shaking from a combination of intense relief and the cold air. Angry tears build behind my eyes, but I blink them back, trying to shake the feeling off. But I can't. This vow was supposed to be about making things less complicated, to stop myself from doing something stupid, to show everyone how much I don't need them. It was about me deciding that if I can't have their forgiveness or their respect, I won't give them anything. All it's done is made me an easy target.

I'm going to get Derek and Lowell back for this. I haven't figured out exactly how, yet, but I have plenty of time to plot my revenge. They'll never see it coming, because they don't expect me to fight back. Well, they have no idea who they're dealing with. I'm Chelsea freaking Knot.

While Derek and Lowell may not have tired of giving me a hard time yet, the good news is Mrs. Finch seems to have resigned herself to my silence.

After class, I stand at her desk, fully prepared for my customary sentencing. Instead of pulling out her detention slips, though, she has the study guide I turned in today in her hands.

"This is very good work, Chelsea," she tells me, and it's enough to bowl me over. She tosses the guide onto a stack of papers and looks at me over the tops of her glasses. "I believe you read the novel. Truly a first."

The truth is, she's not wrong. Usually I just skim the pages and Wikipedia the book summaries. I mean, you can find anything online. A lot of teachers aren't Net-savvy enough to figure that out.

"You have some very...*strong* feelings," she says.

That's probably a reference to the two paragraph rant I did on how much I hate reading about dead puppies, and how much it sucks that the only female character in the book is, of course, a temptress who leads to the two main guys' downfall. Sexist much, Mr. Steinbeck?

"But your criticism stems from an understanding of the material," she goes on. "And it's a marked improvement from your past work. So I have to concede that if this…vow of silence of yours is strengthening your focus as a student, it isn't fair of me to punish you."

Wow. No more detentions? As much as I'll miss sitting in that tiny windowless room every day, I'll find it in me to persevere. Somehow.

"Don't think I'll be letting you slack off from now on," Mrs. Finch warns me. "I expect to see more work of this caliber. You understand?"

I nod fervently. I am so willing to let myself be blackmailed into doing my homework if it means I get my freedom back.

And there's a definite novelty to knowing what my teachers are talking about instead of just zoning out as usual. Like, in geometry, I actually understood the equations Mr. Callihan wrote on the overhead projector. Okay, not all of them, but some. And I even took notes. Detailed ones! Asha is a saint. She really is.

This is what I tell—well, not tell, but write to—Sam while Ms. Kinsey pontificates on the technique behind charcoal shading. He looks at my sketchpad and laughs, and when he takes my pencil, his fingers cover mine for a moment.

yeah she's pretty awesome

Awesome x awesome. $Awesome^2$

$awesome^3$

$Awesome^{99999999}$

$awesome^{infinity}$

What is the square root of awesome?

$\sqrt{awesome}$ = asha

You should be the one tutoring me.

maybe in home ec

Sewing? I already know how to do that.

cooking

Asha said she'd teach me to knit.

tuna melts and scarves. you'd be set for life.

You'd really show me how to make a tuna melt?

if you want. coming to rosie's tonite?

Depends. Am I welcome?

sure

What about Andy?

i talked to him

AND?????

& he's cool

Liar.

o.k. you're not gonna be best friends anytime soon. but he won't punch you in the face or anything. promise. maybe you could talk to him?

...are you kidding?

nevermind

Sam's suggestion for me to talk to Andy sticks with me for the rest of the day. I know he probably didn't mean it literally, but it makes me wonder about what, exactly, it will take for me to talk again. I know I can't stay silent forever, but the longer I don't speak, the less inclined I am to start. Still, that doesn't change the fact that Sam is right. Andy deserves an explanation. An apology. *Something.*

I momentarily consider approaching him when I walk into Rosie's, but the place is a madhouse. There's a line of people waiting to be seated, and before I even get to the counter, Dex leans across it and yells, "Asha, we need you, stat!" Which strikes me as kind of funny, like we're in a hospital emergency room or something. But Dex's face is totally serious.

"Monday nights are always crazy," Asha explains as she pops behind the counter. "The dinner menu's half off."

"Lou's on section two. Need you to start seating," Dex says.

Asha grabs a bunch of menus and hurries toward the greeter stand. "On it!"

"You." Dex points a pair of tongs at me. "I need you on dish duty."

I stare at him with wide eyes. Me? Seriously?

"Seriously," he says. "Andy'll show you what to do."

Andy, in the middle of setting a plate of home fries on the counter, stops dead in his tracks. "What? *Dex,* I'm—"

"Whatever you're doing, it can wait five minutes. Now *go.*"

Dex is really not kidding around. I shrug off my jacket and hang it with my messenger bag on the coatrack before I scoot into the kitchen, up to the big industrial sink. There are dirty pans and dishes and cups stacked all around it, waiting to be cleaned. Andy leans against the sink and irritably blows hair out of his face.

"This—" he starts, grabbing the hose "—is the power spray. It should get anything off of anything, and anything it some-how misses, you use that." He points to a ratty scrub brush sitting on the sink's edge. "Spray everything down until it gets all the crap off it. Set the nozzle to Light when you're doing glass, 'cause this sucker's strong. When you're done, throw as much as you can in here." He pauses to yank open the dish-washer. "It's a sanitizer. Crank the dial back, and the cycle will last maybe a minute or so. Then you put all the clean dishes on the racks, and when they're dry, stack 'em with the rest.

If you don't know where something goes, feel free to bother Sam. Not me. Got it?"

Spray, scrub, cycle, dry, stack, don't bother Andy. I think I can remember that much.

I spend the next two hours on dish duty. Every time I clear the sink, Asha and Lou come by and unload a million more dirty bowls and pans and cups for me to handle, and whenever I do manage to get ahead, I go out and help them bus tables. It's mindless work, but it keeps me busy, and it gives me a better vantage point from which to watch everyone else. Whenever I stack dishes on the drying rack, I get a glimpse of Sam at the grill, stirring and flipping and frying. He's so into it.

It's kind of hot.

I don't know where that thought comes from, but before I let it go any further, I rush back to the sink just as Lou bursts through the swinging door with an armful of messy bowls.

"Chili, chili, chili." She sighs as she dumps them next to the sink. "Everyone wants the goddamn chili tonight."

Even all frazzled, Lou still looks as if she just stepped out of a pin-up calendar, like Bettie Page or something. If Bettie Page wore hot-pink sneakers, that is.

She brushes her thick bangs out of her eyes and looks at me. "You okay? Your face is kind of red."

I just shrug in response. Not like I'm champing at the bit to explain that I don't know if it's the steam or Sam's vaguely erotic cooking expertise causing my cheeks to feel like they're on fire.

The worst of the dinner rush ends around nine o'clock. I start putting away the last of the dried dishes when I discover some kind of sifting bowl that I'm not sure where to put away, so I walk up to Sam, who is sponging down the counter, and tap him on the shoulder.

"Colander," he says, pointing to the bowl. He opens up a cupboard over my head. "That goes here."

I stand on my tiptoes, trying to shove it in to no avail. Sam gently takes it from me and slides it into the cupboard space. His whole body presses against my back for a moment, arm brushing mine, and my breath catches.

"There we go," he says softly. He closes the cupboard but doesn't move back right away.

"I need, like, eight million cigarettes," Lou moans. The sound of her voice startles me, and I quickly duck under Sam's arm and hurry out to the front. Dex and Andy refill and swap out the condiment bottles while Asha sits on top of the counter, legs dangling. It would seem inappropriate, except there are no customers left except this old guy in the corner booth, eating a plate of scrambled eggs with coffee. Breakfast at night. People are weird.

"I thought you quit," Dex says to Lou.

"It's a process." She comes up to him and links her arm through his, leans her cheek on his shoulder. "Besides, I deserve a relapse. Tonight was *brutal*."

"Yeah, but it'll be fun to count the drawer," he points out. Lou rolls her eyes.

Asha kicks her heels lightly against the counter. "Chelsea really helped. It would have been way worse without her," she says, and I shoot a surprised look her way, a little embarrassed.

"I noticed," Dex says, and then to me, "Thanks for jumping in."

"You pretty much saved my life," agrees Lou. "Or at least my sanity, if nothing else. Too bad we can't have you around all the time."

Dex twirls the ketchup bottle around in his hand, considering. "Maybe we can."

Wait—what?

"What do you say?" he asks me. "Want to be our new dish girl?"

The thing is, I *do* like this place and everyone who works here—well, okay, so maybe things are kind of complicated when it comes to Andy—and they all know about the no-speaking deal, so obviously it isn't a concern. It really shouldn't be, since as far as I can tell, the duties of a dish girl don't require much verbal communication, anyway. And maybe it would convince my parents that I'm not only sane but responsible. That I'm displaying maturity. Something they're always saying is oh so important and that I'm oh so lacking.

Not to mention, I could use the money. I just threw out most of the contents of my closet, and I'm pretty sure Mom will be in no hurry to fund an impulsive overhaul of my wardrobe.

I smile slowly at Dex and nod, and Asha's and Sam's returning smiles don't escape my notice. Neither does the way Andy immediately walks out of the room.

"Okay then," Dex says, and I guess that's all there is to it. I'm part of the team.

When I walk through the front door, I drop my messenger bag right there in the foyer, too tired to carry it any farther. I smell like dish soap and the grilled cheese sandwiches Sam made for me and Asha before I took her home ("A congratulatory gesture for your new employment," he explained to me with one of his tilted smiles, and seriously, what is with the sudden somersaults my stomach does whenever that happens?).

I want a shower. I want a nap. Maybe a nap *in* the shower.

But before that I want something to drink, so I head into the kitchen, and I have the refrigerator door halfway open before I realize Mom and Dad are seated at the table.

Whatever they're discussing, it's bad. I know it before either of them say a single word. For one, they always break bad news to me in the kitchen; like when I was nine and our old cat Whiskers was put down, and I came home from school to find Dad waiting in here with a glass of chocolate milk, or when Grandpa Murphy had a heart attack last year and Mom started crying over the sink as she told me.

Second, they always have the same look on their faces. Thinly veiled panic.

I shut the refrigerator and lean against it, unscrewing the top of my bottled water. They both stare at me. Do they expect me to say something? Did they forget already? Maybe they did, because after a minute Dad clears his throat, an awkward and delayed conversation starter.

"Hey, sweetness, why don't you sit down for a minute?" he says without looking at me.

I obediently pull back a chair and sit at the table, watching them carefully. I wonder who died this time.

"I've got some bad news," he tells me, his gaze still focused on the wooden tabletop. I wish he would look at me. But at the same time I'm sort of afraid of what I'd see. "I...I lost my job today."

Mom reaches across the table and grabs his hand. It's weird. My parents have never been very lovey-dovey with each other. Maybe they're different behind closed doors—not that I have ever thought about that, or would ever want to—but the most they ever do in front of me is cuddle on the couch while watching television. So I know this must be really bad.

I want to ask what this means. For him. For us. How did

this happen? He's worked for his company ever since I was born. He's never late, hardly ever takes a sick day. It's like pulling teeth to get him to take his vacation. How could he lose his job, just like that? With no warning? Or was there warning, and they just didn't say anything so I wouldn't worry?

"It's going to be okay," Mom assures me. I can't understand how she can be so calm, but I'm grateful for it. "It'll be tight for a while, but we'll get through it. We can get by for now with me at the shop, and your father will find another job, and..." She trails off, swallowing hard, like she's lost the energy to remain so optimistic.

Dad meets my eyes, his own rimmed red. I've never seen him cry before. Not ever.

"I'm sorry," he says, so soft I barely hear him, and covers his face with one hand.

It kills me to see him act like this. Like he's let us both down. It makes me feel sick inside. I go stand behind him, wrapping my arms around his neck, holding as tight as I can at the awkward angle. He breathes out and rubs his thumb across the outside of my wrist. Mom pushes off her chair with a huff, leans hard against the sink, and I can tell she's barely holding it together by the way she clenches her fists.

"Roger was just looking for any excuse to get rid of you," she spits. Roger is—or, was—my dad's boss. "You should sue. You really should."

"Irene," Dad says tiredly. Clearly they've already gone over this.

She whirls around, wringing a dishcloth in her hands. "It's a conflict of interest! He's that Snyder boy's uncle, for Christ's sake!"

I let go of Dad and look at her. I'd forgotten that Warren is his boss's nephew. It's not something that ever came up, really, only in passing mention. It never mattered before. Does it matter now? Would his uncle really fire my father because of what I did? Yours hurt mine, so I hurt you—that's really what it breaks down to?

I never thought—I mean, my family wasn't supposed to be hurt by this. So many people have been hurt already. It's like a ripple effect. I thought the aftershocks were over, the casualty list limited to Warren, Joey, Noah, Andy. Me. But it keeps growing. And it's my fault.

I want to crawl under a rock and die.

I settle for slipping upstairs into my room. Mom and Dad are too busy launching into another argument to notice my exit. I should take a shower and get the diner smell off, but I'm too tired and too sad, and it's kind of comforting, somehow. To curl up in a ball in the middle of my bed and breathe in Rosie's. To pretend I'm back at the diner, with Sam and Asha and Dex and Lou, where I clicked into their little system like a missing puzzle piece. Where people looked glad to see me. People like Sam.

And that's what I'm thinking about as I fall asleep—Sam, smiling, Sam, standing at the grill, Sam, trading notes with me in art, adjusting his glasses and giving me his default look, skeptical but amused, Sam, his body pressed against my back, Sam, pressed against my front instead, Sam, his mouth near mine, not touching, just breathing, Sam, his hand warm and steady on my hip, Sam, Sam, Sam Sam SamSamSamsamsamsam—

day nine

In the morning, I hit the snooze button on my alarm clock five times before rolling out of bed, exhausted and sore all over, and then I stand under the shower for way too long, take too much time finding something to wear in my meager closet and burn my bagel on the first try and have to start all over again. As a result, I'm almost ten minutes late for first-period geometry. Mr. Callihan is writing something on the board when I slink in.

"Nice of you to grace us with your presence, Chelsea," he says without turning around.

I drop into my seat and lay my head down on my desk. I'm too tired to be embarrassed.

I'm dragging all day, totally out of it, preoccupied with feeling guilty about Dad. And with thinking about Sam, and how much I'm looking forward to working at the diner again tonight, and then I feel even guiltier, because—hello!—this horrible, awful thing has happened to my father, something I am at least partially to blame for. I should not be happy about anything right now.

Asha notices. At lunch in the library, she pokes me in the

elbow with her pencil and says, "Hey, did you even hear what I said? About finding the axis of symmetry?"

I definitely did not. And I definitely do not care. I'm too busy zoning out. A much more productive use of my time than geometry.

She sighs and rolls the pencil between her fingers. "We can work on it later," she says. She pulls out her knitting—the yarn is a mix of green and silver, this shiny, glinting material, and I remember the scarf she told Sam she'd make for him.

I write *Sam?* on my whiteboard and slide it over to her.

She nods and says, "I finished Noah's a few days ago," and then looks at me from underneath her eyelashes. "I'm visiting him this weekend."

I scratch Sam's name off the board with my thumbnail. I don't want to think about Noah in the hospital. What are people like after they wake up from comas? Even I'm not naive enough to believe it's like the movies, where the person just opens their eyes and is perfectly functional. I wonder if he can talk. If the police have interviewed him yet like they interviewed me. If he even remembers that night at all.

"You could come," Asha says, carefully neutral.

Come to the hospital? Yeah, right. I'd probably be kicked out on arrival. There is no way Noah wants me there.

I don't answer. I just take out my sketchpad and doodle absently. Sam and I still have to figure out our project. The last time we talked about it, he mentioned maybe making the characters out of papier-mâché, but the wire netting Ms. Kinsey has doesn't bend well enough for it to seem feasible. So now we're back to square one.

I consider the possibilities. Maybe set the Peanuts characters in a classical painting style? Nah. Too complicated, and besides, we're supposed to mimic the artist's style, not reinterpret it. It needs to be straight-up comic strip style. But how to do it without being completely boring?

There was a really big roll of thick paper in one of Ms. Kinsey's supply closets. What if...what if we recreated a big comic strip with it? That would be pretty cool. A magnified comic. I wonder if Sam will go for it.

I'm still mulling it over when Asha tucks away her knitting needles and says, "I have to go to my locker. I'll meet you after the assembly?"

Assembly? What assembly? She walks away before I can ask what she's talking about.

After lunch I haul ass to art, hoping Sam will be there early, too, but he comes in two seconds before the bell rings. He shoots me a brief smile as he sits down at our workstation. I want to tell him my idea, see what he thinks, but before I can find a way to explain it, Ms. Kinsey announces that we're heading to the auditorium. So Asha's right; there *is* an assembly.

We all file into the empty theater. Our seats are close to the stage, on the left end. Sam sits beside me, his wrist touching mine on the shared armrest, as more students pour in like a tidal wave through the two entrances, all of them talking to each other, laughing, excited to be out of class. It's so *loud*. Was it always this loud, or does it just seem amplified, since I haven't spoken in so long? God, it's obnoxious.

Sam isn't talking, though. He looks distracted. I want to ask him what's up, but I left my whiteboard in the art room, and then it doesn't matter anyway because the lights dim.

People whistle and whoop in the sudden darkness, shifting in their squeaky seats. Someone from the balcony sails a paper airplane toward the stage that makes it all the way to the third row. When the spotlight comes on, illuminating the single microphone stand center stage, the conversation and laughter fades into a hushed swell of whispers. The sound is like rustling insects.

Mr. Fenton, our assistant principal, walks onto the stage and takes the microphone. He spends a minute trying to quiet the audience, saying things like, "Quiet, please," and clearing his throat as he paces a few steps back and forth.

Eventually everyone shuts up enough for him to get on with the program.

"Most of you are aware that recently there was a grievous incident involving a few of our students, one of whom is currently still hospitalized due to an act of violence instigated by a fellow classmate," he says, voice booming out through the room. "Though this did not happen on school grounds, we felt it was important to take some time today to address what has transpired and reiterate our zero-tolerance policy toward any and all harassment, whether it be physical or verbal."

Mr. Fenton goes on, something about counselors being available for support and unanswered questions, and the evils of discrimination and necessity of tolerance, but his words barely register with me. I have this dizzy, sinking stomach sensation, like being trapped in an elevator with the cables cut loose. Nothing but bottomless falling.

He says something else, a final word, and walks off, but I know that can't be it, it can't be over. Just as I'm wondering what's next, Brendon Ryan emerges onto the stage.

This does nothing to help my stomach.

Brendon holds the microphone and looks out at the sea of faces with a somewhat nervous—though still as dazzling as ever—smile. "Hi. My name is Brendon Ryan," he says, "and Mr. Fenton wanted me to talk to you a little about what I've been organizing lately. Starting this week, we'll be forming our own Gay/Straight Alliance chapter at Grand Lake. Any

student is welcome—whether you put the Gay or the Straight
into the alliance. Or even if you fall somewhere in between."
This garners a few titters from the audience, and Brendon looks
down and back up with another smile. "Ms. Kline has been
kind enough to offer us use of her room—A214, it's on the
second floor—Tuesdays after school at three-fifteen. It's really
just a place for us to talk, to have open conversations about this
stuff, you know, answer any questions, so what happened to
Noah Beckett can be prevented from ever happening again."

I swear he's staring straight at me when he says this. I swear
everyone is staring, all eyes on me, blaming, knowing. Everything
I did; everything I didn't do. This is like one of those recurring
nightmares I have, where I'm naked in front of the whole school,
and I'm supposed to ride a tricycle and juggle bananas at the
same time, even though I don't know how to do either. Except
this is for real, not just a concoction of my stupid subconscious.

My legs act of their own volition, and suddenly I'm standing, squeezing my way out of the row, stumbling down the
aisle toward the exit. It's fight or flight, and my brain has apparently chosen flight.

No one stops me. Not as I bolt from the auditorium, Brendon's voice ringing in my ears. Not as I run down the hall,
push through the heavy doors and outside. It is, of course,
only twenty-something degrees, and I have no jacket. I slump
against the brick wall and hug myself, shivering in the cold.

"Chelsea!"

It's Sam.

They always say misery loves company, but right now I
kind of want to be miserable and *alone,* so I can wallow in
my self-loathing properly.

"Chelsea," he says again, out of breath, but I'm too ashamed
to look at him.

So instead I watch as snowflakes cascade down and stick to my wild red hair. Irish red. Red like dried blood on pavement. Like Noah's blood. Like—

"What's wrong?" Sam says, and then, gently, "You can tell me."

But I can't. I don't have my whiteboard.

That is so not what he meant and I know it. I'm not an idiot. Sometimes.

Hot tears well up in my eyes and trace tracks down my cheeks before I can stop them. I'm so tired of feeling like this, sick with guilt and constantly on the verge of panic attacks. And it's like every time I start to feel remotely good about something, life says, "Oh, wait a minute, that's not right," and drop-kicks me back into You Are Made Of Epic Fail territory. It's exhausting. I'm *exhausted*.

"Hey." Sam steps forward, holds my wrist and pulls me off the wall, wraps his arms all the way around me. "Hey, come here. It's okay. Shh. You're okay."

I bury my face in his chest, rubbing my wet cheeks against the worn fabric of his shirt. I can't remember the last time anyone hugged me like this. Like they'd hold me as long as I needed. And I need it right now. I don't try to pretend that I don't. I dig my fingers into the back of his shoulders and cling to him, letting out choked sobs.

I cry and cry and cry until I can't muster up the energy to cry anymore. Even then, I keep my face hidden in Sam's shirtfront, sniffling and taking deep, hiccupy breaths as he strokes the top of my snow-covered hair. My throat is all thick and gross, every breath of freezing air like tiny needles piercing my lungs, and my hands are totally numb to the point where they could snap off like twigs at the wrist.

None of that changes the fact I'd still rather be here than anywhere else in the world.

Once the crying has stopped, Sam offers to go back into the school and retrieve my messenger bag and jacket for me. Thank God. No way can I set foot in there again—at least not today. He lets me warm up in his car, a white Olds Cutlass with torn red leather interior. A few books rest on the passenger's seat, and while he's inside, I take a brief look at the book sleeves. I haven't read any of them—they're by authors I haven't heard of, like Chuck Palahniuk (whose last name I'm sure I mangle trying to pronounce in my head) and David Sedaris—with some comic books stuck in between. After a minute, I put them down on the floor next to my feet and turn up the radio instead. The station is set to NPR; two people are arguing over the estate tax.

If a car says something about the person it belongs to, this means Sam is really into talk radio. And reading books written by dudes. And, if the wrappers on the floor and the half-a-pack in the glove compartment are any indication, eating Twizzlers. Which just so happen to be a guilty pleasure of mine.

Unfortunately Sam does not have any tissues anywhere in his car. I try to make do with some leftover fast-food napkins I find. Even then my eyes are still all puffy and red. I look awful, but at least I feel a little better. More calm. Kind of embarrassed, though, for slobbering all over Sam like that.

Eventually Sam comes back and tosses my coat and bag into my lap. I make an *oomph* sound in surprise and nearly choke on the piece of licorice I'm chewing.

He laughs as he buckles his seat belt. "You know, I think that's the most sound I've ever heard from you."

It's more than a little bizarre that we have never had a real, two-way conversation. With both of us using our voices. I mean, I knew of him before the party, and I'm sure he knew of me. Most people do; it's one of the benefits of being friends with people like Kristen Courteau, if you could call it that. People know who you are. So we knew *of* each other, but we never talked.

Usually there are narcs monitoring the student parking lot to stop delinquents from cutting class, but somehow, thankfully, not today. Sam turns the car out of the lot and drives toward the center of town. He hasn't indicated where we're going. After he let me go, all he said was, "I'll get your stuff, we're getting out of here," and that's all I wanted, to leave, so I wasn't about to object.

"I'll call Asha and let her know we took off," he says now. "She can walk, and after we're done, I'll drive you back so you can pick up your car."

Asha. Shit. I didn't even think about her. But Sam doesn't seem worried, and it isn't a far walk, really. Fifteen minutes, tops. I'll make it up to her later. Somehow.

I notice the cell phone in his hand. It reminds me how I've barely used mine at all since the vow. I take it from him, and he watches bemusedly as I program my number into his contacts list, and then his into mine.

"What's the point of having my number?" he asks. "It's not like I can call you."

I open up a new text message screen on my phone and type in,

it's called texting LOSER.

He grins. "Point duly noted."

He eases around a bend that takes us to the long stretch of road along the lake. I squint out the window at a few figures in the distance. Ice fishers. In the summer, Dad likes to take me fishing at the docks by the yacht club. You can't eat anything you get—they're mostly skinny rainbow trout any-way—so all we do is catch and release, but he likes the sport of it, I guess. I like to sit on the planks, the warm wood dig-ging into the backs of my knees, legs dangling, and cast my line over and over lazily, enjoying the sun.

Snowflakes hit the window and melt, trailing down in tiny rivulets. Summer feels so far away. All there is now is cold and snow, snow and cold.

We end up at Rosie's. Not such a surprise. Sam turns off the engine and says, "Tuna melts."

I raise my eyebrows at him.

"I said I'd teach you how to make them," he continues. "So let's do it."

No one's around when we walk in, except for Dex and Lou, mopping floors and cleaning off tables.

As soon as Lou sees me, she drops her rag. "Oh, sweetie, what happened?"

I must really look like a mess. I shrug and swipe self-consciously at my eyes.

"Do I need to kick someone's ass?" Dex asks. He points the mop handle straight out, wielding it like a weapon. I crack a small, teary smile.

"Just a rough day," Sam says. "You know how it goes."

Lou drags me into the bathroom and helps me clean up, dabbing under my eyes with a damp paper towel, her fingers lightly guiding my chin. When I'm this close, I can see how clear and smooth her skin is. Like a model's. I should ask what product she uses.

"You know, you have killer eyes. Very expressive," she says.

She's only saying that to cheer me up, I know, but I'm still

flattered. Lou has wide-set violet eyes, so light they're almost translucent. Not like mine, which are a muddy-green,
or maybe brown, never settling on one shade.

"You get away with this no-talking thing. All you have
to do is look at someone, and it's all right there." She waves
a hand in the general vicinity of my eye area.

I don't know if I like the idea of that. Having everything
I'm feeling written right on my face. It makes me feel too
exposed.

"So Dex wants to repaint," she goes on, like it's the natural
flow of the conversation. "He gets like this sometimes. Last
summer he did a surfer theme—he put surfboards up on the
wall, and these glass bowls with shells on every table, like this
is Southern California or something. Tacky as all get-out."

I laugh at the thought of it, and she smiles a little, surprised,
maybe. I haven't really laughed around her. Or anyone. It
hasn't been intentional; I just haven't had any reason. Laughing isn't the same as talking, really, so I'm safe. It's not like
anyone's going to call foul. I make up the rules here.

"Now he wants purple," she scoffs. "Jesus Christ, I mean,
purple? Ugh. I'm trying to talk him out of it. I'd ask you to
help, but that wouldn't really work, huh?" She quirks a grin
at me and tosses the paper towel wad into the trash can.

I'm feeling a lot better when I join Sam at the grill. He's
already laid out all the ingredients. He shows me how to
drain the tuna using a colander (which, thanks to yesterday,
I now know the location of), then mix it with other ingredients, sprinkle on cheese and pepper and green onions and this
stuff he explains is called crème fraîche, which is sort of like
mayonnaise but, he claims, tastes better. After that's done, he
stuffs the pita bread with the tuna and some avocado slices,
butters the bread and slaps it on the grill.

He lays out the whole process as he goes. It sounds more complicated than it looks. When he's finished his, I do one of my own. Even under his instruction, it ends up less than perfect—one side is a little burned, and the other a little undercooked, and I used too much crème fraîche.

"Still, not bad for a first try," Sam tells me after he's tried some of mine. "Next time it'll be better."

I smile around a bite of tuna melt, more than a little pleased to hear there will, in fact, be a next time.

The good news is that when Asha rolls in two hours later, she doesn't seem to mind that we ditched her. Well, not ditched. *Ditched* makes it sound like it was purposeful. *Bailed* is the more appropriate word choice.

Either way, she's as bubbly as ever, humming along to the corner jukebox that blasts Otis Redding while she rolls the silverware. I help her sort the forks and salad forks and spoons and teaspoons and knives, and she shows me how to wrap them neatly into cloth napkin bundles.

"My family inherited a set of antique silverware from my grandmother," she tells me. Like most things with Asha, it comes out of the blue. "It's all from India. And there's this teapot—it's really ancient and beautiful. I love it. My mom used to make tea with it all the time."

I stop sorting the forks and give her a questioning look.

"Oh, she's not dead or anything," she explains hastily. "She just ." Asha shrugs a little, looking down. "She's sick a lot. She doesn't do much these days."

I'm glad I have an excuse not to speak, because I don't know what to say to that. I don't think Asha expects anything, though, because the next thing I know she's chattering away about her knitting projects.

Once we're done with the silverware, I join Sam and Dex in the kitchen so I can sweep the floor. Apparently Andy has the night off. I feel kind of bad for being so relieved—but I've had a really, really bad day, and it's like God is cutting me a break for once. Maybe I should start going to church. Earn some points from the Big Man.

"I'd rather have a new milkshake machine than a new coffeemaker," Sam says to Dex. They're in the middle of a discussion about kitchen renovations. "If people want fancy frou-frou coffee, there are other places in town. No one else does milkshakes."

"Hmm." Dex rubs his chin with one hand. "I don't know. What do you think, Chelsea?"

Sam has a point; Rosie's isn't a Starbucks. People don't come here for the gourmet coffee. I point the mop handle toward Sam and nod at Dex.

"Yes!" Sam exclaims. "Team Milkshake Machine for the win." He gives me an enthusiastic high five and we both dissolve into laughter.

"Yeah, yeah, we'll see," Dex says with a grin. "I'll have to shop around." He wanders over to the register and pops it open, counting the money inside.

"That's not going to make you any richer," Lou says as she passes by with a pot of coffee.

"It's not about being rich," he says. "I just like the feel of it. Besides, I'm rich anyway. Spiritually. After all, I have you, darling." He says *darling* with an exaggerated accent, so it sounds more like "dah-link."

She rolls her eyes. "And *that's* not going to get you laid," she retorts, but when he snatches her around the waist and pecks her on the mouth, she kisses him back before shoving him off.

It's quiet tonight, so in between dish duty and busing I finish the sweeping, mop the floor and spend a lot of time lingering around the grill, watching Sam and Dex cook. By the end of the shift, my feet ache and my hands are all wrinkled from dirty dishwater.

"Ready to go?" asks Sam after we've both punched out.

I nod and collect my things, waving goodbye to Dex and Lou before piling into the Cutlass with Sam and Asha. He drops Asha at home, closer to the suburban east end of town; her house is nice, two stories, all beige paint and stone, with a dark green SUV parked in the driveway. I think she told me once that her dad is a doctor.

Sam doesn't say anything as he drives me to the student lot and pulls into the space next to my car. We sit with the engine running for a long time. I don't know what he's waiting for. I should go, but when I unbuckle and reach for the door handle, I think about Mom at the sink and Dad's face and it's suddenly the last thing I want to do.

"Well," he says after a while, like the beginning of a thought, except then he just stops. We look at each other, each waiting for something. Finally I take out my whiteboard.

What is the deal with Asha's mother? She told me she was sick.

Sam looks at the board and then at me. "I think you should ask her if you want to know," he says.

So you know?

"Asha talks to me," he says. "We're friends. If she wants you to know, she'll tell you herself." He shoots me a pointed look. "You really don't understand the concept of secrets, do you?"

Old habits die hard.

He snorts. "Apparently."

Don't look at me like that. I was just curious.

"There's a difference between curiosity and nosiness," he

says. "Don't you have any secrets? Something private you wouldn't share with just anyone?"

I write, *My dad lost his job yesterday*, in tiny cramped letters.

Sam stares at it for a minute, and then at me. "Man. That's really… I'd ask if you're okay, but that sounds like a really stupid question."

I smile a little, because he's right, it would be kind of stupid.

"What did he do?" he asks.

Sales.

Sam nods. "My stepdad owns a car dealership in Westfield," he says. Westfield is the next town over. "He might need a sales guy. Do you want me to talk to him?"

Okay, this is bordering on unreal. There is no way Sam is just that good of a guy. No one is. Not without strings attached.

Don't you hate me?

"No." His brow furrows. "You think I hate you?"

Do I really have to point out the proverbial elephant in the room? Apparently so, because he just sits there, waiting for an answer.

Why wouldn't you? You know what I did to Noah.

Noah, his best friend. Noah, who makes out with guys. Noah, who almost died.

Sam looks at me like he's seeing me for the first time. My heart starts pounding really fast, and I get that elevator-drop stomach again. I shouldn't have brought this up. I shouldn't keep sabotaging the few things that allow me to cling to my ever-dwindling sanity.

I am such a moron.

"I think about what happened to Noah—not just what happened, but *what they did* to him—every day. I was mad

at you. I *am* mad. But—" He stops and sighs. "Asha told me
you didn't know what they were going to do to him," he
says. "Is that true?"

I nod. I didn't know, but—

It wouldn't have happened if I hadn't said anything.

"Probably not," he agrees. "But if you hadn't said anything
to the cops…who knows if they would've been caught. Andy
never saw them. Noah doesn't even remember."

So he has talked to Noah about this. Or someone has,
anyway.

I'm glad the police found the bloody ice scraper in Warren's truck bed. I'm glad he and Joey both confessed. Otherwise it would just be my word against theirs—but now it's
no secret. Everyone knows. I mean, I assume there's probably
going to be a trial, eventually, though it could take months.
And I'm sure I'll have to testify, even if the very idea makes
me want to throw up. I'm not really clear on how all of that
is supposed to go down; Mom and Dad hired a lawyer who
has been dealing with most of the mess. One they couldn't afford before and definitely can't afford now that Dad is jobless.

I still find it unbelievable that this happened at all. I know
Warren and Joey were totally drunk, but it's one thing to joke
about that stuff and another altogether to act on it. To track
a boy down like—like an *animal* and just kick the shit out of
him because of who he is.

"Just tell me—are you sorry?" Sam asks. "And I don't mean
are you sorry for what it cost you. Are you sorry for what you
did? For what happened to Noah?"

I've spent so much time drowning in self-pity. I've been
acting like a total brat. Sure, I lost my friends and my status,
but Noah almost lost his *life*. Andy almost lost his boyfriend.
Sam almost lost his best friend. I wish I could go back in

time and change things, but I can't, and that knowledge will haunt me forever.

I don't understand how Derek and Lowell can be so angry at me, acting like a damn basketball team is more important than someone else's life. They should be angry at Warren and Joey. I am! I haven't even fully realized it until right this second, but I'm *furious*. For what they did to Noah. For thinking they could get away with it. It wasn't my business to tell them what I saw that night, but what they did with that information was their choice. It was their choice to get in that truck and chase him down. Not mine.

I've done a lot I'm not proud of. But that. That much I am *not* responsible for.

I finally meet Sam's gaze and hold up my board so he can read what I've written.

More than words can say.

"Well, then," Sam says. "That's a start."

day twelve

It takes only one minute to compose the email reply, but another twenty to talk myself into sending it.

Bring it.

It's just one line, two simple words, but I still hesitate with my mouse hovering over the send button. One click and that message will go straight to Kristen's in-box. One click and I'll have done something I have never dared to do before: fight back against Kristen.

I've spent the last three days stewing over this decision. If I do this, there is no turning back. I'll have dug myself a hole so deep I won't ever escape it; Kristen will never forgive me, if she ever was going to at all. But I don't want to be forgiven. I want Kristen to apologize to *me*—and the likelihood of that happening is nonexistent. All this time I've been wondering what I can do to make Kristen want to be my friend again, and now I'm thinking maybe it's Kristen who needs to change. And more than that, maybe I need to show her that I'm not someone she can just steamroll over. I have a backbone, dammit.

I click the send button before I can agonize over it any longer. Instead of satisfaction, all I feel is mild nausea, and when my cell phone rings suddenly, I nearly jump out of my skin and scramble to pick it up off my desk. I don't recognize the number on the front screen, but I pick the call up anyway.

"Chelsea?" It's Sam, the sound of dishes clattering and water running in the background. He must be at Rosie's. "It's me. Sam."

I almost answer on pure instinct, but then remember and shut my mouth. Why would he call? He knows I can't speak.

"I know you can't talk," he says, like he's reading my mind, "but Dex has this errand he wants me to run for him... I don't know, he's in one of his moods, he's decided he wants to redecorate and asked if I'd go out and pick up paint samples. I could use a second opinion. You want to come?" He pauses and laughs a little. "Cough once for yes, twice for no."

Well, let's see. It's a Friday night, and my choices are either sit around the house on edge waiting to see if Kristen replies to my email, or go shopping for paint samples. I can't even go downstairs to watch television because Dad is fixing the garbage disposal and making a racket. The answer here is fairly obvious.

I cough once, pointedly.

Sam laughs again. "All right," he says, "I'll be over in a few."

"Oh, God, shut up! You have no idea what you're talking about!"

Sam keeps yelling at his car radio like the hosts on NPR can hear him. I wonder if he does this all the time, or if he's doing it for my benefit to keep this car ride from being dead silent. I'm too anxious to pay attention to his constant grumbling. I stare out the window and watch the buildings slip by, wondering if Kristen's seen my email yet. On one hand, I'd pay to see her face when she reads it—on the other, I'm suddenly feeling like maybe it wasn't such a good idea to antagonize her. Who knows how she'll respond?

"Hey," Sam says. I look over to see him smiling at me, and the knot in my stomach loosens just a little. He turns down the radio volume a few notches. "You okay?"

I plaster on a thin smile and nod, but he keeps staring at me.

"You look...serious," he says.

As opposed to my usual brain-dead ditz look? I just shrug and turn the radio back up, pretending to be acutely invested in whatever the two hosts are discussing all the way until we reach Home Depot. We walk through the sliding doors and straight to the paint aisle, where Sam makes a beeline for the paint sample strips. He starts pulling them from the shelves at random.

"Dex didn't say what color he wanted," Sam explains when he catches my bemused look. "So I guess just grab whatever you think looks good."

I wander over to the neutrals, selecting various shades of taupe and beige. Maybe a deep gold would look nice. Something warm and inviting.

"Chelsea?"

I'm so startled to hear my name that I drop the fan of sample strips onto the floor. When I kneel down to pick them back up, I'm met with the sight of a pair of purple plaid flats I distinctly remember Kristen branding as fugly. Sure enough, when I glance up Tessa is staring down at me with narrowed brown eyes.

I gather the rest of the strips and slowly rise to my feet until we're eye to eye. Tessa frowns like she doesn't know what to make of me. I am, admittedly, not as presentable as I usually am when I go out into public. I'm wearing a pair of dark jeans and a ribbed brown sweater, nothing fancy. Of course, I wasn't expecting to run into anyone but Sam, and it's not like he cares how I'm dressed.

Tessa's gaze shifts over my shoulder, and when she looks back at me, there's the start of a smirk curling around the edges of her mouth. "So you're here with him?" she asks. "Is he, like, your boyfriend now or something? Because if so, someone should tell him he could do better."

I stare back, unmoving, fighting the urge to comb my fingers through my messy hair. It's really not fair that I had to run into Tessa like this without warning, when I'm such a mess and she's so well put-together. Her wispy light brown hair frames her perfectly made-up face; she's learned her lesson about the bronzer, it seems. Looks like Kristen's already started on her, grooming her to be a proper replacement.

"Oh, don't look at me like that," Tessa snaps. There's a newfound conviction in her tone I've never heard before, the kind that comes from having all the power at hand. "Do you really expect me to feel sorry for you, after you went and leaked the pictures of me and Owen?"

I really, really want to inform Tessa that her new BFF Kristen was the one who spread the photos. Instead I set my jaw and stare down at the floor. Times like these I wonder if this vow is worth it, but then again, it's not like Tessa would take my word for it anyway.

Suddenly there's a hand on my back. Sam stands beside me, looking from me to Tessa and back again. "I think I'm done here," he says. "You ready to go?"

I nod, maybe a little more fervently than I mean to, and Sam keeps his hand placed lightly on the middle of my back as we brush past Tessa and head toward the store exit. I don't have to look over my shoulder to know that she's watching me walk away.

day fifteen

The next email from Kristen arrives in my in-box on Sunday evening.

The subject line is FWD: HOT MESS.........MINUS THE HOT, and it takes me a minute to get past my trepidation and open it. And as soon as I do I wish I never had.

There's no text, just a single photo. Of me. Hunched over the toilet, looking like I'm about to puke. I recognize the outfit as the one I wore on New Year's; the plunging neckline leaves my boobs halfway out of my top, and the camera caught me midblink, my mouth open in what looks to be a gag. The flash washes out my already pale skin and catches my monstrous hair in all its bushy, frizzed-out glory.

It's the most unflattering picture of all time, and one I don't even remember being taken. How nice of Kristen to stick a camera in my face when I was drunk and puking into her toilet. I look so completely gross and trashed. When I scroll up to the top of the email, I realize with growing horror that Kristen has cc'ed it to everyone in her contacts list. All of my friends—ex-friends—will have this sitting in their in-boxes when they log in to check their email. Some of them have probably already seen it.

At least I'm not totally unprepared when I walk into school Monday and find a printout of it taped to my locker. Some guy walking by sees it and laughs before I can rip it off and crumple the paper into a ball. I shove it into my book bag, my face hot with shame.

There are more of them taped to the mirrors in the bathroom. And on the inside of every stall. I tear each one to tiny shreds before tossing them in the trash can.

Unfortunately destroying the evidence doesn't stop people from talking. And pointing. And making rude comments. When I go up to Mrs. Finch's desk to turn in my Lit test, I come back to my seat to find another copy of the printout has materialized on top of my desk. Derek and Lowell snicker from behind as I carefully fold it and cram it into my notebook.

Asha catches me at my locker after class, one of the printouts in hand and concern written all over her face. "Um, Chelsea, have you seen—" She takes one look at me and stops midsentence. "Oh, so you have. Are you okay?"

I shrug one shoulder without looking her in the eye. Ordinarily I'd put on a brave face and act like none of it matters, but right now I'm too tired to pretend this humiliating ordeal isn't getting to me at all.

Kristen fights dirty. I *know* Kristen fights dirty. There was no way I could all but invite her to take a stab and not expect something like this. Who knows what other tricks she has up her sleeve. It's like locking yourself in a cage with a tiger and poking it repeatedly with a stick. It'll never end well.

As if she has some kind of psychic link with me or something, Kristen chooses that precise moment to walk by, posse in tow. She looks me up and down as she does with just a hint of a smirk, and she doesn't say anything; she doesn't have to. She knows she's won this round. That pisses me off more than anything, really.

Asha watches me watching Kristen before linking her arm through mine and tugging me down the hall. "Don't pay her attention," she says. "She isn't worth it."

I know Asha's right, logically. Now if only I could make my heart believe it.

Lou is currently obsessed with the soundtrack to the *Rocky Horror Picture Show.* I've never seen the movie, and when Sam rattles off the cast list like he's the living embodiment of IMDB.com, the only name I recognize is Susan Sarandon. Still, I somehow know most of the lyrics to every song because Lou insists on playing it on repeat in the kitchen.

My favorite is "The Time Warp," because every single time it comes on, everyone momentarily pauses in whatever they're doing to sing along and do this orchestrated dance I assume must be from the movie. As an outsider, I am highly entertained.

Tonight the song cues up while I'm in the middle of sweeping the kitchen. Andy sings the loudest while he flips hamburger patties, and Sam mouths the lyrics into his spatula, and Lou and Asha stop busing tables long enough to participate.

As it jumps into the chorus, everyone does the dance— hands on the hips, knees in tight, pelvic thrusts. I lean on the broom handle and giggle at their antics, and Sam laughs back at me, swoops over and grabs me by the hand.

"Come on," he says over the music, "don't just stand there!"

I hesitate, but then he bumps his hip into mine, and I prop the broom against the wall and join in on the dance, awkwardly at first and then looser and looser. I know I must look like an idiot doing this stupid dance with an apron on and sans any makeup and my hair yanked back in a ponytail, but I suppose there's little point in pretending I have any shame after half the school has seen a picture of me practically passed out on the bathroom floor. Sam must've seen the picture, too, I'm sure, but he hasn't mentioned it and he isn't looking at me any differently. So I guess it's not the end of the world.

It's easier to not care about looking like an idiot when no one else does. Dancing this way is like being twelve all over again, flailing around without abandon in my bedroom with Kristen to the radio, and by the time the song is over, I feel flushed and sort of giddy.

"See? That wasn't so bad," Sam teases, drawing me into a sideways hug. It only lasts for a few seconds, but long enough for me to smell the cooking oil on his skin, to feel the comfortable warmth of his side and how perfectly I fit there.

My heart slides into my throat, and when he lets me go, every nerve end tingles. That feeling doesn't go away for the rest of the night.

day eighteen

The week goes by quickly, a blur of classes and the diner and homework. Mom and Dad are too preoccupied to even ask me why I don't come home most nights until almost ten o'clock and reeking of cooking oil. Maybe I should be hurt by their lack of parental concern, but they have enough on their plate right now. Mom's been pulling twelve-hour days at the floral shop, and Dad, in an effort to fill his sudden surplus of free time, has begun various fix-it projects around the house. He tinkers with our dishwasher until it stops making that funky noise during the rinse cycle, varnishes the coffee table in the garage and shovels the driveway and sidewalk in front of our house daily, even when it hasn't snowed.

Neither talk to me about Dad's job (or lack thereof) situation again.

I do my best to keep them from having anything else to worry about, at least when it comes to me. I pay attention in all my classes and to Asha during our lunch study breaks, and when Mr. Callihan hands me back my latest test, I'm shocked to see a B+ written at the top of the page. Seems like all this studying-until-my-eyes-bleed is actually paying off. And Mrs.

Finch hasn't issued any more detentions, so I can only assume she thinks I'm doing okay, too.

Everything seems to be going well—or as well as things get for me these days—up until Thursday at lunch. I'm staked out at our usual spot in the library, chewing on my pen cap as I do my science reading, when Asha storms in and throws a newspaper right under my nose.

I look down to see Kristen's face staring up at me in black and white. Her expression is sad. Pensive. Two emotions I have never associated with her.

GRAND LAKE TEEN SPEAKS OUT AGAINST GAY STUDENT ATTACK, the headline boldly proclaims to the immediate right of her perfectly posed headshot. My heart sinks.

"It's exactly as bad as it looks," Asha says, flinging herself into the chair across from me. As I read the article, I begin to understand why she sounds so appalled.

Most of the interview's content is to be expected. Kristen never thought her boyfriend was capable of such violence. Kristen would have thrown herself in front of the car if she knew what they were going to do. Kristen was absolutely devastated when she heard what happened to her friend Noah Beckett (friend? FRIEND?!). Kristen has a gay cousin. (That part is news to me.) Et cetera.

Oh, but here's the real gem: apparently Kristen cannot *believe* someone would be so insensitive as to publicly out a gay student.

"Have you seen her posters?" Asha asks.

How could I miss them? They're all over the school, purple and pink and sky-blue poster boards with the words *KRISTEN COURTEAU FOR SNOW PRINCESS* written in bright pink marker complete with glitter and intricate paper snowflakes framing copies of her sophomore portrait in the middle. She's kicked off a campaign run for Winter Formal Snow Princess and given an exclusive interview to the *Grand Lake Tribune* defending her integrity—by pointing one perfectly manicured accusatory finger straight at me—all in the same week. What *excellent* timing.

That conniving two-faced bitch. She'd make a wonderful PR person to celebrities someday, spinning scandals into gold.

To top it off, at the very end of the article there's a mention of Brendon and his formation of the new Gay/Straight Alliance club. It quotes him as saying, "It's very important to embrace any student interested in these issues. That's the only way to open minds, by letting them ask tough questions in a safe space."

I find it really strange that Brendon of all people has stepped up as spokesperson for the sexually oppressed of Grand Lake High. Not that I'm against him championing gay rights— I'm glad someone's doing it—it's just unexpected. Though, in a twisted way, also rather brilliant. After all, what better way to disarm bullshit opposition about foisting the "homosexual agenda" on the student body than by recruiting the all-American, wholesome, pretty-faced, straight-as-an-arrow Golden Boy as the face of the cause?

Maybe *Brendon's* gay. It's something I never would've considered before, but hey, stranger things have happened. It'd be a relief, actually, if he was—that would at the very least explain why he wasn't interested when I threw myself at him. My first instinct is to consider the ways I could confirm or deny my theory—asking around the school, seeing if anyone knows—but then I stop myself short. No. I have had enough of outing people for a lifetime.

Asha slides the paper to her side of the table and scowls at it. "What a bitch."

I glance up, surprised. I've never heard Asha swear.

"I should knit her a muzzle," she mutters under her breath, and then I start giggling and can't stop.

Asha's eyes widen and she starts giggling, too. We both laugh so hard we almost fall off our chairs, until the librarian shushes us with a deadly glare. I set my head down on the table and cover it with my arm, wheezing, my shoulders still shaking with silent laughter.

"We're going to that dance," Asha declares, once she's calmed down.

I lift my head off the table and shake it wildly. Has she lost her mind? No. No way. I am so not going to Winter Formal.

"Yes, we are," she insists. "The Wannabe Ice Princess is not going to get away with this. Not without a fight."

It's Snow Princess, not Ice, but I don't bother correcting her. Ice Princess is more fitting for Kristen anyway.

Anyone can run for Winter Formal royalty. You just have to sign up in the office on a clipboard they later give to the dance committee, which arranges the voting via Scantron ballots. The freshmen, sophomores and juniors are all given prince or princess titles, the titles queen and king reserved for seniors only. The senior queen and king get a bouquet of white roses and a gift certificate to the local movie theater while everyone else gets cheap flower bunches and flimsy crowns and tiaras.

It's all lame, if you ask me. I don't see the point. Still, some people get really into this stuff. Like Kristen. But Kristen likes the idea of anything that allows her to be the center of attention. Last year she lost out to Trish Gillepsie, one of the cheerleaders. Which is funny because at our school, cheerleader is not synonymous with popular—but Trish allegedly gave head to half the basketball team, and all the footballers, and even a few guys on the chess team, in order to make it happen.

Or that's the story I heard. And maybe the same story I told a few people. Okay, a lot of people. Everyone and anyone who would listen, basically.

Kristen was positively fuming when she lost out on the crown. I'm sure she's coveting that tiara like crazy this year. I don't know why, it's just a stupid piece of plastic, but when Kristen wants something, she usually finds a way to get it. No matter who she has to destroy in the process.

I'm sort of irrationally pissed that she's running at all, even though I'm not surprised. Sam agrees, evidently, because on our way to the art room—he's gotten in the habit of meeting me at my locker so we can walk together—he stops in front of one of her shimmery glitter posters and grimaces.

"I can't believe people care about this stuff," he says. "And seriously, who would even vote for her?"

A lot of people would. Even now. *Especially* now. All the guys who want to sleep with her and all the girls who want to be her friend will fill in her bubble on the ballot. If anything, she has more of an advantage this year, by having two open slots for a new boyfriend and a new best friend. Also, people are stupid. You can never underestimate that factor.

Too bad Asha can't run against her. Asha's a year younger, still a freshman, so it wouldn't work. And Trish overthrowing her isn't an option, since this year her parents sent her to St. Juliet's, the Catholic school, after they caught her sexing up the starting varsity linebacker in their bedroom over summer.

I really shouldn't be giving this so much thought. I'm not

going to the stupid dance anyway. Let Kristen have her stupid tiara if it makes her feel important. It shouldn't matter to me.

But it does. A little. More than a little.

It just feels unfair that Kristen has gotten through all of this so unscathed. I lost *everything* and she gets to run for fucking Snow Princess. It's such bullshit. High school, the world. All of it.

Sam bumps my shoulder with his. "Come on, we're gonna be late."

We spend the hour in art working on our project. Once Sam understood what I was trying to convey through my written notes, he was totally on board with the giant comic strip idea. Except now we're just doing a mural of all the different Peanuts characters. I sketch the outlines of most of them, since, not to brag, I am a way better artist than Sam; the only one he can draw with any accuracy is Snoopy. I already have most of my part done. All I have to do is finish Schroeder and his piano.

With five minutes left of class, I sit back on my knees and survey our combined work. It won't be long before the outlining is done and we can start painting. That'll be the easy part. Sam's about to roll up the paper when Ms. Kinsey flutters over.

"This looks fantastic!" she says, except since she's Ms. Kinsey, she doesn't just *say* it, she exclaims. Gushes. Like always. "You two work *very* well together."

I glance over at Sam and—is he blushing? He totally is. Either he's embarrassed by the praise, or embarrassed by the last comment. He looks over at me, rubs his hair with a small smile. I swear I would bet good money that it's the latter.

And I really don't know how to feel about that.

★ ★ ★

On the other hand, I do know how I feel about the latest graffiti on my locker.

Disgusted.

This time I know exactly who the culprit is, because Lowell is still topping off the finishing touches as Sam and I turn down the hall. I get a glimpse of a stick figure girl and some poorly drawn genitalia and that's really all I need to see.

Sam says, "What the hell?" His voice is loud enough to make people stop and stare.

I don't want him to make a scene. And I don't want him getting involved. I grab the crook of his elbow and shake my head firmly, silently plead for him to let it go, but he ignores me.

"Knock it off," he says to Lowell, who throws him a bored look over his shoulder.

"Hey, I might not be an art freak like you two, but I think it's pretty good so far," Lowell says. He turns his back to Sam again, taking his own sweet time with his artwork.

Too much time for Sam's taste, apparently, because he pushes Lowell against the lockers. The sound of his back ramming into the metal makes a tinny thud, and heads everywhere turn to see what's happening.

Lowell just laughs. "*Oooh,* you got me, I'm so scared."

"Maybe you should be."

What does Sam think he's *doing?*

"What are you gonna do, make out with me? Sorry, I'm not into dudes. And what would your little girlfriend think?"

"Shut up," Sam says, voice rising. "Just shut the *hell* up."

"Fuck you. We both know you're not going to do anything, fag." Lowell pushes him off and starts to walk away, then throws over his shoulder, "Say hi to Noah for me."

Sam grabs the back of Lowell's shirt collar and slams him into the lockers again, harder than before. Way harder. This time Lowell actually flinches a little.

"You don't get to say his name," Sam growls. "Not now. Not ever. You hear me, you ignorant, piece-of-shit Neanderthal?"

Lowell wriggles under his grasp. "Dude, let go."

"Not until you answer me," Sam replies, shoving him back again.

Some guy down the hall randomly yells, "Oh, snaaa-*aaap!*"

And I, of course, can only stand there, watching along with everyone else. Passive as always. All of us.

Except for Brendon.

He appears out of nowhere and puts a hand on Sam's tense shoulder.

"Don't be stupid," he says, his voice warm-honey smooth and, somehow, infuriatingly calm. "It's not worth it, man."

Sam hesitates, and before the sensibility of Brendon's words can sink in, one of the Spanish teachers pops his head into the hall. He takes in the scene—Sam with his fists knotted in Lowell's shirt, the obscene graffiti on the locker—and frowns. Maybe, I think, this means someone in charge is actually going to notice the crap that's been drawn on my locker and do something about it.

"You two." He points to Sam and Lowell. "In here. Now. I'm writing you up."

Sam reluctantly releases Lowell's shirtfront. Lowell sneers and storms into the classroom without looking back, leaving Sam and Brendon to stare at each other, and then at me.

What, am I supposed to be impressed by this display of unleashed teenage testosterone? Because I am so not. I'm just pissed. Sam has no business getting in the middle of things with Lowell and me. All he's done is make it worse, because there is no way Lowell won't find a way to get me back for this, even though it wasn't my fault.

And what am I supposed to do when Sam isn't there to swoop in and save me from the big bad wolf?

Of course he wasn't thinking about *that*. He doesn't understand how this is all a balancing act. Yes, someday I am going to pay Lowell and Derek both back for the way they've treated me, and it will be a very sweet revenge indeed, but I can't afford to be reckless about it like Sam just was.

"I'll see you later," he says to me, but I just give him a cold look in return.

When he's gone, Brendon puts a hand on my arm and says, "Are you okay?"

Touching. He's actually touching me. Acknowledging my existence. This is new. Even through the fabric of my sweater, I can feel the warmth of his skin. But it's not like before. No butterflies. I feel like I should be more excited about this.

I nod and wonder what's changed.

"How's the whole vow of silence thing going?" he asks.

I shrug, and then I take out my whiteboard and write, *How's GSA?*

"It's a lot of work," he says, "but I think it'll be worth it. My older sister, Dana, is actually the one who suggested starting it to me. She didn't come out until college, but she told me she always wished there'd been something like that for her in high school." He stops for a second, mouth turning down. "Were you…thinking of coming to a meeting?"

I shake my head. I'm not stupid. I know where I'm not wanted.

"Good," he says, relaxing. "I mean, I wouldn't stop you,

of course, but I just think—I think it might be uncomfortable if you did. For everyone."

I realize Brendon's probably right, but the implication still stings. I guess this shows how much he really thinks of me.

I look down at where he's touching me. He's wearing this button-down shirt and a sweater over it, as preppy and clean-cut as ever. The sleeves are rolled up enough to show off his forearms. They look strong, muscular, not at all like Sam's. And even now, in the middle of winter, his skin is all golden tan. He told me he spent Christmas vacation in Miami, and I acted jealous at the time, but really, I thought it was kind of ridiculous. I mean, Christmas is like the one time of the year where it's nice to have snow on the ground. Christmas without snow is like the Fourth of July without fireworks and barbecues, or wearing leggings as pants. Just wrong.

What's really wrong is that I'm looking at Brendon's sexy arms and all I can think about is snow.

"Brendon?"

A heavyset kid with glasses approaches, his hands twisting nervously around the straps of his backpack. He looks from me to Brendon...like he's afraid he's intruding.

"Sorry," he says, "I just wanted to ask you about something about next week's meeting."

"Sure, Garrett," Brendon says with a smile. He turns that smile to me with an apologetic shrug. "See you around, Chelsea."

He squeezes my arm and walks off with Garrett, and I watch him as he goes, but something's off. A few weeks ago I was dying to jump his bones. What is the matter with me?

day twenty

"I can't tell if you're giving me the silent treatment, or if you're just being...you."

I ignore Sam and scrub the pot in my hands. The Friday night special is lasagna. It crusts on the bottom of the dishes so I have to hand wash them.

It's taken Sam two days to catch on to the fact that I'm giving him the cold shoulder. He is right, though; it's hard to let someone know you're pissed off when you're already not speaking. My method has mostly involved avoidance of eye contact and a lot of scowling. Passive aggressive, I'll admit, but it's all I've got unless I want to tell him off via whiteboard.

He steps in front of me when I go to set the pot in the dishwasher. "Look," he says, "about the other day... I wasn't trying to—you know. Overstep. I just *really* can't stand that guy." *That guy* being Lowell, I assume.

I roll the rack in and fold my arms over my chest, waiting to see if he has more to say. He does.

"I know, you don't want me fighting your battles, and I won't anymore. I promise." He tucks his chin to his chest, wiping his hands on his apron, and then looks up at me. "I just want you to know, I'm on your side. Okay?"

I nod a little so he knows I understand. I appreciate what he's trying to do. But he's right. I don't want him fighting my battles. There doesn't need to be another person getting caught in the crosshairs.

Usually the diner closes at ten, but on Fridays, Saturdays and Sundays, Dex keeps it open until two in the morning. It's a haven for the burnouts—clusters of kids filter in after midnight, coming down from their highs and seeking to fulfill their munchie cravings. They all order the twenty-four-hour breakfasts and black coffee.

Things calm down around one or so. Dex and Lou work the counter while the rest of us take a break. Technically, as far as the state of Michigan's child labor laws are concerned, Asha's shift ended at nine, and Sam's and mine ended at ten-thirty, but we've been hanging around helping out anyway. Dex repays us with free food. We sit in the long wall booth, Asha drinking chamomile tea while Sam devours leftover home fries. I squish in next to him and steal a few from his plate. They're mushy and a little cold but still good.

"I need to buy a dress," Asha says.

Sam taps the bottom of a mostly empty ketchup bottle against the table's edge. "What for?"

"Winter Formal."

I groan, and everyone stops to look at me. I can't help it. Is Asha really still stuck on this?

"You want to go to Winter Formal?" asks Sam. He sounds incredulous. I'm glad I'm not the only one who thinks the idea is ridiculous. And bad. Bad bad bad, all around.

She shrugs and licks her spoon. "Why not?"

"Uh, because dances are lame?"

"How would you know? Have you ever even *been* to one?"

"Well, I've never been attacked by a scorpion, either, but I know I wouldn't want to be."

"What does that have to do with anything?" she asks.

He dips a fry in ketchup and points it at her. *"Exactly."*

Asha huffs like she's given up on the argument. I pull my feet into the booth with a yawn. I'm so tired. I really should go home soon. I check my cell to see if either of my parents have noticed my absence, but I have exactly zero missed calls and no new texts. I'd bet anything that Dad fell asleep in front of the television again, and Mom probably went straight to bed as soon as she came home from work. She's been running herself ragged to clock in as many hours as she can.

I lie down and stretch out my legs, resting my head on Sam's lap. He looks down at me, surprised, but doesn't say anything. A few seconds later he sets one of his hands on top of my hair. He starts stroking it, very lightly, like I'm a cat. It feels good. I rub my cheek against his leg and close my eyes. I could fall asleep right here....

Right as I'm drifting off, someone shoves my legs off the booth seat and snaps, "Move it."

I open my eyes to see Andy scowling at me. He has a rag in one hand and a spray bottle in the other.

"Don't be a dick," Asha says to him.

Sam clenches his jaw but keeps his mouth shut. I guess he's afraid I'll get annoyed if he says something. He's right. I would be annoyed.

I *am* annoyed, anyway. But not with him. With Andy. I set both feet on the floor and sit up so fast I get a little dizzy.

Andy makes an irritated sound in the back of his throat as he wipes down the table next to ours. "Oh, grow up, Asha."

She goes quiet and stirs her tea slowly, the spoon clanking against the ceramic mug. Okay, that is not cool. No one should be mean to Asha. She's nice to everyone, all the time.

"Leave her alone," Sam says, and Andy whirls on him.

"Oh, right, let's not hurt the princess's feelings."

"Dude, what is your problem?"

"*My* problem? What's *your* problem?" He slams the spray bottle down on the table and glares at me. "I see Mute Girl here is making herself right at home, isn't she? Putting her goddamn feet on the furniture."

"What are you talking about?"

"I'm talking about how she's Single White Female-ing Noah's ass!" he bursts. "Taking his job when she's the reason he can't even work. And none of you even care."

"Don't tell me I don't care about Noah." Sam's voice shakes, and it makes my heart feel like it's splintering into tiny pieces.

"Oh, really? How many times have you visited him in the hospital, Sam?" he asks. Sam lowers his eyes to his plate, silent, and Andy scoffs. "Yeah. I'm sure you'll be awarded your Best Friend of the Year trophy any day now."

He stalks off toward the back, and we all watch him go. Dex grabs his arm, says something to him, but Andy brushes him off and storms out of sight. We all sit in silence for a long time. Sam won't even look at me.

I push my way out of the booth. As I pass, Asha tugs my sleeve and says, "Chelsea, maybe you should leave him alone. Let him cool off a little."

No. I think it's time we had this out. It's been a long time coming.

I snag my whiteboard from my bag and follow him out the back door. He's sitting outside on an overturned crate, hunched forward, smoking a cigarette. When the door closes behind me, he looks over his shoulder and frowns.

"Fuck off," he says.

I stand in front of him. At the party, when he left with Noah, I remember he was smiling, this wide grin that was too big for his face. He'd had no idea what would happen that night. Neither of us did.

I'm sorry.

I hold the board up so he can see it. He stares at it, and then at me, unimpressed.

"What for?" he asks flatly.

Everything.

"Wow. Thank you. I feel all better now," he says. "I don't care if you're sorry. I don't care what you feel. I don't *care*."

I don't expect you to forgive me. Ever.

He blows out a thin stream of smoke. "Good."

I'm still sorry.

He doesn't respond. I start to write more, but then he stands and says, "Stop it, okay, just stop! You can't be sorry. You don't even know what to be sorry *for*. You have no idea. Noah isn't some stand-in to teach you a moral life lesson. He's a fucking person. Do you even know anything about him?"

I swallow and slowly shake my head.

"Well, let me tell you," he says, not at all nicely. "His favorite color is blue. His middle name is Christopher. He'd eat nothing but macaroni and cheese if he could get away with it. He judges anyone who lists J. D. Salinger as their favorite author. One time he spent an hour explaining to me in specific detail why he thinks *Catcher in the Rye* is a piece of crap. He has a scar on his left knee from wiping out on his skateboard when he was twelve. Sam was there when it happened, and puked because of all the blood. It took five stitches to close it. Noah went as Draco Malfoy for Halloween, and he tried to get me to go as Harry Potter, but I thought it was a dumb idea, so we had a big fight about it. The first time he kissed me, we were standing right over there." He points to the Dumpster. "It was raining, and I was smoking a cigarette as he dumped the last of the trash, and I made a stupid joke about the weather, and Noah laughed, because that's what Noah does—he laughs at any joke, no matter how stupid. Sometimes he just laughs for no reason. He tossed the trash, and then he came over to me, and he flicked my cigarette out of my hand and he kissed me, out of the blue. Just like that. Like it was nothing."

Andy throws out each fact like he's drilling nails into my heart. His stare doesn't waver from mine, rooting me to the spot. I feel like crying, but I think if I did, it'd just make him angrier.

"He's never been out of the country, so we've planned this road trip to Toronto for the summer, just so he can say he's been," he continues. "He wants to become a doctor and volunteer in Haiti, because he saw this documentary about it last year, and it's stuck with him ever since. He's excited about senior year because he makes good grades, and if he gets into any of the schools he applies to, he'll be the first one in his family to go to college." He stops to let that sink in. "Someone almost stole all of that from him. For no reason. And you helped it happen."

I didn't think it was possible to feel any worse than I have, but it is, because in all the thinking I've done, I haven't thought about it like this.

"So forgive me if I don't feel like extending you the hand of friendship," he says. "Everyone else may buy your little act, but I don't. It's pathetic. You're not helping anyone."

I cap the marker and stare at my feet. Maybe he's right.

Maybe I should give it up already. And if I'm going to say any-thing to anyone, I should be apologizing to Andy, out loud.

The problem is that now it's all hyped up in my mind. My first words should be important—and apologizing to Andy is important, but not enough for me to break my silence. Not yet. That moment has to mean something, it has to, but I don't know what.

"Sam says you're getting a lot of shit at school," Andy says. I look up and nod. I wonder how much Sam's told him.

"They're all fucking scum. I hate them so much."

I don't disagree with his assessment. Even if he's including me in that category.

He sits back down with a sigh, ashing his cigarette, and after a minute I sit on the crate next to his. I write, *How is Noah?* and inch the board toward him.

"Why should I tell you?" he says, but then, after a pause, "He's…better. Getting there. He sleeps a lot. Has some trouble figuring out what he wants to say, sometimes. But that could be the painkillers. He's got some broken ribs, so."

It hurts to hear, but it's good that I do. That I don't just ignore the Noah component in this fucked-up equation that is my life.

"He didn't even want me there," Andy says. He's staring down at the cigarette pinched between his fingers. "I had to *beg* him to let me come to that stupid party. I was mad be-cause—I always knew, what I was, you know? It was never a big…thing, with my parents or at school. I was *mad* at him, for not being comfortable with it. Like I thought he wanted to hide us. Me. So I made him take me to that party. I was the one who…started things. In the bedroom. And I didn't lock the door, because part of me wanted someone to walk in, and when you did—" He laughs, but the sound is like shattered glass. "I was glad. I thought, 'Good. Now people will know.'"

I sit there, the cold air heavy in my lungs, absorbing this. Andy *wanted* me—well, not me specifically, but *someone*—to find out, all along.

It sounds like he blames himself as much as he blames me. I want to write *It's not your fault,* underline the words until he believes them, but I know by now it's never that easy.

"You have to stop punishing yourself," he says, so quietly I almost don't catch it.

I don't know if he's talking to himself or to me. I guess it doesn't really matter.

day twenty-one

I wake up the next morning when my phone beeps on the nightstand. It's not a ring, more of a *bloop*. The sound it makes when I receive a text message. I roll over and fumble for it, squint through bleary eyes at the front display. It's already past noon. I flip it open and scroll through screens to my in-box. It's from Asha.

lets go shopping 2day

God, I could just pull the covers over my head and float back into the warm, dreamless sleep I was so rudely interrupted from. Instead I tuck my Nelly under my arm and respond.

im not going 2 wntr frml

I rub my eyes, trying to wake up, and stretch my arms over my head, thinking. Saturday Saturday Saturday. Dad will probably be hanging around the house all day in his pajamas. Mom will be slaving at the shop until later this afternoon. I didn't really have any plans today; Asha and I technically have the night off, but I figured we'd go hang out at Rosie's anyway, just to have something to do.

My phone *bloops* again.

w/e. i need yarn. plz?

Sigh. Might as well. I'm too awake to fall back asleep now.

give me 1 hour.

When I pick her up, her brother Karthik is out in the front yard with some other neighborhood kids, in the midst of a heated snowball fight. I know he must be her brother because he has the same black hair and light brown skin and big dark eyes. Asha squeezes out the front door. I wave to her, and a snowball sails through the air and splats against my windshield. Karthik points and laughs.

Kids these days.

Asha yells something at him I can't hear and ducks into the car. She has this thick blue-and-white scarf wound around her neck. I bet she made it herself. It's gorgeous.

"There's a craft store in the mall," she tells me as I back out of her driveway and onto the street. "I usually go there."

I know where the craft store is; I've been there plenty of times to pick up fabric for my various ill-fated sewing projects. It's funny to realize Asha and I have something in common outside of the diner.

The mall is crazy busy, of course, since it's Saturday, and there's nothing else to do in this town. It takes ten minutes just to find an open parking spot. Blah. Crowds. They never bothered me before, but when we walk through the sliding doors and are met with the swarm of shoppers, my stomach crawls.

We wind our way past the moms with their strollers and packs of preteen girls in their way too slutty outfits. Looking at these girls makes me sad, even though they don't seem to be—they giggle in high-pitched voices, their faces stretched with glossy-lipped smiles. All of them are the same type; girls with overprocessed hair and too much makeup and way too much access to Daddy's credit cards. Girls who, if you took away the designer labels, hair dye and cover-up, wouldn't be more than average-looking, but with all that stuff look too plastic to be pretty.

I know because I used to look just like one of them. I'm wearing next to no makeup now, just a touch of mascara and some clear lip gloss. Compared to them, I'm practically naked. I haven't set foot inside the mall in weeks. Saturday mall trips used to be a weekly tradition. But that's over. Like so many things.

No. No angsting today. Time to cheer up, emo girl.

The crafts store is full of old ladies with too much perfume, and Asha and I are the youngest customers by at least thirty years. She goes straight to the yarn aisle, starts sifting through the shelves. I randomly pick up a roll of scratchy black wool.

"You should get some," Asha says. "I said I'd teach you, right? I have some extra needles you can borrow."

I do have some leftover Christmas money I haven't spent. My grandparents on Dad's side are crippling agoraphobics who live in Maine, and as compensation for seeing me only once every few years, they always send a hefty check. I was saving it for—irony of all ironies—a new Winter Formal dress. Ha ha ha.

Asha ends up with an armful of different-colored yarns,

and I pick out the black wool for myself, since Asha says it's good material to learn on. I try to imagine myself knitting like she does. Maybe I'll fare better with knitting needles than I do with sewing machines.

We're walking toward the food court when Asha grabs my sleeve and says, "Hey."

She points to a window display where there are Barbie-shaped mannequins lined up, dressed in tight, flashy, fashionable formal dresses.

"Can we look?" she asks. "Just a look. Really."

I roll my eyes a little but follow her in. This store, Athena, is a hotbed for teen girls looking to catch up on the latest trends. At least eighty percent of my own wardrobe originates from here.

Asha fingers her way through a rack of dresses toward the back of the store. She pulls some out—ranging from the pretty to the god-awful, and all of them way too big for her tiny frame—and holds the hangers up to her chin. One in particular is just a crime against fashion, and for that matter, all laws of nature—this horrible shade of orange with poofy sleeves and a giant bow at the hip. Tacky to the max.

"What do you think?" she asks, trying to keep a straight face but barely suppressing a grin. "Fabulous, right?" She spins in a circle with the dress pressed to her front, and we both laugh.

My laugh stops short, however, when I turn my head and catch sight of Kristen Courteau all of six feet away. She has a few dresses draped over her arm and is staring at me.

The funny thing—not ha ha funny, but, you know—is that she looks shocked. Upset, even. Only for about two seconds, of course, before she masks her expression with her default bitchy face. The perfect look for an ice princess, I can't help but think nastily.

Except my feelings toward Kristen aren't all nasty. They're… complicated, like everything else in my life. Because, stupidly, I miss her. Even with everything that happened. Even if our friendship was never the same after she hooked up with Warren. All I want at this moment is for her to look at me and smile like she used to. The smile that made me feel important, because Kristen is important, because people want to look like her, date her, *be* her, and she chose me as her best friend, so that had to mean something.

And maybe she meant some of that crap in the article, about how bad she felt about what happened to Noah, and it wasn't just damage control. Part of me wants to believe she does. I want to believe that I wouldn't ever be friends with someone completely heartless.

Tessa steps out from one of the dressing rooms. "You should totally buy the pink one," she says. "It's so hot. Brendon will *die*."

Brendon? That must mean… Kristen is going to the formal with him. As her date. She knew how into him I was.

Maybe she really is that heartless.

Kristen smiles at me, but it's not like her old one—it's more of an "I'm better than you and don't you forget it" smile. The kind that cuts straight through my bones. How many times have I stood where Tessa is standing? How many times have I seen that smile? Too many to count. But this is the first time she has ever directed it at me.

It makes me feel about two feet tall.

Asha steps next to me and says, "We should go."

I'm shaking as we walk to the parking lot. I hate that Kristen can do this to me without saying a word. I hate her. Except I don't. Like I said: complicated.

I almost drop the keys twice before I manage to unlock the car. Asha watches me, concerned, and says, "Are you okay?"

I just nod and stick the keys in the ignition. Even if I could speak I wouldn't have the words right now. I drive out of the crowded lot and shove that nauseous feeling into the pit of my stomach. My phone *bloops* as I roll to a stop at a red light. I pick it up and flip it open. The text is from Sam.

Hey loser. what r u doing rite now?

I smile.

w/ asha. Mall. U?

Rosies. come over.

I hand the phone to Asha and point the car toward the lake.

Sam's practicing ollies on his skateboard outside Rosie's when we arrive. He sees us coming down the sidewalk and glides over, popping to an abrupt stop. He has this grin on his face, big and crooked, so different from Brendon's perfect million-dollar smile, and I don't know why I keep on doing that. Comparing them.

"Look who finally decided to show up," he teases. He pushes his floppy hair out of his eyes and picks up his skateboard.

"Don't lie. You're thrilled we're here," Asha says. She leaps onto his back, throwing her arms around his neck as he staggers forward a step, laughing, surprised by the sudden weight. "Mush," she commands.

He aims that slanted grin at me. "So demanding!"

He gallops her into Rosie's, me tagging after, and carries her up to the counter. The post-lunch lull means the diner is mostly emptied out. Dex is ringing up some takeout while Andy scrapes the grill.

"This is not a playground," Dex says, extending a white paper bag to the pretty blonde girl waiting.

"Yeah, it's a mental institution," Andy says. "Get it right."

Dex reaches a leg out and kicks him in the shin, but he's smiling.

Asha slides off Sam's back and onto a stool. I sit on the one next to hers. Phyllis, the sixty-something waitress whom I usually never see since she works the day shifts, passes by us with a smile.

"Where's Lou?" Asha asks.

"Ohio. Her sister's getting married," explains Dex.

"Which one?"

"Elizabeth. The oldest one." Dex laughs. "You should see the bridesmaid dress she has to wear. Hang on. I made her let me take a picture of it."

He digs his cell phone out of his pocket, presses a few buttons and passes it to Asha. I lean over to take a peek. Sure enough, there's a pixeled image of Lou decked out in some sea-foam-green monstrosity, flipping off the camera.

"Wow, that's bad. But it could be worse. Chelsea and I saw some seriously awful dresses today," Asha says, handing back the phone.

"At, like, the mall?" Sam says in a put-upon Valley Girl accent. He's behind the counter, washing his hands. "Was it, like, totally awesome, like, oh, my gawd?"

Andy snaps a dish towel at him. "Dude, you're creeping me out with that voice."

Sam flicks a spray of water his way, and then they're tussling playfully. Guess the tension from yesterday is a nonissue.

Boys. I will never understand them. Not even the gay ones.

"I give up," Dex says, throwing up his hands in defeat.

"So why were you looking at dresses?" Andy asks, Sam's head locked under one arm.

Sam says, "They want to go to the winter dance...thing."

They? Incorrect plural usage! Only Asha wants to. I draw an arrow pointing toward her on my whiteboard and hold it up. Sam pushes away from Andy—who smirks, victorious—and rubs at his hair.

"Correction. Asha wants to go," he amends.

"From the way everyone acts, you'd think I was offering myself up as a virgin sacrifice," she mutters, then blushes at what she's let slip. To their credit, Andy and Sam don't crack any inappropriate jokes.

My rumbling stomach interrupts the awkward silence. Oops. I probably should've eaten something today. Everyone looks at me and laughs.

"Get that girl some food," Dex says as he walks off into the back.

Sam leans his elbows on the counter in front of me and grins. Imperfect though it may be, it is a damn charming smile. "What can I get ya?"

"I want an omelet," Asha interjects.

PANCAKES, I write. I think for a second, then add, *& eggs, scrambled. & orange juice.* I draw a little smiley face underneath the words.

Andy sees my board and says to Sam, "I call pancakes, bitch."

"Like I'd trust you to make an omelet anyway. Bitch."

Andy can't cook as well as Sam can, or make as many dishes as Sam can, but even I know pancakes and scrambled eggs are easy, and they turn out wonderful. Of course, right now I'm so starved that pretty much anything remotely edible would look wonderful.

He sets the plate down in front of me and says, "I think you should."

Should what? I cut some pancake with the side of my fork and raise my eyebrows.

"Go to the dance thing," he clarifies. "I mean, you shouldn't let those idiots stop you from doing what you want to do."

Asha and Sam trade looks over my head. I know they must be wondering what transpired between Andy and me to make him suddenly care about me standing up for myself.

"Andy does have a point," Sam says carefully from his place at the grill. "If you want to go, go."

I push my eggs around on my plate, thinking. Looking at those dresses...it did sort of remind me of how much fun it is. Wearing the kind of formal wear you can't get away with any other time of year and dancing my ass off to generic pop music.

"You should!" Asha bounces on her stool. "We *all* should."

Sam and Andy stare at her as if she's grown two heads.

"Come on!" she says. "It'd be great! We could all get dressed up and go to the dance and then come back here. You, too, Andy."

"That sounds like a terrible idea," he tells her. "Like, monumentally bad."

Sam runs his knuckles along his jaw. "I don't know, man..."

Oh, my God, is he seriously interested in going to Winter Formal? I almost choke on my orange juice.

Andy must share my incredulity, because he says, "You can't actually be considering this. You were the one talking about how much of a waste of time school functions are."

"I know, but if we all crash it as a group, maybe it would be fun."

"Yeah, and maybe we'd all get our asses kicked."

"You shouldn't let them stop you from doing what you want to do," Sam says back to him with a pointed look.

Andy stares at him, and then he says, "You're going to burn the omelet."

day twenty-four

For the first time in a week, I'm actually home for dinner. The good news is that it isn't tofu. The bad news is that the reason it isn't is because Mom stopped buying organic foods since we're now on a tighter budget. Dad resorted to his old standby: mac and cheese from the box.

"I used to make this all the time when you were a kid," he says as we sit down at the kitchen table.

I remember. That was when Mom was taking night classes at the business school. The idea was that she'd eventually start her own chain of floral shops instead of just managing someone else's, but she ended up dropping out before she could graduate. I don't know why.

"How is school going?" he asks, brushing some lint off his sleeve. I'm so used to him wearing work clothes—button-down Oxfords and ties—that it's strange to see him like this, wearing a flannel shirt and *jeans*.

I give him a thumbs-up that is far more enthused than I feel. I can't lie, though—it has become significantly less torturous now that I can glom on to Asha and Sam. I've memorized their schedules and made a point of meeting them outside their classrooms so I'm not on my own in between classes. There's a safety in numbers. People are less likely to mess with me when I'm around them. The worst I've gotten lately is some shoving in the halls, pointed glares and snickering from Kristen and her minions, and of course the daily locker vandalizing. I guess that Spanish teacher's intervention didn't stop Lowell. Or someone else is picking up his slack. Today through the vent cracks someone slipped in a folded note that read *WATCH YOUR BACK TRAITOR BITCH*.

I promptly tore the note in half and threw it in the trash. Hey, at least that's easier to get rid of than the marker.

As I pick at my mac and cheese, I have to admit, after so much delicious diner food lately, all this bland processed cheese is a chore to eat. But I don't want to hurt Dad's feelings, so I shovel as much into my mouth as I can bear.

"So, you're still not speaking." It's a statement, not a question, and a displeased one at that. The corners of his mouth are pulled down like he's sucking on something sour.

I keep my eyes on the orange clumpy mess covering my plate. My appetite is suddenly gone.

"I'm just wondering," he says. "How long is this going to last? It's been nearly a month now."

Dad is supposed to be on my side, not grilling me about this. That's what Mom is for. I guess, though, that in light of his own problems, mine must look childish and dumb.

"Chelsea," he presses, "I think it's time you—"

I'm spared from more lecturing by the phone ringing. Dad exhales, shooting me a *this-is-not-over-young-lady* look, and answers it.

"Hello?" he says. He pauses for a moment. "Yes, this is he."

I watch him, stirring my mac and cheese around, but he walks out of the room with the phone before I can hear anything else.

I tell myself that Dad is just stressed out. Justifiably so. He's been sending out résumés, applying for jobs online, but the economy sucks, and he hasn't had a single call back. My first paycheck from Rosie's won't come for another week or so, but I'm already planning to give the entirety of it to my parents. It's the least I can do.

I dump the rest of my lukewarm mac and cheese down the garbage disposal and run the tap for a while. I wish I was back at Rosie's. Or at least out of this house. Six o'clock on a Saturday night and I already have nothing to do but kill time before going to bed. My life is so depressing.

I tear off a page from the refrigerator pad and write, *Going out for a drive. I'll be back later. -C.* I stick the note next to Dad's half-finished plate where he'll be sure to see it.

I love driving. I love the feel of the steering wheel under my hands, all of that power. It makes me feel in control. In summer I like to open all the windows, the cool air rushing in and pushing my hair off my shoulders, and take off my shoes so that the pedal grooves dig into my bare feet. It's too cold outside to do that now; the heat is on full blast, the radio low as I try to figure out where to go. Instinct points me toward the center of town and the lake.

I've lived in Grand Lake all my life. It's a small town, yeah, but I've always liked that, that I know it inside and out, the way everyone knows everyone. Something about that is comforting, even if a little incestuous. And everyone knows everything *about* everyone; I should know. I've spent the last few years collecting secrets and gossip the way other people collect butterflies or Pez dispensers.

There are never any surprises in Grand Lake—which I think is why what happened to Noah was so shocking. Because things like that aren't supposed to happen here. Every-

one was so defensive, so desperate to downplay the situation.
I think they all would've been happier if I'd kept my mouth
shut so they could stick their heads in the sand and pretend
nothing had happened. When they couldn't just ignore it,
they were so quick to blame it on Warren and Joey just being
two bad apples, because if they weren't, that meant something
more insidious was going on. That kids who grow up here
aren't raised right. That this town could produce that kind
of hatred in its children. And no one wants to believe that.

I don't want to believe that.

The problem with small towns is the same thing I like
about them—it's so insular. No one's thinking about the big
picture. Derek and Lowell, they don't care about Noah, they
care about winning at basketball, because for them…what else
is there? College, maybe, but we all know they're the kind
of kids who will inevitably end up back here. And they'll be
happy about it. They wouldn't get to feel so big and important in any other place.

I want my life to be more than this. More than just this
town and everything that's happened in it. I don't want my
high school years to be the best of my life. I want to be better
than this, better than the Chelsea Knot who stirs up trouble
just for lack of anything more interesting to do. Andy was
right—I didn't see Noah as a person, the same way I didn't see
Tessa as a person, or anyone else I've helped to spread rumors
about. Their feelings didn't matter, at least not more than my
need for a quick entertainment fix.

I end up at the hospital, underneath the buttery-yellow
light thrown from one of the parking-lot lamps. In the day-
time the building stands stately and inviting, made of warm
red brick, but in the dark it just looks scary. Daunting. Like
it could swallow me whole.

I take out my phone.

u busy?

Sam texts back a minute later.

Not rly. whats up?

Im at the hospital.

R u ok?

Fine. Parking lot. Can u come?

Yes. ten mins.

All I'm doing is sitting there, engine running, my heart beating fast in my throat for no reason, when Sam's Cutlass pulls in next to my driver's side. He gets out of his car and climbs into mine, shuts the door and turns to me.

"What happened?" he asks, worried.

I shake my head. Nothing happened. Nothing new. It's just everything else, weighing on me.

"So no one's hurt?" Even behind his glasses, I see the relief in his eyes, the way it relaxes his shoulders. He breathes out and rubs his face with both hands. "Jesus. I thought..." He trails off instead of finishing the sentence.

My whiteboard is at home. I wasn't expecting to need it. I dig through the glove compartment and find an old gas station receipt and a Jelly pen, use the light from the outside lamp to scratch out some words.

I keep thinking about Noah.

He swallows hard. "Yeah?"

I don't know what to do.

This applies to, like, my entire life, really, not just the Noah situation.

"I know." Sam's voice sounds strange. A little choked. "Andy was right, you know. What he said. I've been...avoiding Noah, because I'm—I don't know. It's too hard."

He swallows, looking away from me. I'm suddenly, brutally struck with how much what I've done has hurt him, too, even though I know he doesn't see it that way. Still, it makes the way he treats me even more baffling.

"I know I didn't have anything to do with what happened, but I still feel all this guilt," he says. "Like I should've stopped it somehow. I have no idea what to say to him."

Maybe you don't have to say anything, I write. *Maybe just being there is enough.*

"Maybe," he says quietly. "I keep telling myself I'll go. I just...I can't make myself do it. I know I should be doing something to help, but I don't know what. I'm supposed to be his best friend, and I can't even bring myself to be in the same room as him. What does that say about me?"

That doesn't make you a bad person, I write.

He laughs, low in his throat. "I'm pretty sure it does, actually."

You are the best kind of person.

He stares at the words like he doesn't understand them. "You really think that?" he says.

I reach out and cover his hand with mine so he knows exactly what I think.

"Chelsea," he says, barely above a whisper. I love the way he says my name, like it's something he wants to keep safe. I sway a little toward him.

And then we're kissing.

It's weird how comfortable it feels. With Joey, it was always awkward, his hands rough on the back of my neck, his tongue wet and weird in my mouth. But Sam is so gentle with me, lips barely brushing mine, one hand lightly cupping my cheek. He pulls back before we've hardly started and looks at me for a long time.

Well. That was unexpected.

I mean, there's kind of been a vibe. But I've never been good at reading these things. It's too easy to confuse friendship with something more. Especially when you're looking for it.

His eyes search mine, and I have no idea what he's thinking. Maybe he's wondering the same thing, about me.

"I should go back to Rosie's," he says softly.

I nod, a little shaky. What we did—it was barely even a kiss, but I feel like I've just finished running a marathon. Completely out of breath, every limb as boneless as rubber.

He gets out of the car, walks around toward his. I roll down my window and am met with a blast of cold air. Sam sees me motion to him and, after a heartbeat of hesitation (*please don't leave, please don't just walk away, please please please,* my brain screams), he comes over, ducks his head to my eye level.

I don't say anything. Of course. I reach a hand out, brushing it slowly through his brown hair. It looks almost reddish under this sticky light. I draw him down to me. We kiss through the open window for a little while, my face cold from the whistling wind, my back warm from the car's heat, Sam's mouth soft against mine.

When we stop—I can't tell which one of us breaks away first—he keeps his forehead pressed to mine.

"So," he says, a smile playing on his lips, "does this mean you'll be my date for Winter Formal?"

days
twenty-eight &
twenty-nine

Discombobulated. It's a word my mother often uses, and one that happens to describe me perfectly at the moment. I feel turned around and pulled inside out, all out of whack. But in a good way. I think.

I also like the way it sounds, even in my own head. Dis-com-bob-u-lated. Every syllable pops.

I'm worried that kissing Sam is going to make everything weird between us, but when I go back to school on Thursday, everything feels the same. I go to art class and we work on the project—we've moved on to the painting phase—and nothing is different; I spend the whole weekend at Rosie's, and nothing is different. It's sort of disappointing. I keep waiting to see if he's going to kiss me again, but we're never alone together, so I'm left to overanalyze every fleeting touch.

The one thing that *has* changed is that suddenly everyone is on board with the idea of going to Winter Formal. Even Andy.

Asha is, predictably, thrilled by this development.

"Six days!" she sings every time she dumps more dishes for me to wash. I glare at her receding back as she prances back through the swinging doors and to the dining area.

Six days. Six days, and I'm going to be facing every person at this school who hates me. I don't even have a dress yet.

Sam hasn't mentioned it since that night at the hospital—am I really going to be his date? For real? Or was he just joking? It doesn't matter. Either way I'm going. I've committed.

Later Asha says, "I know a place to look for dresses," while we're sitting in one of the booths. She's finally showing me how to knit. I suck at it, surprise, surprise. But Asha says if she can teach me geometry, she can teach me anything. Today I actually got an A- on a pop quiz, much to the surprise of myself and Mr. Callihan, so I figure she must be right about that.

I cock a skeptical eyebrow at her as I loop the black wool through the needle. Wherever this place is, it better not be in the mall. No way am I stepping foot in that place again.

"There's this little vintage shop on the west end," she explains.

I don't know the west side of town as well as I know the east end. Every place worth visiting is near the lake, and all of the firmly middle-to-upper-middle-class housing is on the east, including my house and Asha's. But the west side is safe. Mostly it's all apartment buildings and liquor stores and low-end groceries. There's no way Kristen or anyone from her posse would be caught dead over there. The next day after school, Asha and I drive over to the vintage shop, this little place called Recollections. I've never been. The inside smells musty, like mothballs, and so do most of the clothes on the racks.

Asha pulls some ridiculous top hat on her head. "What do you think? Maybe I could show up in a tuxedo," she says, and then sneezes. She sets the hat back down. "Or maybe not."

Most of the clothes here aren't true vintage. There's a lot of crap from the eighties—old KISS band T-shirts, NAS-

CAR sweatshirts, denim jackets, neon-colored track suits. But there is one section, toward the back of the store, a rack of old dresses. I sift through them while Asha looks through some nearby shoes.

Too poofy. Too slutty. Too churchy. Too pink. Crap. All crap.

And then.

It's like the heavens parting, the light shining down, angel choirs launching into jubilant song. It's how I felt when Dex offered me the dish-girl job, how I felt when Mr. Callihan handed me back the quiz I aced, how I felt when Sam leaned in to kiss me in the car. The feeling that this is right. This is exactly how it should be.

I've found the perfect dress.

I'm pretty sure my day can't get any better, but then I get home. I kick the door shut with one foot, careful not to let the plastic bag carrying my new dress drag on the floor.

"Chelsea? Is that you?" It's Dad, calling from the living room.

Before I can make my way over, he finds me. Mom's right behind him, a bottle of wine in one hand. Dad skids into the hall, practically running, and this giant grin on his face. I don't know what's more shocking—the fact that he's smiling, or the fact that Mom is home. On a Tuesday. Before nine o'clock.

"Honey," he says, out of breath, "I got a job."

He grabs me in a hug before there's time for this news to sink in. I drop the bag on the ground and hug him back. A job? A *job*. I'm so, so happy for him. When he lets go, he's still smiling, and Mom is…laughing. Laughing!

It's nice, for once, to be proven wrong.

"It's at the Harrison dealership across town," he says, all

in a rush. "Selling cars. Your friend's dad owns the place. He called Saturday, I interviewed this afternoon, and he offered me the job on the spot. I start next week."

Mom smiles at me. "I took the night off to celebrate. Come on, we're watching movies."

We spend the night on the couch, together as a family, popping in a DVD of Dad's favorite film, *Caddyshack,* one of his arms wrapped around my shoulders and the other around Mom's. Every so often I catch them making eyes at each other.

Sam. This is because of Sam. He put this look on my parents' faces.

If he was here right now, I'd totally make out with him.

day thirty-one

I settle for giving him a huge hug the second I see him the next day in art class.

Of course, the sentimentality of the moment is all but ruined when I nearly knock over the open paint bottles in my exuberance. Sam laughs, catching me around the waist, and I don't care if everyone in the room is looking, I don't care I don't care I don't care, I could kiss him right in front of everyone. But I don't.

"My stepdad told me last night," he says. He keeps his hands on my hips, even after I've released him from my death-grip-monster-bear hug. I like that. "I'm really glad it worked out."

We sit down on the floor, and I pull out a notebook and pen from my bag.

What's your stepdad like?

Sam looks at the page. "What, afraid he's gonna be a bad boss?"

Is curiosity a crime now?

"Sometimes," he says, grinning. "Peeping Toms, for example."

I punch him in the shoulder.

"Ow!" he laughs, rubbing his shoulder. "Violence is so unnecessary."

I write, *I'm SERIOUS!! I know nothing about your family.*

And, by extension, nothing about Sam's personal life. Which, let's be real, is really what I'm getting at.

"Mick's okay." Sam shrugs. "I mean, you always hear these horror stories about evil stepparents, but he's not bad. He has two daughters—both older, one's married and the other's at Mount Holyoke—so he's done this before. Doesn't get on my ass too much." He stops and unscrews a bottle of black paint. "And he makes my mom happy. That's what matters, you know?"

I *do* know, actually. I've forgotten what it's like to feel this way—so *happy,* glowing, lighter than air. Maybe everything is finally turning around. Maybe things are only going to get better from here on out. I mean, I have people now—Sam and Asha and Lou and Dex, and Andy, too, maybe. I have the diner. I have a *life.* A different one than before, but maybe this one is better, because it's totally and completely mine.

And the art project, due tomorrow, has turned out kickass, too. I'm pretty proud of the result. Charles Schulz would be giving us some major props, for sure.

"Hey, didn't they teach you in kindergarten how to stay inside the lines?" Sam teases when I accidentally get a little red outside of Snoopy's doghouse.

I respond by sweeping my paintbrush over the bridge of his nose so it leaves a smear of red.

"Oh, no you *didn't,*" he says with a mock gasp, and retaliates by painting my cheek yellow. I scream and roll away, shrieking with laughter, and when I see Sam laughing, too, all I can think is that it would be so, so easy to tell him everything on my mind.

I can't believe someone as good as you exists. I can't believe you even want to be around me. I can't believe how lucky I am when just weeks ago I thought my life was over.

The words are bubbling up in my chest, I swear I can feel them, ready to spill over, but then…they don't. And the moment is over.

Sam doesn't notice, of course. He wipes his palms on his jeans and offers a hand to help me sit up.

"You look ridiculous," he says, his thumb brushing the splotch of yellow he streaked under one of my eyes.

I could tell him everything, but I don't. And I don't know why. What is my vow accomplishing anymore? Why can't I just speak, say what I'm dying to say?

I don't know what I'm waiting for.

"I'm telling you. Purple. It's the way to go."

"If you paint this place purple, I'm quitting. Swear to freakin' God."

Dex and Lou are arguing about redecorating again. It's not serious, of course, no matter how many times Lou threatens to walk out. For the record, I'm on her side. Yes, the current beige walls are too boring for this place, but purple would look atrocious with the red vinyl booths. Unless Dex wanted to replace those, too. Really he should pick something striking. Gold, or maybe bronze.

"You should go with blue."

Lou and Dex stop their bickering and look over. I swivel on the stool, too, to see a cute boy with spiky hair and the cockiest smirk I've ever seen leaning over the counter. The dark-haired girl next to him rolls her eyes, but from the way they're standing, it's obvious they're together. Like, *together*

together, not together just as friends, or in the weird friends-with-benefits ambiguity sense Sam and I currently are.

"I'm sure they really want your input, Jake," she says dryly.

"What? I'm just saying." He grins at her, and she bats him on the shoulder.

"Actually…" Dex twirls the whisk in his hand around a few times, which is how I know he's considering the suggestion. He always plays with utensils or counts down the till when he's deep in thought. Once I saw him do all these tricks with a spinning egg on a silicone turner while he was talking to Andy about replacing the milkshake machine. "That…that could work."

"Blue…" Lou folds her arms over her chest, looking thoughtful. She nods slowly at Dex. "I like it. Blue would look good."

"See?" the guy—Jake—says to the girl. "*Some* people appreciate my genius."

"Oh, yeah," she says around a grin, "today it's interior design, tomorrow you'll be tackling world peace."

Dex gives them their takeout bag and tells them it's on the house.

Lou comes over and refills my Coke, careful not to splatter any on my open history book. We're studying the Elizabethan era. As far as historical figures go, Queen Elizabeth I is pretty badass—telling the royal court to go screw itself and refusing to marry and shaving her head and declaring herself a Virgin Queen. Even though Mrs. Griffin, my social studies teacher, says the queen still had all of these affairs anyway.

Good for her. Who wants to be a virgin forever? I mean, it's something I've thought about, obviously. People always assume only teenage boys have an obsession with sex, but girls do, too. The difference is that most of us want it to *mean*

something. We're complicated. We need more than magazines and badly acted pornos to get off.

Since Sam and I kissed, sometimes I find myself imagining. Just a little. And for the first time, when I'm thinking
about it, I'm not worrying about how much it would hurt,
or if I'd be doing it right, or how awkward it might be; I'm
wondering if it would feel as comfortable, as natural and *right*
as it did when he kissed me.

Not that it matters—we haven't done anything since. Or
even talked about what happened. Maybe it was nothing more
than a fluke. Maybe he's not even interested.

Lou says, "So I heard you're all going to some winter dance
this Saturday?"

I nod and flip to the next page of my textbook. Andy and
Sam said they've already picked out suits to wear. Asha never
bought anything from Recollections, but she says she has
something else in mind, and she's been all mysterious about it
ever since. This morning I pulled my dress out, laid it on the
table and started making measurements, figuring out where
to take it in and how far to adjust the neckline. I can already
see the finished product in my mind. It's going to be so absolutely perfect.

The urge to whip out my notebook and sketch more ideas
for the dress is tempting, but I force myself to focus on history. There's a test tomorrow, and I've been on a roll with this
academic kick; I'm self-aware enough to know that if I slip
now, I will inevitably succumb to a slacker spiral and never
get on top of things again.

Andy comes over to swap out the condiment bottles
and glances at my open textbook. "You could save yourself the time and rent the biopic," he says. "The one with
Cate Blanchett and Joseph Fiennes at his physical peak." He

pauses. "You should watch it either way, really. Joseph Fiennes alone is worth it."

"He is a dreamboat," Sam agrees, walking up. I'm not sure if he's joking or if he's just secure enough to comment on another guy's objective attractiveness. Maybe some of both. He leans over with his palm right on top of my textbook and grins, his face close to mine, his voice low when he speaks. "You've been studying for over an hour. I'm on break. Come take a walk with me."

That's all it takes. I abandon my books, grab my coat off the hook and follow Sam out the door. He offers his arm as we cross the icy parking lot, and I take it, and if I'm clutching the crook of his elbow a little too tightly, it's only because I'm worried about slipping and cracking my head open on the pavement. Really.

I don't know where we're going, or if Sam even has a destination in mind—I let him take the lead, enjoying the closeness. After a minute I realize he's heading for the lake. We pick our way through the snow to sit on top of a picnic table not far from the water. My ass is freezing and even huddling next to Sam doesn't protect me from the cold wind whipping off the lake, but I'm willing to endure it as long as Sam keeps holding on to my arm like this.

"Can I ask you something?" he says. He's looking straight into my eyes as he says it, and I can feel myself melting toward him. How did it take me so long to notice how cute he is? How did I spend so much of high school not noticing him at all? I was so busy mooning over Brendon Ryan. Brendon, who probably doesn't even like me at all, and certainly doesn't trust me. Brendon, who is taking Kristen to the dance, meaning he's either a total idiot falling for her lies or more concerned with his image than anything. Either way, he's not the guy I thought he was. It's not his fault; it's mine, for building up this fantasy version in my head, putting him on a pedestal, making assumptions about him the way I make assumptions about everyone, the same way people make assumptions about me now.

I am trying so hard not to be that person anymore. I am trying to be the kind of person who deserves to be looked at the way Sam is looking at me now, like I'm someone worth caring about, someone worth knowing. I want to prove that the risk he's taken in reaching out to me isn't for nothing, but I don't know how to do that.

Sam is so earnest it hurts, and he's staring at me with this kindness in his eyes, the kind you can't fake—there's an innate goodness in him, like deep within his soul or something, and you don't even have to hear him speak to feel it. It just *radiates*.

"Do you know when you're going to start talking again?" he asks. "I only ask because—well, I like to be on speaking terms with the girls I make a habit of kissing." He leans forward so our foreheads touch for a moment before backing away with a smile.

I want to remind him that it isn't a habit yet since we've only done it once, though it's nice to see where his mind is at on that subject.

"I know you can't answer me right now," he says quickly, "and I know you have your reasons, however fuzzy they may be. I just think... I don't know, maybe it's time to start...moving on. I feel like this whole thing is wrapped up in all these ugly feelings, and it can't be good, carrying all that around inside you. You know?"

I nod, because everything he's said is true, but I don't know how to explain to him that I'm holding on to this because it's all I have. There are things I can't put words to, and if I even try, I'll screw it up, and I can't afford to mess this up. This is too important. Sam is too important.

His eyes flicker over my face. "I really want to kiss you right now," he blurts out. "If that's okay."

He leans toward me, slowly, inch by inch, leaving me plenty of time to move away from him. I don't. Instead I close my eyes and hold my breath as I wait for his mouth to meet mine, the anticipation tingling all the way from my stomach to my throat. I can feel him coming closer, his breath warm against my cheek in contrast to the freezing air, making me shiver.

Just as his lips hover over my own, we're interrupted by the telltale *bloop* of my cell phone; I push back from Sam and wiggle it out of my pocket. A new text message, from Dad, asking me to come home. He says it's important. I pass the phone to Sam and reluctantly hop off the picnic table. I may be willing to risk possible hypothermia for a make-out session, but after all I've put my parents through, I'm trying to be a better daughter and actually do as they say. In a timely manner, no less.

Besides, if we pick up again now, I'll just be thinking about my dad the whole time, and that's too gross for words.

Sam groans his disappointment, but he's grinning at the same time, so I know he's not actually upset. He leaps off the table and tosses me my phone.

"Fate is a cruel mistress," he laments.

He walks up to me, tipping his head down like he might kiss me again; my breath catches in my throat, aching for it so bad it makes me a little light-headed. I have to stop myself from saying his name or just wrapping my arms all the way around him, no matter how much I want to in this moment.

At the last second he draws back with a smirk and says, "Come on, I'll walk you back."

He starts off across the park without me, and I stand there for a moment on my own, swallowing down that dizziness and trying to regain the feeling in my numb feet.

What a tease.

There's a black sedan I don't recognize parked in my usual spot in the driveway when I get home. The sight of it sets off alarm bells in my head, and the ominous feeling only grows stronger as I slide up to the curb instead and make the perilous trek across our icy driveway. I shoulder through the front door and drop my bag by the foot of the staircase, kicking the door shut behind me and listening for voices. There's bits and pieces of muted conversation drifting in from the living room—I can't make out full sentences, but I catch words and phrases, like *charges* and *police statement* and *testimony*.

I ignore the sinking feeling in the pit of my stomach and poke my head into the living room. There's a man in a navy suit sitting next to Mom on the couch, a manila folder spread open on the coffee table, on top of a brown leather briefcase. They're engrossed in conversation, Dad standing off to the side with a coffee mug in his hands that he keeps stirring without drinking.

Dad's the first one to notice my entrance. He stops moving his spoon and says, "Chelsea," and I try to glean as much as I can from the tone of his voice, but it doesn't give much away. It's serious, but not death-of-a-valued-family-member serious.

When he says my name, Mom and the suited guy both stop speaking and swivel their heads to look at me. The man stands first, stepping toward me with a smile I think is meant to be reassuring and his hand outstretched. I look at him for a long moment before warily reaching out to shake his hand.

"You must be Chelsea," he says warmly. When he smiles,

his whole faces crinkles, and I notice that his hair is streaked with silvery-gray. It gives him a dignified air. "It's nice to finally meet you. I'm Terry Goldman."

"Mr. Goldman is our lawyer," Mom explains, rising to her feet and twisting her hands. "We thought it'd be a good idea for him to meet with you."

Mr. Goldman relinquishes my hand and turns to her. "Why don't I speak to Chelsea privately?"

Mom hesitates. "Is that necessary?" she asks.

"I think it's a good idea," Dad says from his place by the wall. He walks over to Mom and touches a hand to her back. "Come on. We'll wait in the kitchen."

Mr. Goldman waits until they've cleared the room to sit back down on the couch. He gestures to the spot next to him, and I slowly shrug out of my jacket and sit down. I don't know what exactly this is all about, but I don't have a good feeling about any of it.

"Here," he says, handing me a yellow legal pad and a pen. Off of my confused look, he adds, "If you have any questions for me, you can write them down. Your parents told me about your...social experiment. They say you've gone over a month without speaking. That's a pretty impressive feat." He chuckles. "I have two daughters. They're older than you, but I remember them at your age. Could talk your ear off. Still can, really, but back then, there were times I would've paid for just *one day* of blessed quiet."

There's something disarming about his tone, an easy warmth that puts me a little at ease despite myself. I glance over at the open manila folder and the papers inside it. I can't read them from here, but they look like some sort of legal documents.

Mr. Goldman's gaze follows mine, and he seems to get what

I'm thinking. "That's a copy of your police statement," he tells me. "The one you gave when you reported what happened the night of Noah Beckett's assault. Would you like to see it?"

He picks up the paper and extends it toward me, but I shake my head. I don't need to read it; I remember what I said. I don't want to relive that.

"All right," Mr. Goldman says agreeably, setting the paper back down on the stack. "Do you remember what you said in your statement?"

I nod, not sure where he's going with this. I uncap the pen and scribble on the legal pad.

Are they pressing charges against me?

"No," he says. "They felt after their investigation that your story lined up. I just wanted to go over it with you, because there is a chance you'll be needed to testify."

A chance?

"Warren Snyder and Joey Morgan both pled not guilty at the hearing, but that's typical for most initial pleas, even in the case of a confession," Mr. Goldman explains. He says this all very matter-of-factly, and I appreciate how he's speaking to me like I'm an adult instead of a little kid. "The evidence is pretty damning, and this isn't a case that will look good in front of a jury, so I wouldn't be surprised if their lawyers hammer out a plea deal behind closed doors and come to a settlement before this ever goes to trial. In that case, your testimony would not be necessary. However, you should be prepared in case it is required."

I lean back against the couch cushion and silently pray for the option that renders my involvement unnecessary. And the one that punishes Warren and Joey as they deserve. Maybe it's selfish but I want the best of both worlds.

"Your parents are good people," Mr. Goldman goes on. "They're doing their best to shield you from this, and as a father myself, I can appreciate that. But I believe it's important for you to understand what's going on. I think you're old enough."

I hate knowing I've burdened my parents with this mess, that I've disappointed them. It's hard to remember sometimes that I did the right thing. Sometimes it feels like it wasn't the right thing at all, but then I remember Andy and Asha and Sam and the way they look whenever Noah's name is mentioned, and the disturbing, hard glint in Warren's eyes right before he walked out the door that night, and it reminds me that my mistake was not in speaking out.

No, my mistake was staying silent for too long.

Mr. Goldman doesn't stay long after that. He asks me some questions about my police statement, to make sure that everything I said was truthful. It was. Lying to my teachers, my friends, my parents is one thing, but lying to the cops never even occurred to me; I was too freaked out by everything to even consider that an option. I knew as soon as I took that first step—telling my parents what happened—that there was no turning back.

When Mr. Goldman goes to use the bathroom, I steal through the papers in the manila folder, curious as to what else there is. My most interesting find is a copy of Kristen's statement. I'm expecting nothing but blatant lies, but to my utter shock, everything in her account is truthful to what I recall. There's no attempt on her end at protecting Warren or Joey. She was even honest about coercing me to keep my mouth shut, though she claims Warren only implied what he'd done over the phone, and that when she put the pieces together, he threatened her if she said a word.

This revelation makes me sit up a little straighter. I don't know if it's true—maybe Kristen only wanted to cover her own ass—but I can actually believe it. Warren's clearly not the most stable human being around. Kristen makes it sound like she was scared of what he might do to her if she told, something she never let on to me—and if that's really what happened, it makes me wonder how messed up Kristen is that she would still feel any twisted loyalty to him after that. Maybe their relationship was never what I thought it was.

Mr. Goldman returns while I'm still skimming the last page of Kristen's report, but he doesn't seem to mind that I've dug through his papers. Still, I set it back down and pick up the legal pad again.

Are they pressing charges against Kristen Courteau?

I feel like even I, current social pariah, would've heard this news if it were true, but I want to make sure.

"No, they're not," he says, and I'm struck with a sharp sense of relief, one I don't fully understand considering the current state of Kristen's and my friendship and everything she's done to me over the past month. Mr. Goldman starts to pack up his briefcase, popping open the brass snaps and shuffling papers back into the manila folder. "Ms. Courteau is in the same boat as you."

Huh. Funny how after everything, all the bad feelings and severed ties, Kristen and I are still connected.

Mr. Goldman shakes Mom's hand and Dad's hand and then mine before he leaves, and that makes me feel adult, too. Even though it sucks that it's under these circumstances, I still kind of like the feeling, like I'm worthy of being interacted with as a grown-up. Mom turns the lock before leaning hard with her back against the door, eyes closed; she looks so tired and stressed out and when she looks at me again, it makes my stomach hurt.

But she smiles—still tired and somewhat exasperated, but a real one. "You've given me so many gray hairs, Chelsea," she says, and Dad laughs and walks over to her, rubbing her shoulder with one hand.

"Gray looks good on you," he assures her. He presses a kiss to the top of her hair.

They could be mad. They could be yelling at me for what I've put them through—God knows I deserve it—but they're not, and Mr. Goldman is right, they're good people and they're trying the best they can, and I'm suddenly so overwhelmed with gratitude for having them behind me through all this that I catapult myself into them both, flinging my arms around them in a tight hug.

"Whoa." Dad laughs, his arm reaching around my back. "What's this about?"

I feel Mom's hand on the back of my head, gently stroking my hair. The unruly red hair I inherited from her. "I know, honey," she murmurs. "I know. We love you, too."

day thirty-two

When I was five years old, my parents took me to Disney World. I rode the teacups a million times, got Mickey Mouse's autograph, saw the fireworks show at the palace, and it was the best week of my life. I came home sunburned and tired and happier than I'd ever been, and bounced into my room with armfuls of new stuffed animals I'd refused to pack in the suitcase, wanting to check on my hamster, Freddy, and show him my souvenirs.

Except when I peeked into his cage, Freddy was balled up in a corner. Not moving. Dead.

I still remember how fast my five-year-old self went from feeling at the top of the world to crushed in two seconds flat. I guess that's the thing about riding on cloud nine—it can't last forever. And that particular fall was hard and fast.

Much like the one I'm experiencing now, in the art room.

I'm the first to discover it. Our art piece, ripped to shreds. Sad scraps of Lucy and Charlie Brown and Snoopy scattered carelessly over the floor. I'd come in especially early, just to take a final, admiring look, only to find this. All of that work, gone. Torn apart like it was nothing. Like it was there just to be destroyed.

No one else is in the room yet; I can hear the echo of clanging lockers and voices talking over each other in the halls. I don't know how much time passes before Ms. Kinsey walks in and finds me there. When she lays eyes on the paper massacre, she audibly gasps. "Oh, Chelsea—"

She goes to put a hand on my shoulder, but I move away. My throat aches with the effort it's taking not to cry. This shouldn't matter so much. It's just a stupid project. Just a stupid grade.

No. It's more than that.

"I was only gone for a minute," she says, distraught. "I was making a phone call… I didn't see anyone… Maybe—maybe it was an accident?"

I know she doesn't believe that. It's just what she has to say.

I can't stay. I can't stay and see Sam's face when he realizes what happened. I have to get out of here.

Ms. Kinsey says my name again as I rush out of the room, but I don't stop.

This was no accident. I know exactly who did this.

Tracking down Lowell isn't difficult. He's loitering by the vending machine near the science wing, blocking another shorter but heavier boy from putting quarters into the machine. As I approach, I recognize the boy as the one who spoke to Brendon that day in the hall. One of the GSA kids. Gary? Garrett? Something like that. He looks unhappy, and it doesn't take long to figure out why.

"I'm doing this for your own good," Lowell says in a faux-sweet voice. "You need to go on a diet. None of the other boys will want a fatty sucking their dick."

I've seen this behavior from Lowell before, the same way I'd seen it from Warren and Joey and even Kristen, tossing out homophobic slurs like they were nothing. And when it happened I did nothing. It barely even registered; it was like white noise. Sometimes I even laughed along for show. At least it wasn't being said about me—and I know how embarrassed I would've been if it had, because that was how awful everyone I hung out with agreed being gay was. And I thought it was okay as long as I didn't actively participate, that it was enough for me to secretly believe in my heart of hearts that there was absolutely nothing wrong with being gay even if I never dared say it out loud.

I thought it was enough, and it is so far from enough. I can't change what I've done and what I haven't done, but I can change what I do now. I can actually do something. Stand for something.

The boy at the vending machine is shifting from foot to foot, his face beet-red, but he doesn't say anything. He turns to leave just as I come storming up.

I totally can do this. I can.

I *am* doing this.

"Who the *hell* do you think you are?"

The words rush out of me like a wind that can't be contained, up, up, up, until they're out, in the open, and I can't take them back. My heart is beating like it wants to escape my body.

Lowell looks over at me, and for a moment he's speechless. A very, very sweet moment, but unfortunately just that.

And then his lips curl into a smirk. "Is this about your stupid art thing? Because you can't prove shit."

"No," I say, because even though I'm angry about that, what I'm seeing in front of me is making me *furious*. "No, this is about what you're doing right now."

"This isn't your business, freak," he snaps.

I step closer to him, and my fury must be radiating from

every fiber of my being or something because he actually shrinks back a little. Not a lot, but enough.

"Seriously, what is your damage? Did your mom not hug you enough growing up? Is that it?" I shoot back. "In what universe do you think it's at all okay to treat people the way you do? I'd really like to know." I pause, but when Lowell opens his mouth again, I cut him off. "Actually, no. I don't care how you justify this to yourself. No matter what, you're pathetic. And vile."

"What are you, Queen of the Fags? Their savior?" he snarls. He barks out a laugh. "Oh, I get it. You're one of them, aren't you?"

"I'm not gay, but the fact that you think anyone should be ashamed to be makes you a total fucking asshole," I say. "Congratulations on being a miserable excuse for a human being, you ignorant scumbag."

"Fuck you," he says back. "You're nothing but a—"

"No." I hold up a finger warningly. "Do not even. I am done. I am *so* done. I swear to *God,* I am taking you down."

"Oh, yeah?"

"You better believe it."

Lowell rolls his eyes. "Please. You can't touch me."

"Wanna bet?" I snort. "Go ask Warren and Joey how that philosophy worked out for them."

At this, Lowell's face blanches, his scowl falling into a worried line. His eyes narrow like he's wondering whether to take my threat seriously or not.

Behind me, the boy clears his throat nervously. "Can I go?" he asks.

"Get your snack first," I say.

I keep my eyes locked on Lowell, unwavering, and after

a moment he moves aside from the vending machine. And I know in that moment I've won.

The boy hesitates for a moment before hurriedly popping his quarters into the machine and grabbing his snack from the bottom. He scurries off without another word.

I shoot Lowell one last venomous look and turn to go. I walk down the hall, and I keep going, keep going until I'm all the way in my car. One of the narcs tries to flag me down as I floor it out of the student lot, but I ignore him and turn so fast onto the road my tires squeal against pavement.

I'm not good at standing up for myself. Shocking information, I know. I've *never* been good at it. I never had to be— the rare times someone decided to give me a hard time, I had Kristen, at my back, sticking up for me. I always appreciated that about her. Her fierce loyalty. I knew doing what I did, ratting out Warren and Joey, would put me on the other side of it. I knew *exactly* what it would cost.

I still did it anyway. And I'm glad. I really am. Because I was never happy before, and I never even realized it. I know now. You can be surrounded by people and still be lonely. You can be the most popular person in school, envied by every girl and wanted by every boy, and still feel completely worthless. The world can be laid at your feet and you can still not know what you want from it.

And I'm glad because it means I'm different from Kristen, different from Warren and Joey and Lowell and Derek and all of the rest. It means that even then, I knew right from wrong, knew what was really, truly important, knew what I could lose and still, I was willing to give it all up if it meant Noah had some justice. Even if Noah wasn't a friend. Even if Warren and Joey were.

It means I'm not heartless. I'm a decent person. I am.

The second Lou sees my face she fixes me a cup of hot cocoa and tells me to sit down. She doesn't ask any questions, just leaves me alone at the counter to drink and calm down a little while she and Phyllis clear tables. It's weird to be here early like this, without Asha or Sam in tow. I go through five cups of cocoa before Andy shows up. He's always the first—Westfield High gets out twenty minutes before Grand Lake.

He cocks his head at me as he ties on his apron. "You're early," he says. He glances at the clock. "Looks like I have a few minutes before my shift. Gonna go have a smoke."

I stay seated for a minute, gathering my nerve. Before I can talk myself out of what I'm about to do, I push off the stool and follow him into the back alley. He's leaned up against the wall, midsmoke.

I take a deep breath. And let it go.

"I need your help."

"You're sure that's enough brown sugar?"

Andy gives me a strange look.

I cross my arms and stare back, impatient. "Don't look at me like that."

"Sorry," he says, turning his gaze down into the bowl he's stirring. "I'm just not used to…you. Talking. Out loud. It's sort of blowing my mind at the moment."

Honestly, it's blowing mine a little, too. My voice sounds weird to my own ears. It's been—what? Four weeks? Four weeks and not a single word. Not *one*. Pretty impressive.

When I spoke, Andy actually dropped his cigarette out of sheer surprise. Once the initial shock wore off, he just told me to follow him into the kitchen, where he handed me off ingredients and told me how much to measure. He said I could talk to him while we made a batch of Dex's famous brownies, because his best conversations are held while he's baking. Apparently it helps him focus or something. It doesn't exactly make sense to me, but I'm going with it.

"So," Andy says, "does this mean you're done with the vow for good?"

"I don't know what it means. I haven't thought that far ahead." I pick an egg up out of the carton and examine it for cracks, then set it back in its spot. "You're only the second—okay, technically third—let's call it second-and-a-half—person I've...you know. Spoken actual words to."

He pretends to pout. "I'm disappointed I'm not your first."

If I didn't know firsthand exactly and completely how gay he is, I might be offended at the innuendo. As it stands, I just roll my eyes.

"I didn't exactly plan it, okay?" I say. "I...kind of went off on this homophobic jerk."

"Really?" Andy perks up at this. "I want to hear this."

"It's sort of a blur, to be honest, but I'm pretty sure the words *pathetic, vile* and *total fucking asshole* were all used during my tirade."

"Delicious!" He cackles. "What I would have given to witness that showdown. But may I ask, what exactly set this off?"

"I caught him picking on this gay kid," I explain. "Or, I think the kid is gay. Maybe. I probably shouldn't assume. Anyway, I just—I couldn't just watch it happen and not say anything."

"Ah, yes. Where would we poor gays be without straight white girls sticking up for us?" Andy drawls, rummaging through a cupboard until he finds the vanilla extract. He closes it and faces me again, noticing my frown. "I'm kidding. Mostly. I get it. It was a noble gesture on your part. Brava. But none of this explains why you need to talk to me."

I hold up the cup of brown sugar, examining it. "Seriously, are you *sure* you need this much?"

Andy snatches the cup from my hand and puts it on the counter. "First of all," he says, "while I freely admit my culinary skills may pale in comparison to Sam's, I learned this brownie recipe from the master—and by master I mean Dex—and I will not be insulted in my kitchen."

"You know, it's not really *your* kitchen, technically speaking—"

"*Secondly,* if you don't spit out whatever you need to say to me, I'm going to kick you out of *my* kitchen because I'm quickly becoming bored with this conversation. Or lack thereof. And bored of you in general. The speaking novelty is wearing off fast into annoying territory."

"The guy I yelled at—his name is Lowell—we kind of used to be friends, before...well, everything, and he's on the basketball team, so he was pissed about me narcing on Warren and Joey. He's been messing with me for the past month. And he destroyed the art project Sam and I were working on. I can't prove it, but I know he did," I say. "And I really, really want to get back at him. I just don't know how."

"And you think I can help with this...why, exactly?"

"I don't know. You seem more diabolical than anyone else here."

Andy puts his hand over his heart and smiles at me like I've just granted him a wonderful compliment. "That's sweet of you," he says. He hums low in his throat, thoughtful, as he dumps the sugar into the bowl along with two teaspoons of vanilla extract, beginning to mix it together with everything else already in there. "We could make pot brownies, you somehow smuggle them into his locker along with a few ounces, he eats the brownies and gets high as a kite, teachers notice him staring at his hand for an hour during class and conduct a locker search on suspicion of drug possession, and boom. Instant payback."

"Um," I say, "that's a great plan and all, but I was thinking something a little more...I don't know, morally sound? And less illegal? Besides, he's such a pothead anyway that I hardly need to go out of my way to plant anything on him."

"Well, that's no fun," he sighs. He keeps mixing, his face scrunched in thought. "Wait, he's a stoner and he's on the basketball team? Noah had to do mandatory drug tests during soccer season last year. Don't they do the same for basketball?"

"They do, but the team somehow always find out about it beforehand," I explain. "With just enough time to bribe or threaten some freshman into pissing into a cup they can smuggle in." No one outside the select few are *supposed* to know of this practice, but Warren, meathead that he is, is the kind of drunk who will blurt out anything if he's liquored up enough.

"Maybe you can work that angle," Andy says. "Just rat him out or something."

"Maybe," I say uncertainly. "But I need to be careful. What I need is for Lowell to fall on his own sword without getting my hands dirty."

"I stand by the pot brownies plan," he says. "Feel free to take artistic license with that idea, by the way. Maybe you can work it into something that fits your newfound ethical code."

Artistic license. I'm struck with a sudden thought. No, not just a thought. A plan. Oh, my God. "Oh, my God."

"Oh, my God, what?"

"You gave me the perfect idea."

Andy beams. "You're going with the pot brownies?"

"Not that," I say, "but something else. Something so much better. This is legit."

I divulge my plan to Andy, and at the end of it, he offers his hand in a high five, which I gladly indulge. After he's battered up the brownie mix, poured it into a glass pan and set it in the oven, he turns to me and says, "I can't lie. I'm sort of flattered."

"Flattered?"

"That I was your second-and-a-half." He smiles, just a little. "That you came to me for this."

"Oh, really?" I say, skeptical. "Because if *I* remember correctly, not too long ago you called me—and I quote—'pathetic.'"

"I was talking about the vow. Not you," he says evenly.

I shrug, not sure if I believe that, but still wanting to. "Anyway. It made sense. I knew you'd get it. I'm not sure Sam would…you know. Approve. He's not the vengeance type."

"I don't think Sam is as sanctimonious as you think."

"What is that supposed to mean?"

"I'm not slamming him. What I mean is, he's a fucking human being, you know?" he says. "He's just as pissed about what happened. And Noah… Noah is his best friend. Yeah, so maybe he could've handled some things better." He falls silent for a long moment. "We all could've handled things better."

Isn't that the truth.

I take off from Rosie's before Sam or Asha can get there, Eminem blasting at full volume. I sing to all of the lyrics as I drive toward home. I could've waited for them before I left. I could've just stayed at Rosie's and picked up a shift for tonight. But I didn't want to. I don't want to think about what I'm going to say to Asha, or to Sam, God, *Sam,* because things

are different now. I'm talking again. But not just *again*—
because I've *never* talked with Asha, or Sam, or Dex or Lou.
Not for *real*.

I go home and straight to my bedroom, where I lie on my
bed, clutching a pillow to my chest. I stare at my ceiling and
practice what to say to Sam when I see him.

"Hello, Sam," I say to the plastic star in my direct line of
vision. "This is what my voice sounds like, Sam. Sam, I hope
you don't think I'm a total freak, even though I can't stop
thinking about your stupid sexy face, Sam." I say his name,
over and over, testing it out. "Sam. Sam. Sam."

"Is this like a meditation thing? Should I come back later?"

Asha's in the doorway. I bolt upright, flushing bright red.

"You could've knocked," I point out. My heart is beating
fast in, like, my ears.

"Sorry," she says without sounding apologetic at all. "Your
dad let me in." She bounces onto my bed and sprawls next
to me. "Wow, your ceiling is awesome. Is that supposed to
be the Big Dipper?"

I sit up on my elbow to look at her. "That's all you have
to say? *Really?*"

She shrugs. "I don't know," she says. "What did you expect?"

I was expecting—I don't know. A little fanfare, maybe.
More than total nonchalance. I mean, I am speaking! Words!
Out loud! This is a huge deal!

Isn't it?

"Disappointed the world doesn't revolve around you?" Asha
teases.

"That is so not it," I say, and swallow, because suddenly
I'm worried she truly thinks that. Because our friendship so
far has been kind of one-sided. Asha doesn't really talk to me
about anything other than the diner and geometry and knit-

ting, and I've never pushed for more—partly because I don't know if I'm allowed, if she'd be okay with that, and partly because I haven't put in the effort.

Let's be honest. Kristen had a lot of sucky qualities as a friend, but it's not like I don't have my fair share of failings.

"So now that you're speaking," she says, "what do you want to talk about? Let me guess, *Saaaam?*" She makes fake kissy noises until I thwack her in the face with my pillow.

I don't want to talk about Sam. I don't want to talk about boys, or clothes, or shopping, or any of that. That was the problem with Kristen. Whatever we used to have in common, whatever was between us before, it all faded into...crap. Into nothing but gossip and makeup tips and parties and crushes and superficial *crap*. Talking about all that stuff is okay in moderation—but friendships should mean something more.

It's hard to figure out how to explain to Asha that I don't know what my life would be like now if she'd never talked to me that day in detention. How much worse these past weeks would have been. I want to show her how much she means to me—but everything that pops into my head makes me sound like the sappiest sap to ever sap.

Words matter—of course they matter, I know that better than anyone—but just telling her that wouldn't be enough. If I really want her to be my friend, if I really want to get better at this kind of thing, I have to *be* better. Walk the talk, or whatever.

Finally I turn to her and ask, "How's your mom doing?"

She blinks her dark eyes a few times, a little surprised, a little pained. "She's...okay," she says slowly. "Some days are better than others. You know how it is."

"I don't, actually," I say. "You want to talk about it?"

So she does. And I listen the whole way through.

★ ★ ★

The *National Geographic* article is taped to my wall, right above my headboard. I put it there a while ago, after I almost left it in my pants pocket and had to salvage it from going through the laundry for the third time. As Asha's leaving, she runs her hands over the shiny, creased page.

"So that's where you got the idea," she says. She looks over her shoulder and smiles. "I'm so glad you're not *actually* in a cult."

I smile back. What else is there to do? I figure if that's the worst thing people can come up with to say about me, I'm gonna be okay.

After Asha's gone, I finish up some homework—it's sort of fun to imagine Mrs. Finch falling out of her chair with shock as she reads this awesome essay I'm working on, complete with sources cited and embedded quotations and even footnotes—and dick around on the internet. I know, I know, gossip is bad, gossip has consequences, all of that, but it can't hurt to live vicariously reading the celebrity tabloid blogs.

I'm absorbed in a story about some D-lister's botched boob job when I hear this weird tapping on my window. At first I think it's a bird, and then I think I have a stalker, but I peer out the window and see Sam standing below, pebbles in hand.

I lift it open enough to stick my head through and hiss, "What are you *doing?*"

He stares up at me, mouth hanging open. "So it's true," he says. "You're..."

Talking. Yes. And the first thing I've said to Sam has been relayed in an annoyed whisper-yell. Not exactly how I envisioned this going.

"Hang on. I'll be right down," I say, and budge the window closed.

God, it's cold outside. I slip out the front door as quietly as I can so Dad won't hear over the television and run barefoot over the freezing sidewalk, all the way to the side of the house.

"Sam, why are you out here?" I demand. I hop from foot to foot over the snow patches.

"It is true," he says, softer.

I stop in my tracks. The ice bites into the bottom of my quickly numbing feet. "Yeah," I say, and open my mouth to say more, but I'm not sure what. So I just stand there, shivering, looking at him.

"Who else knows?" he asks. I don't know why he's being so quiet. It's not like anyone else is around.

"Um, well, let's see. Lowell was the first—"

"Lowell?"

"Yeah, I know. That's a story I don't want to get into right now," I say. "There's also Asha. Andy. Lou, I'm pretty sure." I press my lips together. "And…you. Think that's the running tally."

"Oh," he says. I don't know what that "oh" is supposed to mean. Like, is he disappointed I didn't speak to him first? Or that other people knew before he did?

I look from him to my window and back. "How did you even know that's my room?"

"I saw you through the window." As if he's reading my thoughts, he cringes and says, "That wasn't supposed to make me sound like such a stalker, I swear."

"What are you doing here, Sam?" I ask. Again. Around chattering teeth, this time.

"The art project…" he starts, and then ruffles a hand through his hair, the way he always does. "I wanted to make sure you were okay."

"And you couldn't use the front door?"

"I don't know…it's kind of late! I didn't want to piss off your parents. Besides, it was pretty cool, right? Very John Cusack, minus the radio playing Peter Gabriel."

I have no idea what he's talking about. "John Cusack? Wait, isn't that the guy from *Serendipity?*"

"Serendipity?" His voice rises with his incredulity. *"That's* what you associate John Cusack with? Come on! You couldn't go for, say, *Grosse Pointe Blank,* or *Say Anything,* or *High Fidelity,* or *Being John* fucking *Malkovich,* or—"

"Sam." I stop him in midrighteous (and totally over my head) tirade. "It is, like, negative five billion degrees out here. I have no jacket. Or shoes. Or socks. Come inside."

I snatch his hand in mine and sneak him in through the side door by the kitchen. At first I start leading him up to my room, but then I stop and sit down on the staircase instead.

"My dad's cool, but he might not be so cool with me having a boy in my room," I explain. "You know. Alone. At night."

"Understandable." He smiles a little and sits on the step below me. "You're really okay?"

I start to nod before I remember I can actually answer now. "I am. I think. I mean—" Man. Talking is hard. I'd forgotten exactly how hard. There's a reason I stopped in the first place. "It's…it's been a long day."

"You talking again," he says, "that's a good thing, right?"

I glance down at my lap. "I don't know. Is it?"

Sam takes one of my hands, and I watch as he plays with my fingers.

He says, haltingly, "I think so. If it felt…I dunno. Like it was the right time. For you." He looks up at me. "How does it feel?"

"Weird," I admit. "But good, too." I curl my fingers around

his. They're all tingly. Probably from unthawing. But maybe not just that.

"I'm sorry about the project," he says.

I shake my head. "Forget it. I don't even care." Sam's face falls a little, and I quickly add, "I mean, I *care*, but—it's not as important as other things."

What's important is the time we spent working on it together. What's important is that Sam is the kind of guy who will trade notes on a sketchpad and teach me how to make tuna melts and drop everything to drive to a parking lot when I need him and throw stones at my window to make sure I'm okay.

And that's separate from the kissing. Okay. Not totally separate. But Sam is my *friend*, the kind of friend I've never had before. Maybe the best friend I've ever had. Is there a way to have that, and the other stuff? The kissing? Can they really coexist? Or is it like asymptotes—two things that can get so close but are never meant to intersect?

I have spent way too much time around Asha if I'm finding love songs in geometry.

"Tomorrow's the dance, you know," Sam says, like it could have possibly slipped my mind.

"I know." I look down at our intertwined fingers. "Were you serious? About being my date?"

"That depends on your answer. See, if you say you don't want to, I can pretend I was just kidding the whole time, you know, ha ha, *oh, that Sam, he's such a jokester,* and thus save a little of my wounded pride, but if you—"

"Yes."

"What?"

"Yes, I'll go with you. Obviously."

Or maybe not so obviously, because the smile he gives me

then is so adorably earnest and pleased that it makes me tingle from the tips of my fingers all the way down to my toes.

"Really?"

"Really."

"Awesome."

"Awesome squared."

"Awesome cubed."

"Awesome to the power of infinity."

"The square root of awesome is—"

"—Asha," we finish at the same time, and laugh.

I quickly push a palm over his mouth to keep him quiet. Really don't need Dad to overhear this little visit now.

He takes my hand off his mouth and holds it, his face suddenly serious. "I just need to know one thing. Very important."

My stomach drops. What now?

"What color is your dress?"

day thirty-three

The thing I mentioned earlier, about cheerleaders not being synonymous with popular? This is true, like, ninety percent of the time. But then there are times they *are* actually the most popular girls in school, at least for a day, because those days are Game Days.

On Game Days, the cheerleaders get to wear their uniforms to school. And boy, are they teeny tiny. The uniforms. Not the cheerleaders. Well, some of them are, but some of them are on the heavy side. Not judging, just pointing out the fact. I mean, when you think about it, it makes logical sense. *Someone* has to be strong enough to throw the tiny ones in the air.

I make my way through the sea of cheerleaders gathered around the watering hole—the lockers of five team members, including Lowell and Derek—carrying all kinds of desserts. It's Game Day tradition for the players to leave their lockers open in the mornings so they can be showered with the gifts they so richly deserve. Namely, goodies. Every cheerleader has something delicious and homemade to present the team members with, cookies and cupcakes and whatnot. One girl even has a custom balloon in the school colors—blue and

red—that says GO RED HAWKS! that she's tying to someone's combination lock.

If I play my cards right today, there'll be no more balloons
or cookies or fawning cheerleaders for Lowell or Derek.

The question, of course, becomes how to bust these two.
There are a few avenues I could take; I could go directly to
the principal. I could call the cops myself. I could break into
their lockers with a nail file and take photo evidence of the
weed they're most likely holding in there and spread it around,
but that tactic is too old-school, and not in a good way. I want
to do this in a way that leaves my hands as clean as possible.
Lowell and Derek will get the message without me linking
myself to it directly. So I've come up with an idea.

Ms. Kinsey.

The one teacher in this school who, inexplicably, likes having me as her student. The one teacher I trust. The one most
likely to agree to my plan.

The art room is empty when I walk in, except for Ms. Kinsey. She's standing on a stool, hanging some art piece made
out of wire and ribbon from a ceiling hook.

"Chelsea!" She sees me and smiles, one part pleased, one
part concerned. "We missed you yesterday."

"Sorry I bailed," I say, and she freezes.

"And she speaks!" *Great deduction there,* I think, and then tell
my brain to stop being rude. Ms. Kinsey doesn't deserve that.

She steps down from the stool and puts her hands on her
hips. "When did this happen?"

"Yesterday." I pause. "Um. It's kind of a long story." I remember what I came for, and hunt through my bag for the
whiteboard. "I wanted to give this back to you."

"Chelsea." She doesn't move to take the board from me,

so I'm left holding it out there between us. "I'm very sorry for what happened yesterday."

"Why? It's not like it's your fault."

"No, it isn't, but that doesn't change the fact."

I get that. It's like how I told Andy I was sorry for what happened to Noah, even though I knew by then I wasn't really the one to blame. Sometimes you just have to apologize anyway.

"I want you to know, I've graded you on the project," Ms. Kinsey says. "I thought I'd seen enough beforehand to give a fair evaluation."

This surprises me. "Oh?"

"Yes. And I think you and Sam will be very happy with it."

"Oh. Thank you."

She eyes me curiously. "So tell me, did you learn anything from this period of silence? Spiritually?"

I don't know if I learned anything spiritually. I'm still not exactly sure what that means. I mean, I didn't spend any of the time thinking about God or faith or whatever. I spent it thinking about how much I hate myself, mostly. Maybe that makes me a major narcissist, I don't know. A self-loathing narcissist, is that even possible?

I do feel like I've figured some stuff out. Not everything. Not even close. But the not-figured-out stuff feels less scary now. Manageable. It's like someone opened my eyes and suddenly I'm seeing everything all new—like when Asha explained to me how to solve for $x,$ and something just clicked, and from that point on I wasn't just looking at a mess of numbers and letters but actual equations with actual solutions. Even if I still couldn't solve every single one.

"Maybe," I say, and apparently that's enough for her, because she nods and takes the whiteboard from me.

"Glad to hear it." The smile she gives kills me with its kindness. "It's good to be uncertain, Chelsea. It's a big world. There's always more to learn."

"Ms. Kinsey, I didn't just come here to give you back the whiteboard," I say. "I need your help with something. It's kind of a...sensitive issue."

"Oh?" She looks more concerned now. "Well, I'll do whatever I can. What is it?"

"I need to leave an anonymous tip."

When Sam comes up to my locker before art period and says, "Let's cut," I'm annoyed.

Not at him. I was already annoyed before he came up to me. I'm annoyed because there was a typo on page two of the essay I handed in to Mrs. Finch, but I didn't have time to dash to the library and reprint it. I'm annoyed because there are some kids down the hall erupting into the school song with plastic mini megaphones in preparation for this afternoon's pep rally. I'm annoyed because I have no idea if the plan has worked yet, or if it will work *at all,* or if it'll somehow backfire and the not knowing is making me all itchy and anxious.

"The narcs," I point out, but Sam grins and shakes his head.

"I'm parked in the teacher lot," he explains.

"You're not supposed to do that."

"I'm not supposed to do a lot of things."

It's such a cliché response, but he makes it work. Maybe it's because right after he says it, he slips one of his thumbs through my belt loop and pulls me close to him. Close enough that I can see his clear blue eyes perfectly. And his not-so-perfect mouth, a little crooked, a smile that goes up farther on the left than the right, but is somehow even more alluring for that. Perfection is overrated.

I hesitate. I already cut once this week....

"Hail to the Hawks!" the kids chorus. "Hail, hail, hail to the red and blue! Hail to the conquering heroes, proud and true!"

Screw it.

"Let's go."

Sam lets me drive the Cutlass. Not that I really ask. I snatch the keys from him the second we hit the teacher lot and jingle them in my hand as we walk. I'm nervous and I don't know why.

That's a lie, I totally know why I'm nervous. Stupid Lowell and Derek and their stupid faces. Their faces are genuinely stupid, not like Sam's—Sam's is just stupid cute. Especially when he's looking at me like he is now.

I buckle myself into the driver's seat, adjust the mirrors and say, "What?"

"You know how to drive a stick?" he asks.

"Please. My dad taught me on an old-ass Camry."

I throw the car into first, ease up on the clutch and tap on the gas. The Cutlass bucks a little and jumps forward, and we're off.

I don't know where we're going. Rosie's would be the obvious choice, but I kind of just want to drive around for a while, getting used to the feel of the car. It's hard to relax, though, with Sam sitting next to me, playing his fingers over the seat belt, stretching it in and out. I keep thinking about his hands. It's so distracting that I accidentally let the clutch out too much and stall the car at a stoplight.

I'm waiting for Sam to yell at me for screwing up his transmission, but he just waits for me to restart the car and says, "You've got it."

He is so nice it *hurts*.

We drive around in silence. Funny how now that we're both talking, we have nothing to say to each other. Or maybe it's just habit. As far as silences go, it is pretty comfortable— it's the kind of quiet shared between two people who don't feel the desperate need to fill every second with the sound of their own voices.

Eventually I pull down into the park by the lake, take the gear down to First and cut the engine.

"Good," he says when I set the parking brake. "We don't need to pull a *Risky Business*."

I blink at him. "Huh?"

"You know, the movie? With Tom Cruise? When the Porsche rolls into Lake Michigan?" he says, like I should know this. At my uncomprehending stare, he shakes his head. "We really need to make a list of every classic you haven't seen and Netflix them all."

"I can't look at Tom Cruise the same ever since the Oprah incident," I say, and he gives me a blank look. I scoff indignantly. "The couch? And the jumping? And the Scientology craziness? Come on, you have to know about that!"

He doesn't have a clue, of course. I sigh and rest my forehead on the steering wheel.

"We don't have anything in common, do we?" I say in a small voice.

"That's not true."

"It is! I mean, I tried listening to NPR the other night, and my eyes glazed over, like, five seconds in. And you read all these books—" I gesture to the stack between us, the top title staring up at me—*Ham on Rye,* is that a cookbook or something? "—while I just follow stupid shallow internet blogs mocking celebrity fashions, and I've never even *been* on a skateboard, or in-line skates, for that matter—"

"Whoa, Chelsea, slow down." He puts his hand on the back of my head, and I stop midsentence. "What about Rosie's? We have that."

"I wash dishes. Big whoop. I can't cook *anything*—"

"You know how to make tuna melts."

"I made one, once. And only because you showed me."

"Well, then I can teach you more. You can ride my skateboard. I'll listen to your music. I usually stick to political blogs, but I'll read your celebrity gossip ones, if you want. But, Chelsea, all that stuff…it's just *stuff*. It doesn't matter."

"Of course it *matters!*" I sit up and rub my eyes. "Mutual interests! It's what ties people together! You're going to get *bored* of me, because I'm so shallow and stupid, you don't even know."

"I really don't think that's a concern." He's still smiling, and it drives me a little crazy how completely unworried he is. Does he not hear what I'm saying? "So you like reading about celebrities. So you like clothes and stuff. So what?" he says. "And don't give me this crap about how shallow and stupid you are—we both know you wouldn't be hanging out with Asha and all of us if that was true. You'd still be friends with Kristen and that crowd." He pauses, and the smile fades. "Is that what you want? To be friends with them again?"

"That's not an option."

"What if it was?"

"No." I don't even have to think about it. "God, no."

"Why not?"

Because I don't even miss Kristen anymore. Okay, I miss the idea of Kristen, a little, but not the cold, hard reality of what it means to Kristen's best friend. Because what I thought was important to me then doesn't feel so important anymore. Because I don't have anything in common with them, either, and all of that *stuff* didn't really mean anything in the end, anyway, did it?

Maybe Sam's right. Maybe when it comes down to it, what we're interested in doesn't mean so much—it's who you are that ties people together.

"You asked me before, why I wasn't mad at you," he says. "It's because you turned Warren and Joey in. You did that. Now I just want to know...why? What made you do it?"

No one has asked me point-blank before. Not my parents, not Kristen, not Asha. No one.

I take a deep, shaky breath. "When I was seven, I had to get my tonsils taken out," I tell him. "I was in the hospital, totally freaked out, because I'd never had surgery before or anything. And my dad showed up with this stuffed dog. He sat next to me the whole time, holding my hand, and that stupid dog—it made me feel better. And after...what happened, with Noah, I kept remembering that. How scared I was, and how much it meant for my dad to be there, so I wasn't alone." I have to stop for a moment because my throat is constricting with tears. "Noah must've been so scared. He was by himself. He didn't have his dad, or his mom, and I just—I couldn't. I had to. No one should have to go through that. It's not *fair*."

Sam reaches over and brushes away the lone tear that's trailed down my cheek with his thumb. "Yeah," he agrees softly. "It definitely isn't fair."

"I was so stupid," I say. "I never want to go back to that. I am so much happier around you guys."

It's the truth, and not only that, it is also so *totally* the right thing to say, because Sam lights up with a smile, like I not just made his day, but his *life*. I grab his shirt collar and kiss him, hard and long. Then I sit back and put my hand over the dangling key ring, thinking.

I'm at a crossroads. If I drive west, I'd be going toward Recollections and liquor stores and gas stations. If I drive east, I'd be going toward the nice houses, including mine. And it would take only a minute if I decided to drive to Rosie's.

We could go anywhere.

I turn to Sam and say, "I have an idea."

The last time I was in a hospital, it was last year when Grandpa Murphy had his heart attack and no one was sure whether or not he was going to make it. Mom let me miss two days of school to stay with her, and Dad actually called out of work the first day, which was how I knew it was serious. Mostly I hung out in the waiting room, making prank phone calls to 1-800 numbers on the payphone with my cousin Bree while Mom and Dad and Mom's crapload of siblings were too busy talking to three different doctors and each other to notice our shenanigans. Grandpa Murphy was okay in the end, even though it was touch and go for a while.

But that was in a different hospital, not this one. The last time I was in *this* hospital, I was eight and fell off the jungle gym, and Mom was convinced I'd broken my arm from the way I was screaming my head off. Turned out to be only a bad sprain. The nurse wrapped it in an Ace bandage, presented me with a lollipop (which shut the tears off instantly) and sent me home with an ice pack and a recommendation for Children's Tylenol.

I don't have any traumatic memories associated with hospitals, really, and I'd like to keep it that way. As Sam and I step into the elevator in Van Buren Memorial, somehow I'm not so sure that'll be possible.

Sam knows where he's going, of course. I follow him out of the elevator, down the squeaky linoleum hall, and to the nurses' station.

"We're here to see Noah Beckett," he says to the woman at the desk. She smiles and gives him a room number.

I know I suggested coming here, but I'm still numb with fear as we walk down toward some rooms. Am I really ready for this? I'm about seventy percent committed in my head to spinning on my heel and fleeing the hospital when Sam reaches for my hand.

"It's gonna be fine," he says, and squeezes, and it helps, a little.

A short blonde woman stands outside of Noah's room, talking to a doctor in hushed tones. Sam and I hang back until the doctor says a final word and walks away. The woman stares after him, and Sam says, "Mrs. Beckett?"

When she turns at his voice, the woman's distracted look is replaced by a genuine smile. "Sam," she says warmly. "It's so good to see you."

He drops my hand and hugs her, and she pecks him on the cheek.

"How is he?" he asks softly.

"He's improving," she tells him. "They're saying we can take him home next week."

"That's great news." Sam squeezes her shoulder. "And how about you?"

"I'm holding up all right." Her smile is a little wobbly around the edges. She looks over his shoulder at me. "Who is your friend?"

I'm embarrassed to be drawn into this conversation, like I'm intruding on some private moment. I hold my hands behind my back and look to Sam.

"This is Chelsea Knot," he introduces.

"Oh. You're Chelsea?" Noah's mom pauses, and in that pause, a million horrible scenarios race through my mind: she knows who I am, and she's going to yell at me, right there. Or start bawling. Or tell me what a horrible human being I am for what I did to her son.

She steps toward me, and oh, God, I brace myself to be slapped, or spit on, but instead she puts her arms around me and holds me close, and—oh. A hug? She's actually giving me *a hug?*

"Thank you," she says in my ear, and I'm too bewildered to do anything but stand there. "If it weren't for you, who knows if those boys would've gotten away with it." She pulls back and smiles at me, her eyes shining like she might cry. "It was a very brave thing you did."

Not only am I receiving a hug, but *gratitude?* My mind, it is blown.

I'm not sure what to say. "Um, I—I d-don't—" I want to explain why, exactly, she should be angry with me, but Sam shoots me a look, and I understand I'm supposed to just accept this. So I attempt a smile and say, "It was nothing."

My first lie since I started talking again. Sorry, God.

Mrs. Beckett says, "Why don't you go in and see him? I think he's awake now."

Sam and I enter Noah's room. It's crowded with balloons and flowers and gifts, and I'm shocked, a little, to see such an outpouring of support and love. It's such a contrast to the ugliness I've seen at school. But the row of cards tacked to the wall are all from students, so maybe I just was too caught up in my own bubble to realize how much people do care.

"I'm pretty sure I'm single-handedly keeping Hallmark in business."

The voice takes me by surprise. I jump away from the wall and whirl to see Noah, in the bed, propped into a sitting position by pillows. He looks…rough. There's an IV attached to one of his arms, a line of stitches across one cheek and his lower lip is split and bruised. A patch of his white-blond hair has been shaved off and covered with a bandage.

"Hey, loser." Sam sits down on the side of Noah's bed. "How do you feel?"

"Like shit," Noah says, but he's smiling.

"Yeah, I bet. Giving the nurses a hard time?"

"No. They're all in love with me."

"Sucks for them, huh?"

They both laugh; Noah's all wheezy and gasping. He stops and takes deep, pained breaths, squirming uncomfortably, and then his eyes lock with mine, and I feel all light-headed with nerves.

"Easy on the ribs, there, kid," Sam says.

Noah ignores him. "Chelsea?"

This was such a mistake. I shouldn't have come, but it's too late to back out now, isn't it?

"Hi," I say timidly. He just stares at me like my presence isn't fully registering, so I glance toward the door and say, "I can go, if you want. I didn't mean—"

"No." He wheezes for a few breaths. "Stay."

Sam looks from me to Noah. "I'm going to wait outside, okay?"

Noah nods, and when Sam passes me, I want to latch on to his arm and say, *don't leave me,* but I know I really shouldn't. I know I have to do this, because no matter how painful it is for me, it's ten times worse for Noah, and he stills wants to talk, for whatever reason. He deserves the opportunity to tell me how much he hates me to my face.

My eyes are still on Sam walking through the door when Noah says, "I thought you were taking a vow of silence?"

The question startles me. How did he know about that? "I am. Well, I was," I begin to explain, but of everything there is to say, that seems so unimportant. I can't sit here and pretend to make small talk with him. "I know you hate me," I blurt out, all in a rush, and then stop because I don't know what comes next.

Noah blinks at me, surprised. "I don't—" he starts, before dissolving into a racking coughing fit. The sound is like someone stabbing me in the heart. Repeatedly. "I don't...hate you," he says between harsh breaths.

"What do you mean?" Tears spring to my eyes, hot and fierce, and my voice is shaking, my whole body is shaking. "Don't you know? I was the one who told Warren, and I—I ruined *everything,* and I'm—" I collapse onto the edge of his mattress, my hands over my face. "I'm so sorry, Noah. There's no excuse."

"No," he agrees after a minute. "There's not. It was a shitty thing to do."

"I didn't know what would happen," I say. "But I know that doesn't change anything."

"It changes some things," he says. "You...you know what you did wrong. You don't need me...to point that out." He's still breathing a little hard, but his voice is steady, calm. "Asha's talked a lot about you."

I peek at him through my fingers. "She has?"

"At first I thought you kind of deserved what was happening to you," he admits. "Some days I still do. I mean, I woke up and first thing got to have a very awkward one-sided conversation with my mother. 'Hi, Noah, so happy you're not going to die. By the way, everyone knows you're gay now.'"

He pauses, a slight smile touching his lips. "That's a joke. You can laugh."

Except I don't find it funny at all. "I took something important away from you. I had no right."

"Would it make you happier if I told you to go to hell?" he asks. "Look. I've spent the past month with nothing to do but think. Try to figure out what's worth being angry about. It's a long list. I could be angry about all of it and I'd probably be justified. I don't know if I'll ever stop being mad about what happened. About what Warren and Joey did. I don't even know if I *should* stop being mad. But I'm trying not to hate them, even if it's what they deserve, even if no one would blame me for it. I don't want to live like that. I'm not going to spend my life hating you, either. You're apologizing, I'm accepting."

"But *why?*"

I don't understand. I need for him to make me understand.

"Chelsea. Look at me."

I lower my hands into my lap and look up at him through my blurry vision.

"Hate is…it's too easy," he says. His face is calm, calmer than it has any right to be, his eyes not wavering from mine, like he's so completely sure of what he's saying. "Love. Love takes courage."

day thirty-four

The mirror in my bedroom isn't big enough for two people to use, so Asha takes her dress—carefully concealed in white plastic—and holes up in my bathroom. We have one hour before we're supposed to meet everyone at Rosie's. One hour is just enough time to get ready.

I pull my dress out from the closet and slip into it, sliding the thinned-down straps over my shoulders, smoothing out the wrinkles. The deep emerald fabric looks amazing with my red hair; I'm wearing it in loose, long curls that spiral down my back. The gauzy chiffon skirt is just long enough to trail when I walk, even when I try it on with my black heels.

I look in the mirror and feel…good. Sexy. Sexy like I do when I solve a geometry problem right on the first try, or when I flipped over the tuna melt at the grill. This is even better because I did this—I made the dress look this way.

Asha emerges from the bathroom, and I'm honestly stunned when she appears in my doorway. She's dressed in a traditional Indian gown, ruby-red and embroidered with gold, matching gold bracelets all up and down her wrists.

"Oh. My. God," I breathe, and Asha smiles shyly.

"You like it?" she says.

"Are you kidding? It's *amazing,* Ash. Where did you get that dress?"

"It's my mom's." She comes into the room, bracelets jangling as she walks, and beckons to my cosmetics bag. "Could you do my makeup? I tried doing eyeliner and almost poked out my eye."

I sit her down on my bed and get to work. Asha may know geometry, but I am the resident cosmetics expert. Smoky-black eyeliner, mascara to extend her lashes, a touch of gold glittery eye shadow, some dark dramatic lipstick—I explain everything as I put it on her.

She pauses to blot her lips on a napkin and says, "So, Lowell and Derek."

"Yes?" I prod, wanting to see where she goes with this.

"Rumor has it they've both quit the basketball team."

My heart jumps. "Shut up. No way!"

"According to the girl who sits in front of me in chemistry, there was a last-minute scheduled mandatory drug test, and this time they actually made everyone on the team leave the stall door open so they couldn't dupe anyone. Four guys walked off the team instead of doing the test—including Lowell and Derek."

Oh, my God. The plan worked? The plan *worked.* I have no idea how Ms. Kinsey worked her magic and talked the administration into that; all she'd told me was that she would express my concerns anonymously and try to make it happen. I really need to send her some kind of fruit basket. Or maybe bring her a plate of Dex's special-recipe brownies.

"What a shame," I say, doing my best to keep a straight face.

"You can drop the innocent act, Andy told me all about your plan," she says. "For the record, I approve." Asha rubs more gloss on her lips. "Do you think they'll figure out it was you?"

I grin. "They can't prove shit."

I kind of doubt they have that much combined brainpower between them, but it's possible. If it is, and they try to get me back…I'll deal with it then. I'm not worried. They don't hold that power over me anymore.

I'm feeling amazing, lighter and more *free* than I have in weeks, as Asha and I descend the stairs to get our jackets and leave for Rosie's. I'm blocked from the door by Dad, who is armed with a digital camera. The flash blinds me as he snaps a picture.

"*Daaaaaaaaad.*" I roll my eyes at him.

"Indulge me," he says.

"It's our official duty to embarrass you at every given opportunity," Mom adds from behind him.

They're both thrilled that I'm talking again. I sat down at dinner Friday and spilled everything over tofurkey sandwiches (yes, we've upgraded again, to my combined delight and dismay): the fact that I'd broken the vow, my job at Rosie's, my friendship with Asha and Sam, visiting Noah in the hospital, my plans to attend Winter Formal. I figured if I threw enough curveballs at them, they wouldn't be able to freak out about each individual one.

To my utter shock, they took all of it alarmingly well. I guess the fact that I'm speaking again was enough of a relief to overlook everything else.

Asha throws her arm around me, and we pose for more pictures on the staircase, making ridiculous faces. Finally Dad's satisfied and lets us go, but not without smacking kisses on top of my head until Mom pulls him off me.

"All right, Frank, I think you've embarrassed her enough

for one night," she says with a laugh. "You girls look beautiful. I want you to have a good time, but be safe, okay? Oh, and Chelsea, check in with us if you're going to be out past one."

"I will."

"I mean it. If it's one minute past one and that phone doesn't ring—"

"I *will,* I promise!" I hug her quickly. "Love you guys."

"Have fun!" she calls as we scoot out the door to escape their smothering.

Asha says, "Your parents are so cool," as we load into the Beetle.

I almost say *smothering,* but then think better of it. Asha's right. My parents are pretty amazing, all things considered. I have *nothing* to complain about tonight.

When we waltz into Rosie's, Dex leans over the counter and whistles.

"My, my," he says, "look at you ladies."

Lou comes out with a tray of drinks and stops dead in her tracks. "Okay, seriously? You two look fucking fantastic."

"I have to agree."

I whirl around to see Sam behind me, grinning hugely. He's decked out in this retro navy sports jacket with patches over the elbows. It's totally dorky, but like most things, he pulls it off.

"Sam the stud," Asha teases.

"You clean up nicely," I tell him, biting back a smile.

"Likewise." He digs in his pocket and pulls out a small white box. "Here. For you."

I open the box. It's a yellow rose corsage.

"I'm no Marc Jacobs—" he starts, and when I raise my eyebrows, he says "—and yes, I may have done a search for 'famous fashion designers' earlier solely so I could make that reference and impress you—but I figured the yellow would look okay with green. It does, right?"

"It's perfect," I assure him, sliding it over my wrist. I kiss him on the cheek and ignore Dex's whistling behind us.

"So where's Andy?" asks Asha.

"He said he'd meet us at the school. Some kind of a surprise?" Sam shrugs. "It's Andy, so who knows what he's up to."

"You know," Lou says, leaning against the counter, "I don't remember anything about my prom, except that I woke up the next morning on someone's bathroom floor with a tiara in my hair, my shoes on backward and the words *GLITTER WINNERS* were written on the mirror in purple lipstick."

"And, kids, that's the story of how Lou learned tripping on acid is bad," Dex jokes. Lou smacks him with her empty tray.

"I see Dex is on a roll," I say to Sam. "I think that's our cue to leave."

"I heard that!" Dex shouts, but then Lou wraps a hand around his neck and yanks him into a kiss, and he's otherwise distracted from his indignation.

It seems the whole school has decided to attend Winter Formal this year. The parking lot is packed full, and we have to park in a far corner and walk over icy pavement. Asha and I clutch each other's arms and try not to fall.

"That's what you get for wearing insane shoes," Sam says, and then slides over an ice patch. Ha.

Whatever. Impossibly high heels are *designed* for formals.

Around us, everyone is heading toward the school the way Muslims travel toward Mecca (metaphor courtesy of me paying attention in Comparative World Religions for once, thank you very much). Everyone is dressed up, girls in glamorous snazzy dresses, boys in clean suits, all of them looking a little uncomfortable and out of sorts but also a little giddy. The girls are probably excited-slash-nervous at the prospect of intimate slow dances and the boys are probably excited-slash-nervous at the prospect of getting laid.

I, for one, am only excited, not nervous. Or, okay, at least any nerves I have come from being around people who hate me, not about whether or not I'll be having fun sexy times. I sneak a glance at Sam beside me and wonder if he's worrying about that stuff—he doesn't look like it, but really, who can tell with boys?

His cell phone rings. He smiles as he pulls it from his pocket and looks at the caller ID.

"Hey, man," he answers, then pauses for a moment. "Okay. We'll meet you there." He snaps the phone shut and looks at Asha and me. "Andy says he's waiting by an 'old white dude statue.' I assume he means the Covington one."

The Covingtons are the oldest money family in Grand Lake, and somewhere way back in the family line, Gerald E. Covington donated a ton of money to the school, so in return they erected a bronze statue in his honor, complete with a fountain, in front of the main entrance. It's pretty ugly, but tonight the fountain is lit up, so it looks less ugly than usual.

As we come closer, I spot Andy under the fountain lights. Not alone.

With Noah.

Asha shrieks and breaks into a run, insensible shoes be damned, and tackles Andy with a giant hug. Noah watches from his wheelchair. Someone cleaned him up, too—he still has the bandage, but instead of a hospital gown, he has on a nice button-down shirt and pressed slacks.

"Holy crap!" Sam puts his hands over his mouth, apparently at a loss for words. Finally he looks to Andy and says, "How the hell did you pull this off, man?"

"I pulled some *major* strings and got us a one-night pass. And Noah here has to be back before midnight or he'll turn into a pumpkin."

"Pumpkin." Noah laughs. "I want pumpkin pie. Can we get pie?"

Andy says, "Maybe later."

Sam shakes his head. "Dude, you look totally high." It's true. Noah looks way out of it.

He keeps smiling his loopy smile. "Only on life, Sam."

"And a fuckton of Vicodin," adds Andy. "He's on some hard-core painkillers right now." He starts rolling Noah toward the school. "We're going to sit on the sidelines and watch you kids live it up."

Living it up, indeed. The gym's decorations are as mediocre as ever—leftover silver Christmas tinsel and plastic glittering snowflakes everywhere—but the place is packed, reeking of sweat and cheap cologne and teenage hormones.

"Smells like teen spirit," Andy quips as he guides Noah to one of the empty side tables.

Asha wastes no time in dragging me onto the floor. I had no idea the girl could dance like she does. My initial self-consciousness vanishes from the sheer, overpowering force of her shamelessness. A few minutes later Sam abandons Andy and Noah to join us; he dances like your typical boy, all minimal feet shuffling and head bobbing, but he looks like he's enjoying himself, and that's what really matters. Having fun. And I am. We get a few strange looks—I'm not sure if people are weirded out by Asha's dress, or by the fact I've dared to show my face here—but I don't really think about it. Who cares? Let people stare.

After a few songs I take a quick break to use the bathroom, and when I come out, I see Brendon by the water fountain. He smiles when he sees me.

"Hey, Chelsea," he says.

"Hey," I say, and grin at the surprised look on his face.

"You're speaking again," he says. "When did this happen?"

I shrug. "It's a recent development."

"Uh-huh," he says. "I saw you come in with Noah and Sam. Are you guys having a good time?"

"More than I'd hoped for," I tell him. I tilt my head at him. "Where's Kristen?"

"Around," he says vaguely. He bites on his lower lip for a moment, like he's considering what to say next. "You know, I almost thought about asking you, but—"

I wave him off midsentence. "It's good that you didn't."

"It is?" He frowns.

I could tell Brendon all the reasons why—that I've realized he doesn't know me at all, and I don't really know him, either, and that I don't think he's my type anyway. My type has brown hair and glasses and a crooked smile and a dorky sense of humor and can cook the best damn tuna melt I've ever tasted.

I could tell Brendon all of these things, but some things are better left unsaid.

Instead I just smile and say, "Good luck with the Snow Prince thing," and waltz back into the gym.

I find Asha and Sam on the floor again just as the music dies down. People groan with disappointment, and a spotlight appears on the front stage. Mr. Fenton hops up the steps and grabs the microphone, a stack of envelopes in hand.

"Good evening," he says. "I hope you're all enjoying yourselves tonight."

Someone yells, "TURN THE MUSIC BACK ON, DICK-FACE," and people look around and laugh.

Mr. Fenton ignores the disruption and clears his throat. "I know you all want to get back to your dancing, so I'll make this quick. I have the pleasure of announcing your elected Winter Formal Court." He doesn't *sound* very pleased about it.

"Oh, goody," Asha mutters under her breath, and I grin at her.

"What?" Sam teases. "You're not *quivering* from the anticipation?"

I'm not *quivering*, but I do want to hear this. First, Mr. Fenton calls out the freshmen Prince and Princess; a beaming brunette with boobs half spilling out of her tight strapless dress prances onto the stage, accompanied by a tall boy with a long face. Some junior from the dance committee hands out the awards: a tiara and roses for the girl, a crown and staff for the boy. When Mr. Fenton turns his back, the boy holds the staff between his legs and thrusts his hips in a seriously perverse juvenile display, and everyone cracks up.

Oblivious, or maybe just wanting to get through this torturous exercise as quickly as possible, Mr. Fenton forges on. "Now, for the Snow Prince and Snow Princess for the sophomore class..."

I know what that envelope's going to say. Sam and my rendezvous to the hospital yesterday meant we skipped out on the voting at the end of the day, but it didn't really matter—it wasn't like two protest votes would make the difference.

But that doesn't mean my heart doesn't twist a little with disappointment when Mr. Fenton rips open the envelope and says, "Your sophomore court is...Brendon Ryan for Snow Prince and Kristen Courteau for Snow Princess!"

Big shock there.

Everybody except Sam, Asha and I claps as the two of them make their way onto the stage, Kristen towing Brendon eagerly by the hand. Kristen looks radiant, of course, the beaded purple dress she's poured herself into shining like diamonds under the lights, her smile glossy and perfect. She takes the rose bouquet in one arm and uses the other to adjust the tiara so it sits straight on top of her elegant up-do.

Brendon accepts the crown and staff, holding it awkwardly at his side, but instead of standing next to Kristen, he steps forward and whispers something to Mr. Fenton. Mr. Fenton listens for a second and then shrugs, handing over the microphone.

"Hello?" Brendon's smooth voice echoes through the gym. People shift around, impatient for more music, but then the clamor quiets down. "Hi," he says. "So, uh, I'm really honored that you guys in my class voted for me…but I think there's someone here tonight who deserves this title way more than I do."

Asha and Sam both look at me like I should know what's going on. I'm just as clueless as them, of course, so I half shrug and shake my head then turn my eyes back to Brendon. He's looking out across the gym, over our heads.

"Noah Beckett is here tonight," he continues, "and if he'll accept it, I'd really like him to have my crown."

What. The. Hell. Is. Going. On?

I twist around to find Andy and Noah. Andy's staring at the stage, wide-eyed and gob smacked, while Noah just grins his doped-out smile. And then, snapping out of it, Andy stands and maneuvers the wheelchair to the front of the gym, the crowd parting to make a pathway. Brendon hops off the stage and places the crown on top of Noah's head, hands him the stupid plastic shiny staff, and he says something, too, but the microphone is away from his mouth so I don't hear. He squeezes Noah's shoulder with a smile, and everyone is just *staring*.

Everyone still stares, even after Mr. Fenton ends this weird little interlude by announcing the rest of the upperclassman court. Everyone still stares when the music kicks on again, a slow pop ballad, the dance reserved for the Court winners. Everyone stares as Andy slowly, slowly helps Noah stand.

They don't really dance—they just hold each other, swaying from side to side, Noah's face buried in Andy's chest, Andy holding him up, their arms encircled so tightly around each other.

No one is looking at Kristen. But I am. I stare across the room at her, her rose bunch clutched in one limp hand, her mouth slack as she gawks at Andy and Noah, the Snow Princes, the belles of the ball, the center of attention. I wonder if she's thinking what I am. How it seems so impossible that someone could look at them, see how plainly they care for each other, and find anything ugly or shameful or worthy of hatred in it, when all I see is something beautiful.

I can't tell. I hope she is. I hope that's what she sees.

"Best. Winter. Formal. Ever."

This has to be at least the eighteenth time Asha has made this same declaration in the past hour.

"It was your *first* Winter Formal," I point out. I lean against the counter as Sam rummages around for an extra colander. We're having some serious tuna melt cravings.

"I don't care. Nothing can top tonight's." Asha does a giddy twirl on her toes.

I can't disagree—we bailed not long after the announcements, because there was just no way things could get any better. Plus, Noah's curfew will be up soon, and he kept talking about wanting pie, so we figured we'd all head over to Rosie's to unwind and celebrate.

Rosie's is empty at the moment; dinner hour has long ended, and it'll be a while before the post-formal stragglers and hungry burnouts wander in. Andy feeds Noah forkfuls of Dex's pumpkin pie in one of the booths, their heads bent close together as they talk between bites. Lou fiddles with the jukebox until it blasts "Love Shack," and she and Dex and Asha do this funny synchronized dance all in a line.

"I've still got the moves!" Dex crows and Lou bumps her hip against his while Asha dissolves into giggles.

"Are you going to help, or am I expected to do all the grunt work?" Sam asks.

I tear my eyes away from the group scene and face him. He looks so ridiculous in that diamond-patterned sports jacket, spatula in hand, and even so I want to just throw him in the supply closet and do all kinds of dirty things to him.

We stayed at the formal long enough to have one slow dance together, my arms wound around his neck, his slid around my waist. It was amazing, the two of us like that, so close, spinning around and around under the swirling lights. Even if the music sucked, even if no one was looking, it didn't matter because *Sam* was looking, like he couldn't stop, like he couldn't believe I was actually there with him, when really I was the one who should've been in disbelief.

Now we stand next to each other in our fancy outfits and flip tuna melts on the grill. Mine turns out better than it did last time, and we make home fries to go with them, and then slide in across from Andy and Noah, eating off each other's plates.

When Sam kisses some ketchup off the corner of my mouth,

Andy says, "*Awww.* As much as I'd like to stick around with you two lovebirds, Cinderella's gotta get his ass back to bed."

Noah pouts. "An*dy*—"

"Don't you 'An*dy*' me. If we're a second late, your mother will shove her foot so far up my ass I'll be eating Crocs for a week."

Andy helps Noah into the wheelchair, and everyone waves them off. Asha and Lou clean off tables while Dex juggles measuring cups and talks about all of the blue paint he picked up yesterday.

"I'm closing tomorrow so we can get a first coat done," he says. "I can count on you guys to help out, right?"

"Wouldn't miss it for the world," Sam tells him, leaning against me.

I lean back and close my eyes. I could stay here forever and be happy.

He pokes me in the ribs. "What are you smiling about, girlie?"

I didn't even realize I was. I open my eyes and smile wider. "Life's just weird sometimes, that's all," I say, and then I yawn, and Sam grins.

"Maybe we should get you home, too. Do you need to call your parents?"

I check the time on my phone. "I've got a while." I look up at him. "Do you…want to come over?" I ask, and yeah, I'm blushing a little.

He looks at me for a minute and then says, "I…could do that."

Lou offers to give Asha a ride home. Before we leave, I grab Asha tight, hug her until she laughs.

"You'll be here tomorrow?" I ask.

"Of course." She glances at Sam and then at me with a

knowing look and says, "Have *funnnn,*" snapping her dish towel at my shoulder.

In the parking lot, Sam impulsively picks me up and twirls me around and around as I shriek with laughter, kicking my heels, my gauzy skirt floating all around us. He sets me down, and I press my mouth to his, dizzy, breathless.

When I pull back just to look at him, it's like the world is spinning and standing still, all at once. And I'm happy.

Sam is the first boy to ever set foot in my room. Well, the first nonblood relative, at least. Mom and Dad have this whole "boundaries" thing going on, and I've never had a real boyfriend before, so it was never an issue I had to deal with. I manage to sneak him in through the side door, and then herd him straight into my room while I check in with my parents. They're in bed—Dad's already fast asleep, and Mom's reading some thick book by the light of the muted television. When she sees me, she slides a bookmark between the pages and takes off her glasses.

"I didn't hear you come in," she says with a smile. Thankfully that means she didn't hear the second set of footsteps, either. "Did you have a good time?"

"The best," I tell her. "I'm pretty tired. Guess I'm gonna head to bed now."

I go over to kiss her good-night, and Mom touches the side of my face and says, "You look very happy. That's all I care about, you know?"

I smile back. "I know."

I'm a lucky girl. I really am. To have parents like this, ones who care enough to worry, who care enough to smother. I need to remember that.

I slip back into my bedroom and close the door, and when

I turn around, I see Sam, his back to me as he looks around the room. I'm suddenly totally self-conscious. Even though ever since The Great Purging there isn't much to see.

He faces me, my Nelly dog in his hands. Oh, God. That's embarrassing.

"I met your friend," he says. He cups the back of Nelly's neck and bobs her droopy head up and down. "Arf, arf."

"I think she likes you."

"Well, we've been bonding."

I let out a fake gasp. "Uh-oh. Does this mean I have some competition?"

"She's cute, but I don't think so. There's only one girl for me," he says. His smile is like floodlights, lighting up everything.

I all but pounce on him, and he laughs when we kiss. "Shh," I hush against his lips, "we have to be quiet."

"I'm sorry, I don't have as much experience in that arena as you do," he says. He laughs again, soft and breathy, trying to stifle it by pushing his face into my shoulder. "Teach me?"

"No."

"No?"

"I like you talking."

"Fickle, are we?"

Instead of answering, I pull him down on the bed and swing my legs so I'm straddling his lap. My dress, of course, makes it awkward. I lean down and kiss him again, longer, slower.

"You're going to rip your dress," he points out.

Is he kidding me? "A girl has you in her bedroom, on her bed, and *that's* what you say?" I shake my head, clucking my tongue.

"What? It's a nice dress!"

"Hmm, okay, I changed my mind. Maybe no more talking. More—" I touch my mouth to his to finish the thought.

"I can do both at the same time." He punctuates each word with a quick kiss. "I'm—" Kiss. "Very—" Kiss. "Talented—" Kiss. "That—" Kiss. "Way." Kiss kiss kiss.

And that's all we do. Kiss. Sam could try to unzip my dress, or run his hands underneath it, over my legs, but he doesn't. Every time the straps slip off my shoulders, he carefully slides them back into place. He doesn't try anything else, and I like that. How he doesn't expect anything just because I invited him into my bedroom and shoved him on my bed.

Eventually I start yawning between kisses, and he draws back. "I should probably go," he says.

"No." I gently push him back into the pillows and lie with my head on his chest. "I'm pretty sure it's imperative you stay."

"'Imperative.' Big word there for a redhead."

"Wrong stereotype. Blondes are the dumb ones." I run my hand through his hair so it sticks up. "And brunettes are the judgmental dorks, apparently."

"I like how you call me 'judgmental' and 'dork' in the same breath."

"It's one of my many charms."

We lie there for a while, but even as tired as I am, I'm too wired for sleep. My head is buzzing with everything that's happened. And I do mean *everything;* the weight of the last month settles over me like a blanket.

"You asleep?" Sam says softly. I wonder if he's thinking about everything, too.

"Not yet." I snuggle against his chest. "Tell me a story?"

"Hmm. Did I ever tell you about how Dex got Rosie's?"

"No! I wondered how he ended up there."

"It was his mom's place. She died a few years ago—cancer,

I think—and she left it to him. He was living in Toledo with Lou, and so they moved up together to take it over."

"Do you think they're going to get married?"

"Dex and Lou? I don't think they believe in marriage."

"Really? Why not?"

"I dunno. Some people don't need that, you know? I think they just believe in being together."

That makes sense, I guess. Actually the more I think about it, it's kind of romantic. The fact that they don't need a piece of paper for their relationship to mean something. I slide my arm around Sam and nestle into his chest, closing my eyes, half-asleep. Yes. Yes, I can definitely see how being together would be enough.

day thirty-five

When I open my eyes and stretch, Sam's chest still serving as my pillow, it's light outside.

Oh, shit. Shit! Light!

I shake Sam awake and hiss, "Oh, my God, you really have to go, like, right this second."

He rubs at his eyes. He never even took off his glasses. "Right now?" he mumbles sleepily.

"Unless you want my father to castrate you on sight, yes."

This is enough to fully wake him. He tumbles out of bed, hopping around as he yanks on his shoes. He starts for my door when I grab his elbow and jerk him back.

"Are you crazy? You cannot go down there!"

"How am I supposed to get out?"

I look around wildly, channeling my well-honed Jason Bourne instincts, and then my eyes land on the window. It'll have to do.

"You can climb out my window," I explain. "There's the tree, right there. Climb down it and hey, you're home free!"

Sam stares at me like I'm insane. "What am I, Spider-Man?"

"It's totally easy! I've done it, like, *millions* of times."

Okay, that's an exaggeration. I did it once, last summer, when I was grounded and Kristen convinced me to sneak out

so we could drive over to the lake and get drunk with Warren and Joey. I almost twisted my ankle in the process. Totally not worth it.

But what other option is there? A broken foot would be
far preferable to whatever my dad will do to Sam if he finds
him in my room.

He goes to grab his jacket and the green-and-silver scarf
Asha knit for him, stuffed at the foot of my bed. As he tugs
it out, he frowns and pulls at something else.

"Your sweater must've got caught in here," he says, tossing it to me.

I look down at the soft pink fabric in my hands. "This
isn't mine."

It's Kristen's. A sweater she lent me ages ago and I forgot
to return. How did I miss this?

Sam comes over and kisses me softly, and I'm distracted
from the memory. "I can walk to Rosie's from here. Meet
you there later?" he says.

I nod, and then watch as he crawls out my window, giving me a salute before reaching for the nearest tree branch. I
hold my breath and don't let it out until he's scaled all the way
down to the snow. He lands on his knees but gets up quickly,
waves up at me with a grin and runs off. I wave back as he
disappears around the corner.

I shut the window and lean against it, staring at the pink
sweater in my hands. Everything feels so close to perfect—
but this is a glaring reminder of why it's not. Of everything
that's still unresolved. Not every chapter of my life is going to
have a happy ending, but they all do need endings, regardless.

So…so maybe it's time to make that happen.

I could drive to Kristen's house with my eyes closed. Of
course I wouldn't—hello, dangerous!—but I've made the drive

so many times before that it's just ingrained in me. Her house is only blocks from mine. Go down Patterson, turn left on Woodcliff, third house on the right.

I sit in the driveway and stare at her house for a while. I haven't been here since New Year's. Obviously. It's so big and inviting, the hedges perfectly trimmed, Christmas lights still strewn in the tree in the front yard. Looking at it, you'd never know what happened here. How much my life changed right inside.

Except that night didn't change my life. *I* changed it. I have to stop acting like I have no control over these things. Like I'm letting them just happen to me. These are my choices. For better or worse.

I ring the doorbell and wait, huddled in the cold, the folded-up sweater in my hands. Winter can be over any day now, thanks.

While I'm waiting, I realize maybe this wasn't the greatest idea. What if Kristen isn't even home? What if she's at—oh God—Brendon's? What if—

Before my thought process can go any further, the door opens and it's Kristen.

We stand there and stare at each other. She still has bobby pins stuck in her hair, some of last night's makeup on her face and she's wearing a too-big University of Michigan sweatshirt and grubby pajama pants. She looks out of her element. Even though she's standing inside her own home.

I wait for her to slam the door in my face, but she doesn't. She just looks at me and says, "What do you want?" in this brittle voice, like she's ready to crack.

It's so not what I was expecting.

I extend the sweater toward her. "I found this in my room," I explain. "I wanted to give it back. Sorry I didn't wash it, I—"

I stop, aware I'm rambling. It's not like it matters if I washed it or not. Kristen frowns at the pink sweater like she doesn't know what it is. Or if she wants to accept it.

But eventually she reaches out and takes the sweater from me. "Oh," she says. And then she says something I never, ever thought I'd hear: "Thanks."

When it becomes apparent she isn't going to immediately slam the door in my face, I decide to be brave. Go big or go home, right? "I'm not sorry for what I did," I say. No preamble necessary—she knows what I'm referring to. "I mean, I wish I'd done some things—a lot of things—differently, but not telling the cops. It was the right thing to do."

I'm not expecting her to apologize, or for her to even agree—but it still needs to be said.

Her face goes hard. "Warren and Joey will probably go to jail. You ruined their lives," she accuses.

I don't know yet if there will be a trial. If there is, and I have to testify, I'll do it. Happily. I'm not scared of that prospect anymore.

"They did that on their own," I reply. "I think you know that."

For a second I think I see something register in her eyes, a truth hitting home, but her expression glosses over again a moment later. Maybe one day she'll be able to admit it to herself. Maybe not. Today is not that day, and I know now that what she thinks doesn't matter. Not as long as I know the truth about my own culpability. As long as I have Noah's and Andy's forgiveness. As long as I've forgiven myself—I've only just started to, but I'm getting there. Where Kristen believes the blame lies is no longer my problem.

"Congratulations on the Snow Princess thing," I tell her, and to my own surprise, I actually do mean it. "I'm glad you got what you wanted."

I walk to my car without looking back, and as I drive away,

I'm hit with a sudden wave of sadness. But it's a distant kind of sad—like when you look at your Barbies and realize you don't want to play with them anymore, because you're growing up and you've moved on, and in your heart you know it's time to make room for other things.

Noah's words keep running through my head. *Hate is easy, but love takes courage.*

He was right. Hate is too easy. It was easy, back when I used to spend so much time and energy spreading nasty rumors about people—if I was a better person I'd say I felt guilty when I did it, but mostly it made me feel, stupidly, like I had importance, or superiority, or something, when really I was just...pathetic. It'd be easy to hate Kristen, too, for not being the best friend I thought she was. It'll probably always hurt a little, but that's okay. I can deal.

I still hate Warren and Joey for what they did, and I'm not ready to forgive them yet. Maybe I never will be. But I can't let it control my life.

The truth is, the person I've been hating more than anyone is myself. It is so easy. So easy to look in the mirror at all my imperfections and think of all the ways I fall short of someone like Kristen. To struggle with geometry equations and underlying meanings in novels and know I'll never be smart the way Asha is. To realize how much I've screwed up and to obsess over all of the terrible ways I've wronged so many people.

But.

But even though I know my flaws are many (many many *many*), and there are always ways I could be better, and I should never stop working for that—I also need to give myself a break. I can cut myself some slack sometimes. Because I'm a work in progress. Because nobody is perfect. At least I acknowledge the mistakes I've made, and am making. At least I'm *trying*. That means something, doesn't it?

And just because I have room for improvement doesn't mean I'm worthless, or that I have nothing to offer to, like, the world.

Or to Sam.

I'm thinking about this when I push through the doors into Rosie's, ignoring the Closed sign. As soon as I step inside, Dex tosses me a paintbrush and says, "Nice to see you, Chelsea. Now get to work!"

Lou rolls her eyes. "Don't be such a slave driver."

"You better be repaying us with food," Andy says as he runs a foam roller over the wall by the counter. "I'm thinking burgers."

"Veggie burgers," Asha adds from beside him. Andy gives her a look, and she dips her roller in the blue paint and says, "*Someone* has to represent the voice of the nonmeat eaters, okay?"

"Yeah, all one of you."

I look past them toward Sam. He's standing in a corner, detailing the trim with a small brush.

I want to run up to him. I want to tell him exactly what I'm thinking—what his grin does to me. How I didn't think my crazy, upside-down, discombobulated life could ever make as much sense as it does right now. That hate is easy, but sometimes love is easy, too. When you find it.

But then Sam turns around, eyes lighting up when he sees me, tilted smile spreading over his face, and it's like he knows everything. Everything.

And I don't have to say a word.

★ ★ ★ ★ ★

Acknowledgments

Thank you to everyone at Harlequin TEEN, most especially my wonderful editor, Natashya Wilson, and also to my agent, Diana Fox, whose insight and advice for this book was invaluable as always.

Thanks also go to Jen Dibble, Gabriella Marroque, Alexis Kuss, Krista Benson, Lisa Behrens, Sarah Dunworth, Olivia Castellanos, Shoshana Paige and Kaley Wagner for the support, suggestions and, above all, friendship.

SPEECHLESS
READER GUIDE

QUESTIONS FOR DISCUSSION

1. Chelsea Knot starts this story as a gossip whose words wind up hurting others both mentally and physically. What do you think about her vow of silence? Was that an effective way to deal with what happened? How hard might it be to not speak at all for four weeks?

2. At first, Chelsea calls Kristen her best friend. Do you think Chelsea acted as a best friend toward Kristen? Did Kristen act as a best friend toward Chelsea, until events came between them? What makes someone a friend? What makes someone a best friend?

3. Asha is kind to Chelsea from the moment they meet. Why do you think she showed friendship rather than anger toward Chelsea? What might have made Asha give Chelsea a chance when people Chelsea thought of as friends ostracized her?

4. There are many instances of bullying and harassment in *Speechless*. What kinds of intolerance have you witnessed or experienced? What are some steps we can all take to

stop this kind of behavior? What effect do you think the Gay/Straight Alliance club will have in Chelsea's school?

5. When Chelsea takes her vow of silence, her father is supportive. Her mother is not. Why do you think her parents react as they do? In what ways might you support or not support someone in your life who takes such a vow?

6. When Chelsea begins speaking again, she worries that Sam will find her boring and shallow. Do you think Sam and Chelsea have a chance as a couple? How important are common interests, and how much of that is just "stuff," as Sam says?

7. When Chelsea visits Noah in the hospital, Noah forgives her. Do you think Chelsea deserves forgiveness? Why or why not? Who, if anyone, is to blame for what happened to Noah? Why?

8. Stay silent for one minute. For five. Listen. How difficult is it to not say a word? What do you hear that you might not otherwise have noticed? When might it be more powerful to stay silent than to speak up?

Q & A WITH
HANNAH HARRINGTON

Q: Chelsea gets the idea to take a vow of silence from a *National Geographic* article. Where did you get the inspiration for Chelsea's story?

A: I remember in high school how once a year some students would take part in the National Day of Silence, which is a one-day vow of silence designed to raise awareness of anti-LGBTQ bullying and harassment in schools. I always thought it was a great exercise, and it had me thinking what it would be like for someone who is very verbal to voluntarily give up their speech for an extended period of time—how they might cope and what could lead someone like that to that decision in the first place.

Q: What advice do you have for those targeted by harassment?

A: Talk to someone—a parent, a teacher, any trusted adult. If for some reason you can't, or you have and it hasn't helped the situation, there are other resources available to you that can provide support, either online or by phone. Know that there are people who care, who will listen, and who can help. Everyone has the right to a safe environment, whether at school or home.

Q: Chelsea and Kristen have what one might call an unhealthy friendship. Part of Chelsea's transformation is realizing that and coming to value the new friends in her life. How did you approach these relationships and show that Chelsea was worthy of redemption in her new friends' eyes?

A: The most important step for me when it came to Chelsea's redemption was to show her doing something selfless. When we meet her, she's dealing with the immediate fallout of her actions as it directly affects her and she's somewhat self-involved, but at the same time you know there must be something more to her if she is willing to risk her social status to do the right thing—even if she isn't fully aware of the consequences. I think the first sign of her selflessness is the way she sticks up for Asha in front of Kristen, before they're very close friends. One of the most effective ways to make a character sympathetic is to have her do something for someone else that doesn't benefit herself in any way. It's through Chelsea's friendships with Asha, Sam and Andy that she gains perspective. The more they get to know her, the more they each are able to see the good in her and how, at heart, she's not a malicious person but rather someone who made a thoughtless, terrible mistake. These are the people you'd expect wouldn't be able to stand being around her. By showing glimpses of the guilt she's dealing with and that she cares about what happened beyond how it affected her personally—that allows her to transition into getting their acceptance and support. The final step—the one that allows her to literally find her voice again—is when she intervenes when a former friend harasses a stranger. She takes an active role in stopping a cycle she once, if only tacitly, perpetuated—an act that shows the reader how much she's changed throughout the story.

Q: The name Chelsea Knot is a bit different. How did you come up with it, and do you have a method for choosing your characters' names?

A: I don't have a particular method, but I try to pick names I like or that have a personal meaning, and that sound memorable. I've always loved the name Chelsea, and it's not one I've seen used a lot in fiction. I also once met someone with the last name Knot, which I thought was unique. I just liked the way the two names together rolled off the tongue.

Q: Chelsea's mother is upset by her silence, and her father is more supportive. How do you create your adult characters and come up with their motivations?

A: I wanted Chelsea's parents to have differing ways of handling her decision just because it was more interesting than having them on the same page. Plus, having at least one of them be supportive would make it easier for her to continue the "experiment." Her father is a little clueless and indulgent, but also easygoing and very loving, and there's more closeness between him and Chelsea than there is between her and her mother. However, I think her mother's upset stems from her having a better understanding of what is going on with Chelsea and where it's all coming from. They both care about their daughter's well-being, but they're also distracted by other concerns—their financial situation, the legalities of what happened—which is part of why Chelsea is able to get away with her vow for so long.

Q: Once Chelsea reveals what she saw to her parents and then to authorities, she's kept mostly out of the court proceedings against Warren and Joey. Why did

you choose not to have her confront them face-to-face? What might have happened if she had?

A: I wanted the focus to be on the victims and their feelings over what happened, since they deserved to be prioritized. We'd like to think something of that magnitude would be a wake-up call for everyone involved, but I don't think in real life that's always the case—while it was for Chelsea, for example, it wasn't quite for Kristen. I didn't include Chelsea's confronting them because I didn't feel it was necessary for her growth; she wasn't the one who needed to seek justice from them, after all. And I don't think they would've had a change of heart from any kind of confrontation with her. It was more important to me to show her connections with the people who'd been emotionally (and physically) harmed from what happened and to have that be the source of her catharsis and redemption.

Q: What do you hope readers will take away from *Speechless*?

A: Words matter—how we use them and how we don't. Sometimes it is really difficult and even scary to speak up for what you believe is right, but it's important to do. At the end of the day you answer to yourself, no one else, so you'll be happy that you did.

Love is Louder when we use our words to help, not hurt

Our words and actions are powerful. They can hurt people...or they can help people. If you or someone you know is going through the same struggles as Chelsea Knot, check out **loveislouder.com**.

The Love is Louder movement was started when The Jed Foundation, MTV and actress Brittany Snow decided to do something to help those feeling mistreated, misunderstood or alone. Now hundreds of thousands of people around the world have joined the Love is Louder movement and are using their actions to make their communities and schools better places for everyone.

COME JOIN THE LOVE IS LOUDER MOVEMENT WITH US.
Get started now at LoveisLouder.com/SPEECHLESS

LOVE IS LOUDER
A PROJECT OF THE JED FOUNDATION AND MTV

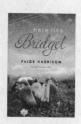

confessions of an ANGRY GIRL

Rose Zarelli has just lost her father. Her brother is off to college, and her mother has checked out on parenting. To make matters more confusing, she's starting high school, and her best friend seems to have become an alien more interested in losing her virginity than having a normal conversation. Then there's Rose's secret crush—unattainable, dangerous older boy Jaime, who might or might not have a scary, vengeful girlfriend. It's enough to make anyone a little bit angry...and store up a whole lot of explosive secrets....

Available wherever books are sold!